TEAROOM
mysteries

Dear Reader,

Recently, I had the joy of visiting with a dear high school friend I had not seen in 42 years. It was an incredible blessing to pick right back up as if we hadn't been apart for so long, and it reminded me of the work I was doing on this book, which has immersed me in "reunion" memories.

As a college student, I received my first batch of Amish friendship bread starter. At the time, I lived in a house with ten other girls, some of whom probably remember the scent and taste of friendship bread permeating our abode. (I'll have to ask them!) When I began brainstorming story ideas, the recipe seemed like a natural fit to help Jan and Elaine celebrate the weekend of sisterhood. "Blest Be the Tie That Binds" also seemed like a natural fit for this story. My mother has belonged to an organization of women for many years, most of whom graduated together. Every year at the annual Mother-Daughter banquet, we form a circle, clasp hands, and sing the first verse of that beloved old tune.

The story takes place in a charming old hotel and is reminiscent of a writers' retreat in Harpers Ferry, West Virginia that I used to attend. It was a magical weekend that gave us memories never to be forgotten, as I imagine the cousins feel about the weekend upon which they embark in this book.

Please consider this my gift of memories to you.

Anne Marie Rodgers

Tearoom Mysteries

TEAROOM
mysteries

Whispers from the Past

ANNE MARIE RODGERS

Guideposts
New York

Published by Guideposts Books & Inspirational Media
110 William Street
New York, New York 10038
Guideposts.org

Acknowledgments

Every attempt has been made to credit the sources of copyrighted material used
in this book. If any such acknowledgment has been inadvertently omitted or
miscredited, receipt of such information would be appreciated.

Scripture references are from the following sources: *The Holy Bible,* King James
Version (KJV). *The Holy Bible, New International Version.* Copyright ©1973, 1978,
1984, 2011 by Biblica, Inc. Used by permission of Zondervan. All rights reserved
worldwide. www.zondervan.com

Cover and interior design by Müllerhaus
Cover illustration by Ross Jones, represented by Deborah Wolfe, Ltd.
Typeset by Aptara, Inc.

Printed and bound in the United States of America
10 9 8 7 6 5 4 3 2 1

Whispers from the Past

CHAPTER ONE

Tea for Two was slow on the last Friday in March. So slow, in fact, that right after lunch there wasn't a single patron in the lovely old restored Victorian on the shore of Chickadee Lake in central Maine.

The two elegant rooms where Jan Blake and Elaine Cook served tea and tasty pastries stood empty. The cousins, however, were in high gear as they prepared to leave for the weekend, something they had never done at the same time before.

Jan carried a large sealed plastic bag with tissue-thin sheets of phyllo dough to the refrigerator and carefully laid them flat on a cookie sheet in the freezer. For Monday's daily special, she planned to bake apple strudel using the phyllo. She would not have time to make the dough this weekend, so she had rolled it and placed it between layers of waxed paper for quick thawing.

She glanced out the window of the back door at Chickadee Lake, where patches of dark water were beginning to show as the deep freeze of winter receded. Some years the lake ice stayed thick much longer, but the cold hadn't lasted as long this year. The ice fishing season was drawing to a close as the ice became unstable, and all of the ice shanties that had dotted the flat surface of the lake had been removed. It was a good thing too. She recalled an incident last week when someone drove a truck onto the ice. It slowly began to sink as the day passed, and the owner had been forced to call for a tow from shore before the lake swallowed his truck completely.

Walking into the dining room, she glanced at the time. "It's almost three, and we need to leave in about forty-five minutes," she said to her cousin Elaine, who was the co-owner of their home and business.

Elaine's mother, Virginia Willard, had invited both Elaine and Jan to attend a mother-daughter retreat for the coming weekend at a lovely old hotel close to the other end of Chickadee Lake. Virginia and many of her high school friends who belonged to the same chapter of her service guild, Delta, would be gathering to revisit their school days together with their family members. Elaine's daughter, Sasha, had flown in from Colorado and was to join them as well. The theme was the Victorian Era, and the program chair had asked the cousins to serve and hold a short talk on Victorian tea rituals during the Sunday-morning break.

Jan had been looking forward to the weekend for some time. She still was. Except that Bob Claybrook, her beau, had just returned to Maine from Baltimore after deciding that it was too difficult to make their relationship work long distance. It gave her a warm glow to hear him say that she was more important to him than his job in the mid-Atlantic region. Additionally, he seemed excited about his plans to open his own local law firm, and she was sorry that she would be gone all weekend just when they were weaving the threads of their relationship into a new and stronger emotional fabric.

Maybe, she thought, she could sneak away for a short time during the retreat and spend a little time with him. She felt positively adolescent about her desire to be with him as much as possible. Grinning at herself, she refocused on her task.

The antique cherry table was covered with an assortment of items Jan and Elaine would need for their talk, and Jan mentally reviewed all of the supplies to ensure they hadn't forgotten anything. "What else do we need to pack?"

Elaine screwed up her face as she registered Jan's question. "I wish the tea had arrived," she said, frowning. They had ordered from a company they hadn't used before. "Maybe I shouldn't have taken a chance with a new vendor, since we need it for a specific event."

The tea, Jan knew, was called Friendship and Memories. They both had thought it was a perfect fit for the weekend. The women in Virginia's group had been friends now for roughly sixty years, and the tea's name had been so evocative Elaine had not been able to resist it.

"Oh, but it will be so perfect. Have you tried tracking it online?" Jan asked.

"Not yet. I need to go do that right now," Elaine said.

"If it doesn't arrive until tomorrow, one of us can run home and get it," Jan assured her. "Thank goodness this retreat is so close to Tea for Two."

Elaine hitched a thumb over her shoulder. "I'll go check on the status of the delivery."

Jan nodded. "And I'll get this stuff packed up."

As Elaine left the room, Archie Bentham, the Englishman who worked for them, entered. "Need some help?" he asked Jan in his charming accent. "I'm bored to tears. If we don't get more customers today, I may be reduced to dusting." Archie was a retired expat from the UK who had applied for work at the tearoom to keep himself busy, but more importantly, because he loved tea. Polished and well-traveled, Archie had become an indispensable member of their little team.

"I'd love some help. We need to get all this into Elaine's car," Jan said, indicating the piles of intricately folded cloth napkins, the stacks of vintage teapots, cups, saucers, sugars and creamers, the boxes of sweeteners, and jars of honey. "Did you hear Elaine say the tea she was expecting for this weekend hasn't arrived yet? If it shows up after we leave—"

"If it shows up later, I'll be happy to run it over," Archie said. "It's not as if you're heading off to Siberia."

"Bite your tongue," Jan said with a grin. "I hope we are done with those kinds of temperatures for this year. I'm ready for spring."

Archie chuckled. "Bit early for that. There's nothing on the radar for the next week, but you know we're going to get snow a couple more times, and at least one of those will be a doozy."

"As long as it melts quickly, I can stand it," Jan said.

The sound of the house telephone interrupted their casual banter. Jan set down the teacup she was about to place into a small compartment in the divided dishware box she'd put together. "I'll get that." Heading into the foyer, she crossed to the table that held the house telephone in its cradle. Lifting the handset, she said, "Hello?"

"Hello, Jan, it's Gloria. Is Archie close by? I tried his cell phone, but he didn't pick up."

Jan already had recognized the voice of Archie's wife. There was an odd note in her voice, perhaps one of urgency. "Hi, Gloria. He probably left it in the kitchen on vibrate. I don't believe he keeps it with him when he's working. I'll get him for you. Hold on."

After returning to the dining room, Jan quickly sent Archie to the foyer when he confirmed that, as she'd suspected, he didn't have his cell phone in his pocket. She resisted the urge to follow him to see what was going on. It might be human to be curious, but it was bad manners to eavesdrop, she reminded herself.

She didn't have to wait long to have her curiosity satisfied. Mere moments later, Archie's hurried footsteps could be heard coming back to the dining room. "Do you mind if I take a few minutes?" he asked. "Rose says she can handle things temporarily. Something's come up." Rose Young, their other employee, was still in one of the parlors restocking clean linen.

Jan was alarmed. "Go, go," she said, making shooing motions. "Is Gloria okay?"

"Oh, it's nothing like that." Archie looked sheepish, but there was no mistaking the excitement in his voice. "No real emergency. It's just that we finally heard from the art authenticator. They've confirmed that the painting is, indeed, one of my father's works. And it seems the fellow's found some sort of note tucked in between the painting and the frame. He's got some questions for me."

Jan's eyes widened. "So he believes it's original?"

"Yes, and he told Gloria he believed the note dates to the time the painting was done," Archie said.

Jan could hear the exhilaration rising in her voice "Maybe it's something your father wrote! You'd better call him right now."

Archie shrugged, trying to appear calm, although she could tell it was an effort. "I have to think that's a possibility at least. If it's handwritten, I might recognize his handwriting. Or at least be able to compare it to other things that were written by him."

"How exciting!"

"What's exciting?" Elaine stepped back into the room from her office, just as Archie left the room.

Jan told Elaine about the telephone call. "Oh, it would be wonderful if it helped Archie learn more about his father," Elaine said. "Or if he finds confirmation that he and Geraldine are sister and brother."

"I know." Jan nodded. "So what did you find out about the tea?"

Elaine sighed. "The shipping order says it was delivered yesterday."

"It was not." Jan was indignant.

"That's what I said. I e-mailed the company and asked them to track it from their end, since I didn't receive it. Unless I hear from them in the next half hour or so, I'll just have to stay on top of it and keep checking my e-mail after we get to the retreat."

Jan frowned. "Well, that's frustrating."

"Very," Elaine agreed. "I'm hoping we can straighten it out. If it arrives tomorrow, Archie or Rose can bring it over."

"Archie already volunteered to run it by," Jan assured her.

They had debated about the wisdom of them both leaving the tearoom on a Saturday, but Archie and Rose had assured them that they could handle it for one day. Elaine and Jan had accepted Virginia's invitation, knowing that the tearoom would be in good hands.

Jan's parents were both deceased, so when Virginia had told her fondly that "I consider you an honorary daughter, and I'd be delighted if you could attend," Jan had gotten a little teary for a moment.

Each of them had a small wheeled suitcase packed and waiting in the front hall. A garment bag held two of the Victorian-era costumes they wore for special days at the tearoom; they would don those before their presentation on Sunday. A small, orderly stack of supplies also waited to one side.

In addition, Jan had two boxes containing the ingredients for a "friendship bread" she intended to make in the hotel's kitchen to be served with the tea. As soon as they got the rest of the dishware packed, they would be ready to go.

"I apologize for making this a working weekend," Elaine said. "When I said we'd give a tea presentation, I wasn't thinking about you having to make the friendship bread."

"It's no problem," Jan said. "I called over on Thursday and the kitchen manager said I could use their ovens either Saturday evening or before they begin their breakfast preparations Sunday morning."

"When are you going to do it?"

"I'm not sure yet," Jan said. "I wanted to take a look at the schedule and see when might be the best time."

When they were finished packing the dishes and other things they needed, Elaine got her keys, and soon the cousins began loading their supplies and personal luggage into her

Chevy Malibu. Earl Grey, the long-haired "stray" cat who loved to sleep on their back porch, came around the corner of the house to say his farewells. He consented to petting and cuddles from both women before extracting himself to return to his snooze.

Fortunately, the weather had cooperated for the folks who would be traveling some distance to attend the retreat. Both cousins luxuriated in the mid-fifties temperature, which felt positively balmy compared to the below-zero chill in which they had been frozen last week.

Elaine had just closed the trunk and started up the steps to get her handbag when Archie stepped out the door.

"What's the scoop?" she called.

"I don't know," he said. "I tried to call him back but the line was busy twice, and then the third time I had to leave a message. Did you still need me to help you pack?"

The cousins chuckled. "No," Jan said, "we took care of it. We're taking off now, so thank you again for standing in for us tomorrow."

"You're most welcome," Archie said. "And best wishes with your presentation on Sunday. I'll let you know when the tea shipment arrives and bring it over as soon as Rose and I get things in order after closing." He greeted four women who were coming up the sidewalk to the front porch. "Hello, ladies. Welcome to Tea for Two. Please come in."

"Great," Elaine said. "We'll see you then. Thanks, Archie."

After adding a few last-minute items, the cousins climbed into Elaine's car, and she pulled the sedan onto Main Street. After a few hundred yards, she took the eastern side of Cottage

Road around the lake toward the small town of Penzance, roughly three miles away at the far end of the lake. Just outside the Penzance town limits lay their destination, the Whisperwood Hotel.

It took less than fifteen minutes to travel to the hotel.

"I hope it's as pretty inside as it is outside," said Jan as Elaine pulled into the circle that fronted the sixty-odd-room building. "I've always thought this place was so picturesque and lovely, but I've never stayed here. This will be a treat."

"It would have been more of a treat thirty years ago," Elaine pointed out. "It's a little run-down now."

"I remember coming to the dining room for a birthday party once when I was a child," Jan said. "It was quite charming, and dozens of wealthy summer people stayed here back then."

The Whisperwood was three stories high, with a wide, columned front porch where inviting rocking chairs waited. Shallow stone steps led up to the porch. Painted a soft sky blue with white trim, the main building put one in mind of a wedding cake. At one side, a rectangular addition with a handicapped ramp led into the dining room, giving guests in wheelchairs or with rolling luggage easier access to the main porch, from which they could access the front entry. Jan had attended a wedding reception and a retirement dinner in the restaurant more recently, which she estimated seated about a hundred and fifty people when all the partitions were opened.

East Cottage Road passed between the lake and the hotel, so all the "best" rooms at the front of the historic structure had a lake view. Elaine was right about its faded, shabby appearance.

Built in 1898, the hotel had been a thriving, bustling tourist destination for many, many summers, but in the last thirty years, business had fallen off. Both cousins could remember the hordes of summer tourists who hiked and swam, canoed on the lake, and browsed through little shops in Penzance and Lancaster. Many of the families had come back year after year; the "regulars," locals had called them.

Elaine put the car in park. "Why don't we just unload our personal stuff for the moment? We can ask at the desk where they'd like us to bring our supplies for the Sunday presentation."

"Okay." Jan gave her a thumbs-up and climbed from the passenger seat. Elaine popped the trunk and came to help her, and the cousins efficiently unloaded their suitcases and costumes onto the sidewalk in front of the steps.

"Back in a minute," Elaine said. After moving the car to a nearby parking lot, she returned, and the cousins gathered their belongings and headed up the steps to the deep-red front door.

Inside, the lobby was filled with quaint groupings of floral-upholstered chairs and loveseats, paintings of the lake and the hotel from yesteryear, and several large and thriving potted plants. The check-in desk was charming, composed of age-darkened wooden panels with three Tiffany-style glass hanging lights overhead featuring swooping dragonflies. Behind the desk hung an antique key rack containing large numbered keys.

Women clogged the room in groups, most with pieces of luggage and handbags the size of small suitcases. The noise level was at a high decibel, a distinct cacophony of female voices punctuated by the occasional shriek as old friends found each other in the crowd.

"...going to be a great-grandma! Can you believe it?" A tall woman grinned, looking thrilled.

A graying blonde rushed across the room and embraced a shorter woman with flame-red curls. "CeeCee! It's so wonderful..."

The gabble of excited voices was deafening.

Blazing a trail to the desk, Jan and Elaine waited to check in, smiling at each other in a "What have we let ourselves in for?" way.

"Welcome to the Whisperwood." An older woman with white-blonde hair and lots of blue eye makeup stood behind the desk, looking as if her smile might hide slightly gritted teeth. After checking them in and giving them directions to the kitchen, where she assured them they could leave their boxes for Sunday's tea, she handed Jan a key.

"You're in number 26 with Sasha Cook, and you," she said, offering another key to Elaine, "are in 28 with Virginia Willard. Those rooms adjoin, as she requested. My name is Heloise Invers. Just ring this desk if you need anything, and we'll see to it."

She held on to the key for a moment as Elaine attempted to remove it from her hand. "I can see you're related to Virginia. You look a lot like her." She leaned forward conspiratorially. "I went to school with all these girls."

Elaine smiled at the characterization of her mother and her classmates as "girls," and the manager released the key. "I'll consider that a compliment. Thank you."

"Elaine! Jan!" A voice behind them prompted the cousins to turn.

CHAPTER TWO

Elaine's mother Virginia Willard was crossing the lobby toward them, arms outstretched. Almost the same height as Elaine, Virginia wore her silvering brown hair in a stylish short crop that swept back from her face. She was dressed in slim khaki pants with dressy heeled boots and a navy-and-beige striped twinset.

"Hi, Mom." Elaine accepted a warm hug and stood aside so Jan could receive the same treatment.

Jan smiled as she backed out of Virginia's arms. "You two look more like sisters than mother and daughter. And the clothes really help."

Elaine looked down at her khaki pants, brown boots, and ivory twinset, and she couldn't help but laugh.

"That's a lovely compliment," Virginia said. "I'll take it. Oh, I'm so glad you were able to come. I'm excited about introducing my family to some of my oldest and dearest friends."

"I'm sure everyone is looking forward to meeting you," Heloise inserted.

Elaine half-turned to include the hotel manager in their conversation. The comment didn't seem to require an answer, and there was an odd pause in the conversation.

"I'm so pleased the Whisperwood could accommodate our old crowd," Heloise chirped, beaming at Virginia.

"It's a lovely facility," Virginia said, "and we're really looking forward to the weekend." She took her daughter and niece by the elbows and gently steered them to a window, where they could see a bustle of activity as other retreat attendees unloaded and prepared to descend on the hotel. "So you already know the theme for the weekend is the Victorian Era, since you've been asked to present a tea program. There will be a variety of different workshops and presentations on what life was like in Victorian England in the last half of the nineteenth century. And it's a mother-daughter event, so a lot of my friends will have family members with them as well."

A squeal from the direction of the desk interrupted her words, and all three of them turned. Heloise, the desk manager, was greeting another guest. She appeared to be overjoyed to see the woman, and she leaned across the desk to throw her arms around the new arrival.

"Heloise graduated with us," Virginia said, smiling gently at the woman's enthusiasm, "although she was not in my guild."

"Why not? Did people have to be invited?"

"Oh no," Virginia said. "It was an open club. But I believe her family had church on Wednesday evenings, and that's when the guild met." There was a wry quality to her smile. "She's very excited to see everyone."

"I'm surprised she isn't retired," Jan said, thinking of the work it must take to manage even a small hotel.

Virginia nodded. "She always did have a lot of energy, and I heard she lost her husband some years ago. I suspect she just likes to keep busy and feel needed."

"Mom," Elaine said, "we need to take our boxes of things for Sunday's tea back to the kitchen. Maybe we should do that now before Sasha gets here."

"Sure," Virginia said. "I can help."

Jan and Elaine left their suitcases stashed in a corner where a lot of other luggage was accumulating, and the three women went back out to the car. Jan and Virginia walked around to the kitchen door while Elaine brought the car around.

"Let me run in and ask where they'd like us to put it," Elaine said.

As she entered the kitchen, she saw a young woman in black server's pants and shirt. "Hello," she said, then introduced herself. "I'm giving a presentation Sunday morning, and I have a few boxes I need to store in the kitchen until then. Is there a good place where they'll be out of the way?"

"I'm Crystal," the girl said. "Right over here's a good place for it." She indicated a narrow table along the inner wall. "This table here is where we always put holiday decorations, and since it's not in use, your things can stay right here all weekend."

"Thank you." With a warm smile, Elaine headed back outside.

It took only minutes to unload their things, and then the cousins and Elaine's mother returned to the lobby, which was crowded now with women and their belongings. Above it all, Heloise Invers's high, trilling laugh could be heard. She had come out from behind the desk, leaving another receptionist to hand out keys, and was rushing around hugging people. Of course, Elaine thought, grinning, there were women hugging all over the room, so she fit right in.

"Mom! Grandma!" A hand appeared across the room, waving high above the crowd.

"Oh, there's Sasha," Elaine said to the others as her daughter forged a path through the crowd and flew into her mother's arms.

"Hi, honey." Elaine hugged her younger child hard, savoring the contact. Sasha lived in Colorado, and Elaine didn't get to see her nearly as often as she wished. She'd been lucky that Sasha had come east several times last year for vacations as well as her biathlete training. Perhaps Elaine could get away from the tearoom in April or May for a few days before tourist season really kicked off and fly out for a short visit. Maybe Nathan would come with her. She really wanted Sasha to get to know Nathan better.

"You look terrific," Jan said, giving her young cousin a peck on the cheek.

"I'm so happy you could join us," Virginia told Sasha, arms outstretched for a hug of her own. "Having my girls with me is wonderful. I invited Corrie, but she couldn't make it, and of course, Lucy's a little too young yet to enjoy a weekend like this." She was speaking of Sasha's sister-in-law and young niece, who was nearly twelve.

"This retreat coincided perfectly with a competition at Sugarloaf, so I was already in the area," Sasha told her. "It was the last one of the season."

"And how did you do?" Virginia held her at arm's length.

A wide grin split Sasha's face. "I took gold."

Elaine couldn't hide her pride in her daughter's achievements. "And she's second in points."

"That's great." Virginia paused. "And what does that mean?"

Sasha laughed. "It means I have a pretty good shot at the national title if I can keep it up."

Virginia clapped her hands together. "I'm rooting for you, sweetheart." Then her attention focused on a woman crossing the lobby. "There's Eleanor. Eleanor! Over here."

As the woman approached, Virginia introduced her. "Everybody, this is Eleanor Mungo. Eleanor and I were cheerleaders together way back when. She just celebrated her fifty-seventh wedding anniversary to her high school sweetheart. Oh, and we go to church together."

Eleanor was a cheerful grandmotherly type, short and plump with pixie-cut gray hair and enormous hoop earrings. "Yes, we're older than dirt," she said, laughing. "It's hard to believe that many years have passed. We sure had a lot of fun back then, didn't we, Virginia?"

"We still do," Virginia replied, grinning.

"Oh, and don't forget Betty Lee. The three of you were thick as thieves!" The merry, slightly-too-loud voice came from Heloise Invers, who was standing just behind them. Elaine, who hadn't seen her, started slightly.

"Yes," Virginia said. "Betty Lee should be here soon, and you'll meet her too."

"I'll never forget the time the three of you got fussed at in the library for giggling," Heloise said. "Funniest thing I ever saw. Remember that?"

Virginia looked a little puzzled. "I'm afraid I don't."

"Remember that, Eleanor?" Heloise repeated.

Eleanor spread her hands regretfully. "I don't, to be honest."

"Which doesn't mean it didn't happen," Virginia cut in. "We got called down all the time for talking too much in class." She turned to Sasha. "Have you checked in yet? We should probably take our bags upstairs and unpack. Dinner begins promptly at five."

"And my daughters just came in," Eleanor said, motioning toward the door. "We'll see you at dinner and I'll introduce you."

Heloise had moved on to another group, Elaine saw as she followed her mother, daughter, and cousin up the wide steps that led to the first floor of guest rooms. Their rooms were on that floor, although they were near the far end, she realized as she checked the room numbers.

A housekeeper with a stack of towels was knocking on a door as they passed. "Hello," she said. "I'm Adrianna. Welcome to the Whisperwood." The woman was tiny and dark-haired and hugely pregnant. She looked exhausted.

"Oh my goodness," Virginia said. "You look like you need to be off your feet, honey, not running up and down these stairs."

Adriana summoned a tired smile. "That would be wonderful, but unfortunately, the bills don't stop coming just because a baby's on the way."

"Is this your first?" Elaine asked. "I was excited with both my pregnancies, but I can still recall the anticipation I felt waiting to be a mother for the very first time."

The young woman nodded. "I can't wait to hold her—it's a girl. I just wish everything wasn't so expensive. They don't tell you how much babies cost until you're in a position to need to know." She smiled, but then her expression faded to a wistful look. "I guess it's enough that she'll be very loved."

Jan smiled tenderly. "When are you due?"

"Three weeks." Adriana's pager beeped, and she glanced down. "Oops. Gotta go. You be sure to call me if you need anything, and I'll take care of you." She waddled off toward the stairs.

"I wouldn't ask her to do anything extra for a million dollars," Virginia said, looking after the housekeeper. "I'd feel ridiculous making that young woman walk one additional step."

"I know exactly what you mean," Jan agreed.

The foursome proceeded down the hall toward rooms 26 and 28. Jan was rooming with Sasha, while Elaine and her mother were just next door.

The old-fashioned key clicked loudly as it turned the lock, and Sasha giggled. "This is totally old school. I love it."

"Oh, how pretty," Elaine heard Jan say. Elaine poked her head through the door that connected their rooms. There were two big beds in the room Jan and Sasha shared, a wide dresser, an overstuffed chintz armchair with a matching footstool, and a big window with curtains that matched the armchair. The color theme was a subdued green and soft peach, and although it was clearly dated, the effect was charming.

"Looks like your room is as pretty as ours. Isn't this just adorable?" Elaine asked.

"What color is yours?" Sasha bounced through the door into Elaine and Virginia's room as Jan efficiently began to unpack the few outfits she had brought.

"Ours is pink and blue," Elaine said for Jan's benefit, since they could hear Sasha exclaiming in the next room. "Your Victorian dress is hanging with mine in my closet."

"Thanks," Jan said.

Sasha came back through the door. "Grandma says I have to unpack fast because she doesn't want to be late for dinner."

They all chuckled as Sasha unzipped a large duffel and began pulling things out and piling them in a drawer.

"Is that all black?" Elaine asked, blinking.

Sasha nodded. "Yeah. It makes traveling easy when I don't have to worry about matching colors."

"Makes sense to me," Jan said. "I'm ready to go down as soon as I brush my hair."

THE DINING ROOM was off to one side of the hotel in a rectangular room with large windows that featured lovely lake views. French doors opened onto a covered side porch, currently not in use but probably very pleasant during the summer, Jan decided. The meals were served buffet style, with extensive offerings that included soups, salads, breads, entrees, vegetables and fruits, and desserts. There was even a soft-serve ice cream machine for those who couldn't resist.

Jan, Elaine, Sasha, and Virginia were assigned seats just inside the double entry door from the hotel proper. The large round table seated eight, and there already were three people at the table when they arrived.

Jan recognized Virginia's friend Eleanor, who promptly introduced her two daughters, Rae Burns and Roxanne Everly. Both looked to be close to Jan and Elaine's age, and both had their mother's warm smile.

Jan took a seat beside Rae, the elder of the two sisters. As they chatted, they learned that they had a great deal in common. Each of them had three children. Rae had five grandchildren to Jan's four. Both had lost their husbands about a decade ago. Rae attended the same church that Virginia and Eleanor attended.

A few minutes later, sharp clapping interrupted their chatter. The club president stood at a small, flower-filled podium along the non-window side of the room. After a short speech featuring a few reminiscences that caused ripples of laughter among the guild members and their guests, she asked everyone to bow their heads while she offered a prayer for the meal and for the weekend fellowship about to commence. Then she said, "Tables one and two, you may proceed to the buffet. The rest of you will be called momentarily."

As they waited for their table to be called to the buffet, a person dropping into the empty seat at their table stopped all the conversations that were picking up again. Another woman with whom she had entered looked around for a moment before spotting the waving hands at the table where she was assigned and heading in that direction.

"Finally made it," the woman said, draping her coat and handbag over the back of her chair. She was tall and heavy-set with steel-gray hair scraped back into a bun. "I had a wedding rehearsal that ran a little late."

"Hi, Betty Lee." Virginia motioned to the table. "This is Betty Lee Krahn, the other member of our high school trio. She's the music director at our church, Cushnoc Community Chapel." Quickly, she introduced Betty Lee to the cousins and Sasha, the only ones she didn't know.

"'Cushnoc'? What an interesting name!" Sasha commented. "I've never heard it before."

"It's an old Indian word," Betty Lee informed her. "The original trading post that predates present-day Augusta was called Cushnoc. I believe it means 'head of tide' and refers to the Kennebec River."

"It's a wonderful place to worship," Eleanor said. "And Betty Lee has done so much to enhance the music program. We have senior and junior handbells and three different choirs. The music brings so much to the service."

"Betty Lee taught vocal music at the high school for more than thirty years," Virginia informed them, clearly proud of her friend. "And the traditions she established there still remain."

"Tables seven and eight." The president's voice interrupted her. "You may proceed to the buffet now."

As they pushed back their chairs and rose, another late-comer scurried into the room. Like Betty Lee, she wore a coat and carried her handbag. She also had a rolling weekender suitcase that she left just inside the door. People at one of the tables yet to be called hailed her.

"There's Ida's daughter Jeanice," Virginia said. "I believe everyone is here now. I can't wait to get started!"

The buffet had quite a variety of food, and Jan loaded her plate with far more than she would eat at home, although she consoled herself that she had kept the portions small. She was determined not to regain the extra weight she recently had lost. Waitresses came around offering coffee, water, and hot or cold tea, and as the guests finished their meals, there was a steady stream of women heading for the dessert area.

Groaning, Jan pushed her plate away when she had finished. "I simply cannot eat like this all weekend," she declared.

Virginia chuckled. "We have about forty minutes before the welcome reception and game night begin. I may go up to the room and relax for a while."

"I think I'll come with you," Elaine said. "I want to brush my teeth, anyway."

"We'll all go," Sasha said.

"See you a little later," Jan said to Rae as her family departed.

It was a relief to return to the room and rest for ten minutes or so. Only, Jan assured herself, until her meal had a chance to settle.

She had just relaxed on her bed when she heard Virginia's agitated voice from the other room saying, "I have no idea, but why don't you have one?"

CHAPTER THREE

A moment later, Elaine appeared in the doorway connecting their rooms. She held a small envelope with a piece of ribbon dangling from her fingers. "Did either of you find an envelope on your pillow just now?"

Jan shook her head, as did Sasha. "What's that?"

Virginia elbowed Elaine aside. "Am I the only one that got one of these?" She was waving a dollar bill in the air.

Jan sat up. Actually, she realized it was a two-dollar bill. That was unusual.

"Was that on your pillow?"

Virginia nodded. "Yes. In that envelope tied with ribbon. But Elaine didn't get one." Her brows were drawn together, and Jan realized her aunt was distressed rather than pleased or excited. "It's very upsetting to know that someone was in my room—and possibly yours, since the connecting door is open—while we were downstairs at dinner."

"Who could have gotten in here?" Sasha asked. "We have the only keys."

"I'm sure there's a master for housekeeping, or maybe they have extra copies," Elaine said. "There would have to be a way for management to get into a guest room in case of an accident or something."

"Oh, I imagine that's it," Jan said, hoping to calm Virginia. "Maybe the hotel management let someone in specifically to lay that on your pillow. It could be a head start on a game or something."

"I bet you're right." Elaine looked relieved as she scanned her mother's face.

Virginia seemed to relax a little, although she still looked troubled. "Maybe you're right."

Jan's cell phone, recharging in the other room, dinged loudly, signaling an incoming text. "Excuse me," she murmured.

Checking her phone, she saw that the message was from Bob. In the last couple of months, they had talked through the rough patch they had suffered during his time in Baltimore. Now he wasn't any more ready to be parted from her for an entire weekend than she was from him, she saw with pleasure as she read his message. *Want to take a walk this evening?*

Smiling, she texted back, agreeing to meet him on the front porch at eight thirty. Hopefully the evening's formal entertainment would be over by then, and she could sneak away for a few minutes.

A short time later, the foursome headed downstairs to a spacious enclosed side porch which had been set up for their evening's entertainment. At the back of the large space, a table was set up offering tea, lemonade, water, and a mouthwatering selection of fresh fruit and cookies. Toward the front, there were a dozen large folding tables with chairs.

Currently, everyone was gathering near the food, helping themselves to drinks.

A woman standing alone turned to greet Virginia when they entered. Jan was pretty sure the woman was one of those who had come straight to dinner after arriving late.

"Hi, Laurette," Virginia said. "This is my family." Quickly she introduced Elaine, Jan, and Sasha. "This is Laurette Martel, another of my guild members," she told them.

"Nice to meet you," Jan said as the others said hello.

"You too." Laurette was about Elaine's height, plump, with short gray hair that was choppy and uneven, as if perhaps she had snipped at it herself. She had been digging in her handbag, but she looked up and acknowledged them when Virginia spoke. "Did you see all those cookies over there?"

Virginia groaned. "It's been less than an hour since dessert. I can't even look at those cookies right now."

Sasha laughed. "I can. But I better not. Training starts again on Monday."

"Sasha is a skier and runner, among other things," Elaine said to Laurette by way of explanation.

"No training this weekend?" Jan asked Sasha.

"No official training," Sasha told her. "I'm going to get up early tomorrow and Sunday and try to fit in five or ten miles, but that's about it. I'm taking it easy."

"Running five or ten miles is easy?" Laurette looked taken aback. "Walking down to the lake and back would do me in."

Elaine laughed, shaking her head fondly. "I can't imagine considering a five or ten mile run 'not official training.'"

"Hey, Virginia." It was Eleanor Mungo, trailed by her daughters, as well as Betty Lee Krahn. "Look what I found on my pillow after dinner." She held up a postcard. "What do you suppose this means? Rae and Roxy didn't get them. Did any of you?"

"Was there a note in a little envelope tied with a pink-and-green-striped ribbon?" Virginia asked.

Eleanor nodded. "You got one too?"

"Yes. Mine wasn't a postcard, though. It was a two-dollar bill."

"That's weird," Rae said, looking perplexed.

"What did your note say?" Eleanor held up a small piece of paper in her other hand. "Mine's kind of strange."

"Note?" Jan took the postcard and the small piece of pale-pink paper that Eleanor offered. The postcard was a scene of the main street of Augusta from roughly fifty years ago. Boat-sized automobiles with large rounded fenders lined the street, and the lone pedestrian was a woman who wore both gloves and a hat as she window-shopped the five-and-dime department store that was prominent in the hand-drawn image.

The note itself was no more than three inches by five, the size of a small index card, although it appeared to have been torn out of the sort of notepad that had gum across the top, because a thin sliver of the rubbery substance still clung to the top edge of the paper.

"*In over your head? There's still time to save yourself,*" Jan read aloud.

"What?" Sasha looked dubious. "If this is a game, it's a pretty odd one."

"It doesn't sound like much of a game," Laurette said, frowning. Jan had to admit she was right.

"Mom didn't get a note." Then, slowly, Elaine turned to her mother, whose expression was the very picture of guilt. "Or did you, Mom?"

Virginia sighed. "I did." She fished in the stylishly tooled handbag slung over her shoulder and came up with a piece of pink paper like Eleanor's. "I didn't understand it, and it made me feel a little...I don't even know what the word is. Unsettled? Uncomfortable? At any rate, I didn't think it was important, unless we needed it for some game."

Elaine took the note, which had been folded in half, from her mother. Unfolding it, she read, *"You must have been out of your depth. Have you found your footing now?"*

"That's even stranger," Rae said.

"I can't believe you both got one and I didn't." Betty Lee sounded disgruntled. "If it's a game, we all should have gotten one too, right?"

"I guess it depends on the game," Jan said.

Betty Lee shrugged. "Eleanor said hers was on one of the pillows on her bed. I ran to my room and dumped my bags, and I tossed my book on the bedside table, so I know I'd have seen it if it was there before I joined you for dinner. And I went back up afterward and didn't see anything."

"Mine was on my pillow too," Virginia said.

Laurette had taken Eleanor's note and was looking at it. "I believe I have paper like this," she said. "I can't remember where

I got it, though. Probably at some guild function, I think. It's in a little purse-sized notepad with a paisley design on the front."

"Oh," Betty Lee said. "If you're thinking of the one I'm thinking of, we each got one of those as a favor when Delta went to that talk and luncheon at the Bates College Museum of Art."

"The whole guild attended?" Elaine asked.

Eleanor and Virginia both nodded. "There may have been one or two absentees, but most of us local members don't miss many events," Eleanor told her.

So that meant most of the guild members would have had the notepads, Jan realized. "How long ago was that?" Jan asked.

Virginia thought for a moment. "Not last year—I believe it was spring two years ago. Probably right around this time."

Eleanor nodded along with the others. "That's right," she said.

Jan thought her aunt's eyes looked disturbed. Virginia exchanged what looked like a troubled glance with Eleanor, whose grandmotherly warmth seemed to have melted away and left her looking equally concerned.

"I wonder if anyone else got one of these," Sasha said. "Maybe it's like a murder-mystery weekend and these are clues."

"Except there has been no murder or anything we need to solve," Elaine pointed out.

"Yet." Sasha grinned. "Thank goodness. But you see what I'm getting at, right?"

"Maybe as soon as game night begins, we'll find out what these mean," Virginia said hopefully.

"...and it was on my pillow when I entered my room after dinner," another voice said from behind their group.

Jan and the others turned to see an attractive older woman with a cap of sleek blonde hair holding up a brochure of some kind. "Do you know her?" she asked Virginia.

"Of course. That's Kinley Devore. She's one of the guild members."

"And obviously," Elaine murmured, "she also received something. I wonder if it was in an envelope with a note."

"I suspect it was. Interesting that none of the 'gifts' are the same." Jan edged forward to get a closer look at the brochure.

It was just a black-and-white trifold brochure advertising a 1K race. A 1K? That was weird. Jan had never heard of anything less than a 3K, and even that was less than two miles. A 1K would be...Jan took a second to recall the distance. That would be only about three-fifths of a mile. Hardly a challenge for a woman like Kinley, who was as slender as a whippet and was wearing a skirt that barely hit her knees, showing off slim, muscled legs that clearly got some sort of regular exercise.

"Was there a note with it?" Jan asked, unable to contain her curiosity.

The woman turned to her with a lifted brow, and Virginia said, "Kinley, this is my niece, Jan Blake. Jan, Kinley Devore, one of my guild friends. And this is my daughter, Elaine Cook, and her daughter, Sasha Cook."

"How nice to meet you all." Kinley shook each one's hand and then nodded in answer to the question. "There was a note with it. Something about...holding my breath, I think. Can't recall it exactly. It was kind of weird. I left it in my room."

"Was it on pink paper?" Laurette asked.

Kinley nodded. "Sure was."

Another woman holding a photo spoke up. "Did I hear you say you found a gift on your pillow after dinner?"

"Did you get something on your pillow too?" Kinley asked.

"This is Babette Parture," Virginia said for the benefit of her relatives. "Another guild member. She and Kinley both attend our church."

After the cousins introduced themselves, Babette said, "This is just plain odd." Her forehead wrinkled in perplexity. She was a short, stout woman with blue eye shadow and artfully colored and styled platinum-blonde curls that looked as if even a high wind wouldn't dislodge a single hair. "I got a picture of a speed limit sign."

Jan took the photo she held out. It was a 35-mile-per-hour sign, and it had been cropped so closely that there was no way to see background details. It could have come from any rural road in the state.

"There was a note with mine too. Did you get a note?" Babette asked Virginia and Kinley.

"We both did," Kinley told her.

Babette still looked confused. "Mine didn't make any sense."

"What did it say?" Virginia anticipated Jan's question. "May we see it?"

"Oh, I can't remember exactly. It's in my room," Babette said. "Sorry. It didn't seem important. I'll show it to you at breakfast."

"If we don't need them sooner," Kinley said. "I think it's part of some elaborate game. Maybe we'll find out more tonight."

Jan intercepted a skeptical glance Virginia and Eleanor shared between them. Neither of them thought these "gifts" related to a game, she felt certain. And what's more, she suspected that they had an idea what the clues really meant.

Betty Lee sniffed, looking narrow-eyed and annoyed. "I still can't imagine why I wouldn't have gotten one if they did." She swept a hand toward her two friends. "Everyone knows the three of us were like glue."

As the reception wore on, Jan looked around for others who might have received gifts on their pillows, but it appeared Virginia, Eleanor, Kinley, and Babette were the only ones so far. Or at least, they were the only ones who had advertised the odd things they had received.

The noise level in the room rose as most of the roughly ninety women joined in. All of the guild members and their guests appeared to be present.

Heloise Invers, neither a guest nor a guild member, Jan recalled, was right in the thick of things, mingling with almost manic desperation. As Jan watched, Heloise clutched one woman by the elbow and engaged in her conversation. After looking around as if in need of rescue for several minutes, the woman finally excused herself and vanished in the direction of the ladies' room. It made Jan feel sad for the hotel manager. There was a neediness about her actions.

Elaine and Sasha approached, and Jan greeted them with a smile.

"We sound like a gaggle of geese," Elaine commented.

Jan chuckled. "Good description. I guess these folks are happy to have the chance to spend some time with each other."

"I remember my last class reunion felt far too short, and I imagine that's how this feels," Sasha said. "Only even more since they were so close."

"Considering that a lot of them probably saw and spent a good deal of time with each other every day during high school, you're probably right. But if I hear one more conversation about how to make your manicure last longer, I may scream." Elaine chuckled.

Jan laughed aloud.

"Girls? Girls, I'd like to introduce you to someone." Virginia appeared at Elaine's elbow with two women who looked so alike they must be a mother-daughter pair, Jan decided.

She was proven right a moment later.

"This is Ida Karlen, another of our guild members," Virginia said, "and her daughter, Jeanice Evanak. They also go to church with several of us."

"It's nice to meet you," Elaine said. "I believe I was introduced to you both when I visited last year with Mom."

Ida was a sharp-angled woman of average height. She had silver hair, and her face was etched with lines of what appeared at first to be deep discontent. But then she smiled, making her look noticeably younger and more attractive. Her daughter, Jeanice, looked much like her except that her facial lines were not as deep and her hair was dyed a deep, dull black from which silvery roots peeked. It seemed to Jan that the lines were simply a hereditary trait rather than an indication of temperament.

Everyone dutifully exchanged greetings.

"I was nearly late for dinner," Jeanice said. "I had an appointment that ran late, but I am so glad I didn't miss that food." She patted her tummy, and everyone smiled.

"I know," Sasha said. "I'm going to have to handcuff myself to my chair to avoid the desserts."

Jeanice laughed. "I know. The ice cream, the cake, the pie... where do I stop? I just wanted to go back again and again and again." She looked at Virginia. "How lovely that both your daughters and your granddaughter could join you for the weekend."

"Jan's my niece," Virginia reminded her. "But yes, I'm thrilled to have them all here."

Ida spoke up. "Jeanice's daughter, Mary Jane, isn't here. She couldn't get away."

"She works for a brokerage firm in Manhattan," Jeanice said quickly. "She's indispensable." She looked at Sasha. "She's about your age, I imagine. What do you do, dear?"

"I'm a fitness trainer at a gym," Sasha said, smiling.

"How nice. It must be very... rewarding."

Sasha nodded, appearing unfazed by what Jan felt was a slightly patronizing tone. "It really is. I enjoy working with people, so it's a good fit for me."

"Mary Jane gets her love of numbers from her mother," Ida said proudly. "Jeanice has always had a head for figures. It drives her crazy when she can't balance her checkbook. Even as a little girl, she was always determined to make sure all the numbers added up. She's like me, quite obsessed with whatever it is she undertakes.

Jeanice retained her smile, but Jan could see that beneath the cheerful expression, she seemed annoyed, possibly at being labeled obsessed.

Before anyone could respond, a shout from Betty Lee turned everyone's heads.

CHAPTER FOUR

L isten up, girls!" The choir director's stentorian tones silenced the chatter immediately. "If you all will proceed to the dining room and take your seat at your table, it's time for our game night to begin. We're going to be playing a game of Jeopardy."

Murmurs and cries of delight greeted the announcement. "I love Jeopardy," Virginia said. "I wonder how she's going to manage it. Wouldn't we need a big game board?"

"Mom," Elaine said, "you've known Betty Lee longer than I have, but I have never seen her plan anything that didn't work out. I'm sure she's got it covered."

"We have a game board," Rae informed them as they made their way into the dining room with Eleanor and her daughters. "Mother made it. And you should have seen me trying to jam it in the back of my Suburban. Thank goodness she made it in two sections that were Velcroed together after we arrived."

"It even has an adorably authentic-looking Jeopardy logo on it," Roxanne added with a proud grin.

"Oh my goodness." Virginia clasped her hands together. "Eleanor's an artist, Sasha—did I already tell you that? She's enormously gifted. That watercolor of Mount Desert Island that hangs in my dining area is hers."

"Wow." Sasha looked impressed. "I've always loved that painting. You're very talented."

"Thank you," Eleanor said comfortably, as if she'd heard that many times. "That particular painting is one of my personal favorites. Don't get too excited about this game board, though. It wasn't a highly artistic endeavor." She chuckled.

As everyone settled at their tables in the dining room, Jan studied the giant board Betty Lee had placed at one side of the space. Made of two huge canvases stretched over frames, the board probably measured eight feet high by ten feet wide after the two sections Rae had mentioned were set side by side and joined together. Its surface had been painted a dark blue with a stylized title across the top bearing the Jeopardy logo and the name of the guild. Beneath it was the large grid that comprised the Jeopardy board, six columns wide by six rows high. Across the top row were listed six categories. Beneath each category were five clues with cash values attached to the board with Velcro. The first clue was worth $100, the second $200, and so on until the fifth clue down, which was worth $500. Eleanor might have downplayed her artistry, but Jan was thoroughly impressed with the quality of her effort.

Beside the game board stood a blank dry-erase board. "We're low-tech," Betty Lee told them. "The answers are printed on the backs of the index cards. Once you select a question, I'll read it aloud."

Jan reviewed the categories. Some appeared to be general enough that anyone might have a shot at answering, while a few were more specific and might be answered only by one who lived or had lived in Maine, or by one of the guild members.

"Welcome to Jeopardy!" Betty Lee boomed. "Here are the rules for tonight's opening round. Just like the TV game show, we will also have Daily Doubles and a Double Jeopardy round. Each table will comprise a team. Go ahead and choose a team name now, and we'll list them on the scoreboard."

Virginia leaned forward. "How about Family Friends?"

"Not bad," Elaine said, grinning.

"Mother-Daughter Mania?" Eleanor offered.

"Delta Daughters," Rae suggested. The guild's full name was the Delta Philanthropic Guild, though the members typically shortened it to "Delta."

"Oh, I like that," Virginia immediately said.

"Me too." Eleanor nodded. "Do the rest of you like it?"

"Sounds good to me," Jan said as everyone else nodded, so when Betty Lee asked the name of their team, "Delta Daughters" was printed neatly in one of the score columns, along with ten other groups. A few other guild members had been recruited to stand around the edges of the room and be spotters for the first team to raise the white flag they'd been given, while one would be the scorekeeper. Strategically, Betty Lee had chosen one from each table to assist, so that all the teams had seven members rather than eight.

"Most of you have watched the show on television," Betty Lee went on once all the team names had been recorded. "The rules are the same. The first team to respond must come up with the question that corresponds to the answer. If they answer correctly, they get the points and the chance to choose the next question. If they're incorrect, another team gets a chance. The spotters around the room will do their best to let me know who raised their flag first in each case. Once this round has concluded, we'll take a brief break and then begin Double Jeopardy.

"So here are the categories for our first round. The first one is Book Club. This refers to books that are considered good choices for book club selections. Nature, 4-Letter Words, and Food & Drink are self-explanatory. Local Yokels refers to people from our high school who went on to some kind of fame, even in a minor way. Note that they are not necessarily from our graduating class. And our last category, Manners, Please, is a nod to our Victorian theme. The questions to these answers will refer to that era."

Next, Betty Lee held up a basket. "This has all the team names in it now. I'll choose one at random to get us started." She fished in the basket and came up with a slip of paper. "Mainely Loons gets to choose first," she called. "What category would you like?"

The team chose Book Club for $100. Betty Lee reminded everyone their answers had to be phrased in the form of a question, and they were off.

The first round was fast, fun, and hilarious, with teams needing repeated prompts to phrase their answers as questions and giving a fair number of incorrect answers. Jan decided she would not want to be one of the spotters noting which team's flag rose first, second, or third, since there were invariably a few competitive souls who mounted highly vocal challenges in an effort to get their team a chance to answer.

At the end of the first round, Delta Daughters stood in third place behind Ladies of the Lake and The Weekenders.

"Not too bad," Virginia said approvingly to their table. "Next round we're going to stun them with our brilliance."

"We already did," Sasha opined. "Eleven teams and we're in third. Not too shabby."

"It helped that Jan and Elaine know so much about Victorian manners," Roxanne pointed out, grinning. "Hopefully, there'll be another Victorian-themed category in the next round, and you two can master that as well."

After a few moments, Betty Lee called the room to order. She reviewed the teams' point totals and then said, "Now we're on to our Double Jeopardy round. Here are the categories. High School Hijinks, which of course will take our club back to high school days. Before & After is when a common word must appear before and after others. An example would be the answer: 'Romantic comedy movie from 1993 starring Tom Hanks and Meg Ryan, and professional football team based in Washington state.' The question would be 'What is *Sleepless in Seattle* Seahawks.'"

Laughter rippled through the room.

"Clever." Sasha nodded approval.

"I'm terrible at those," Roxanne said.

Betty Lee went on. "Flowery Phrases, which refers to the Victorian use of flowers as a language to convey a message; State Capitols; Maine Events, which are facts about our lovely home state; and Opera."

"Oh boy," Sasha muttered. "I'm going to be deadweight on this one."

"You and me both," said Roxanne with a chuckle. "Opera and state capitols are not my forte, and as for the rest, let's just say I'll probably be more of a spectator than a participant."

As they all laughed ruefully, Betty Lee said, "Buncha Bobcats, you are currently in last place, so you get to select the first answer." Bobcats were a native species to the state, but Jan had learned the name also was the mascot of the guild's high school.

Buncha Bobcats' spokeswoman said, "Before & After for $200, please." There was a collective groan, as many regular watchers of the game show knew the category was often challenging.

Betty Lee plucked the card from the board and read, "A potato and an event that took place in the Klondike."

There was a moment of suspended silence in the room, and then Jan grabbed the white flag that lay on their table and thrust it high in the air.

"Delta Daughters?" Betty Lee prompted.

"What is Yukon Gold Rush?" Jan said triumphantly.

"That's it." Betty Lee smiled. "You get to pick next."

Jan considered the board.

"Flowery Phrases," urged Elaine.

Jan shrugged. Her knowledge of the Victorian language of flowers was basic at best. She hoped her cousin could pick up the slack. "Flowery Phrases for $200," she said.

Once again, Betty Lee plucked a card from the board. "The red rose."

A number of flags shot into the air, but Jeanice Evanak from Mainely Loons was first with theirs. "What is the flower that means 'love'?"

"Correct. Loons, you choose."

Mainely Loons chose Flowery Phrases for $400—and it turned out to be a massive mistake. The answer was "Hemlock," for which Elaine's question of "What is death?" was accepted, and she went on to run straight through the rest of the category with forget-me-not (true love), white heather (good luck), and for the $1,000 answer, "Pink carnation," Elaine responded, "What is 'I will never forget you'?"

Several people clapped, and Kinley Devore called, "Good job!" from three tables away, making Elaine blush.

Their run of luck ended when Elaine chose Maine Events. Several of the "girls," as Virginia called her friends, were history buffs, and there were even a couple of librarians in the crowd, so those clues were picked off rather quickly. Shortly after that, they started on the High School Hijinks category. The $400 answer was, "Student council president."

Guild members' flags shot into the air all over the room, and a woman, practically bouncing in her seat, squealed when she was called on. "Ida Karlen," she blurted. The room fell silent, and she quickly said, "Who is Ida Karlen?"

Everyone chuckled, and Ida smiled.

Virginia said, "Ida always was a force to be reckoned with. Our student council got a lot of things accomplished when she was our leader."

Eleanor, to her left, snorted and said in what sounded like a not-entirely-complimentary tone, "It was always her way or the highway, wasn't it?"

"But you can't deny that she got things done," Virginia said, clearly striving to be kind. She caught Eleanor's eye, and they both chuckled ruefully.

"I'll take Hijinks for $600, please," the woman with the correct answer said.

This time, after removing the card from the board, Betty Lee held up a supersized photo that apparently had been blown up from their high school yearbook. It showed three girls bent over a table, apparently deeply engrossed in what appeared to be some type of art project, while a fourth girl hovered in the background looking over their shoulders. "The answer is," she said, "the three Mouseketeers worked on this day and night."

Everyone laughed, and guild members' hands grabbed for their white flags. The winner shouted, "What was the yearbook?"

As the women continued to chuckle, Jan overheard a woman at the next table explain to her daughter, "That's Virginia, Betty Lee, and Eleanor in the picture. They used to be inseparable. *The Mickey Mouse Club* was a big TV show back then." With that in mind, Jan recognized that the rulers and photos on the table did, indeed, show a yearbook layout in progress, as it had been done before the advent of computer programs.

But as she glanced at Virginia, Jan noticed that neither she nor Eleanor had grabbed for their table's white flag. Instead, both women were completely frozen, still staring at the large photo that Betty Lee had propped against the dry-erase board for the moment. Virginia's eyes sparkled as she blinked, fighting tears.

"Mom?" Elaine leaned toward her mother, whispering. "What's wrong?"

Virginia appeared to make an effort to shrug off the moment. "Oh," she said, blinking rapidly, "you know. Memories of yesteryear, when we all were so young, so carefree..."

Elaine patted her hand, looking confused and troubled as her gaze met Jan's.

Beside Virginia, Jan noticed Eleanor Mungo taking deep breaths. Her chin was quivering. The two women's obvious distress seemed an overreaction to the photo. If the threesome were such good friends, why were two of them fighting tears right now, while the third appeared oblivious or unaffected?

As the second round ended, Betty Lee reviewed the team standings. Next, the Final Jeopardy question was revealed. "The Victorian Era," Betty Lee intoned.

While all the teams digested that, she and Ida turned the Jeopardy board around. To everyone's surprise, a large piece of poster board was affixed to the back, which also was canvas-covered and painted like the front. "Ready?" Betty Lee asked as Ida walked through the room distributing one piece of white paper and a marker to each table. "All teams will have thirty seconds, timed by Ida, to write down your wager and your answer on your paper."

Once each team had received its paper and marker, Betty Lee said, "Here we go. I am going to remove this poster board and read the Final Jeopardy answer."

She carefully removed the poster board taped to the back so that she could read the clue beneath it. "The formal term for a means of cryptologic communication through the use or arrangement of flowers and associated plant matter."

There was a hush in the room, quickly filled by whispers as the various teams attempted to talk without their opponents overhearing. Elaine quickly flipped to a clean sheet on a yellow notepad on the table. On it she first wrote, *Anyone have the answer?*

Everyone looked at it, Rae and Roxy leaving their seats to stand behind their mother and Virginia so they could see better. Each of them shook their heads.

Next, Elaine wrote, *Related to language of flowers?*

The Delta Daughters indicated by shrugging or by spreading their hands that they had no idea. Again, Elaine put pen to paper. *Then wager nothing?*

Emphatic nods from the group.

Aware that time was running out, on a clean sheet of paper Elaine wrote down a dollar sign with a large zero behind it. Below, she wrote, *What is the language of flowers?*

Then she turned the paper face down and shrugged, grinning.

A loud phone alarm bell rang, and Betty Lee said, "Drop your pens or else, people!"

Everyone laughed as the few who had still been writing complied.

"All right," Betty Lee said. "Ida, do you want to go around and reveal each wager and answer?"

Ida walked to Mainly Loons' table and picked up their sheet of paper. "Their answer was 'What is fluorography?' She

44

turned around their wager paper, so everyone could see it. "They wagered everything," she said, sounding surprised.

Betty Lee held her impassive façade for a long moment. Finally, she said, "That answer is...incorrect, Loons. I'm sorry. That takes you to zero."

"What?" Jeanice Evanak protested. "I was sure that was the correct term."

Betty Lee shook her head. "I'm sorry." While Jeanice flopped back in her chair with narrowed eyes and a frown, Jan felt her shoulders relax.

"Whew," Jan said. "They could have beaten us if they'd been right and doubled their winnings."

Ladies of the Lake, Moose Tracks, Buncha Bobcats, and several other groups went next. No one, as it turned out, had the correct final answer. Some, like Jan and Elaine's team, had wagered nothing, but others had wagered some or all. Most had left the question blank, having no idea before they ran out of time. They were down to two teams now, just Delta Daughters and The Weekenders.

Thanks to Elaine's streak of winning answers in the Flowery Phrases category, Delta Daughters had amassed a solid point total. Since they had not wagered anything, their points would stand as they were. The Weekenders had somewhat fewer points, but if they had doubled down and bet all their points— and if they gave the correct answer—they could still win.

"Delta Daughters," Betty Lee said, "what was your answer?"

Ida picked up their paper from the table. "*What is the language of flowers?*" she read.

"Hmm." Betty Lee's eyebrows rose. "And what was your wager?"

"Zero" Ida said, flipping the paper over for all to see.

"That is incorrect," Betty Lee said. "And we're down to the final team. Weekenders, what was your answer?"

Ida moved to the last table and confiscated their paper. *"What is floriography?"* she read and proceeded to spell the word, which Betty Lee wrote on the bottom of the dry-erase board.

The room erupted. The Weekenders had wagered all they had and if they were right…

"If they have the right answer, they'll beat us!" Jan exclaimed.

Elaine grinned. "Yep. But wow, hasn't this been fun?"

"I'll tell you after I see if we win or lose." Jan smiled at Elaine's amusement.

Betty Lee silenced the room with an upraised hand. "Weekenders, what is your wager?"

Ida cleared her throat. "Two thousand dollars," she said.

Jan snapped her fingers. "That's right. I've seen it before," she said, just as Betty Lee bellowed, "That's *correct*! Weekenders, you are the Delta Jeopardy Champions. Congratulations!"

Everyone surged to their feet, clapping and cheering, as Betty Lee approached the winning table and distributed a candy bar to each woman. Jan and Elaine applauded with them. "What fun that was," Jan said. "We should remember that in case we ever need something special for the tearoom."

"Do you know how much work it would be to make up all the clues and create a game board?" Elaine demanded.

"Yes, but if we made it to last, we could use it again and again, and all we'd have to do is come up with new clues," Jan argued. Then her face fell. "Your mom didn't seem to enjoy the game very much, did she?"

"No. And neither did Eleanor. At least, not after that picture was revealed."

Jan turned to look at her aunt as Virginia and her friend huddled together in a corner. "That photo really seemed to upset both of them. I wonder why Betty Lee chose it, and if she had any idea it would make them feel bad."

"I think this all started when they received those gifts on their pillows earlier," Elaine said. "I don't think those items were part of a game at all."

"No one's mentioned a word about them being part of something organized for the retreat," Jan pointed out.

"And surely something would have been said by now." Elaine looked perturbed.

"What are the odds that one of the guild members still had the notepad they received at that outing and had used it for this without thinking about it?" Jan wondered. "I think the person who left those gifts is probably in this room with us right now."

Elaine nodded. "I want to know who left those weird notes and what it all means."

CHAPTER FIVE

I'm in," Jan said immediately. The memory of Aunt Virginia trying not to cry wouldn't leave her mind, and she was just as determined as Elaine to get to the bottom of the mystery. As Elaine turned toward her mother, Jan checked the time. Almost eight thirty. Perfect. She was right on time to meet Bob.

Leaving the dining room, she walked into the lobby. The gifts were still on her mind, and as she saw the registration desk to her left, she realized she had an opportunity to learn something more about them. Perhaps.

Approaching the desk, she said, "Hello. May I ask you a question?"

The clerk was one she hadn't seen before, a very young-looking blonde with red-framed glasses and her hair twisted up behind her head in a messy bun. "Certainly. How may I help you?"

"I was wondering if you knew who was permitted access to several guest rooms during the dinner hour. A couple of retreat attendees found gifts left on their pillows, but we don't know who they were from."

The clerk looked blank and then she frowned. "I'm not aware of anything being left in the guests' rooms, ma'am. We often have retreat groups here and we encourage them to leave little bags or gifts on the doorknobs rather than entering guests' rooms. That would be a departure from our usual policy." She brightened. "But Heloise, our manager, could tell you more. She left a little while ago, but she'll be back in tomorrow. Maybe she authorized something and forgot to mention it to me."

"Thank you for your help," Jan said. "I'll talk to Heloise tomorrow."

Turning from the desk, she then hurried up the stairs to the room she shared with Sasha to grab her coat. Her three suitemates still were chatting with others and hadn't even left the dining area yet. Just in case, she checked the pillows in both rooms, but there was nothing out of the ordinary to be seen.

After slipping on her peacoat and grabbing a scarf, she headed back downstairs. Her timing was perfect. Bob was walking toward the hotel just as she exited.

"Hey there!" he called.

She hurried toward him, eager to be back in his arms. He didn't disappoint, and they shared a long hug and kiss before he enfolded her in the warmth of his arm and drew her away from the hotel along the sidewalk.

"How's your retreat?" he asked. "Off to a nice start?"

"Oh, we just played an amazing game of Jeopardy." She went on to describe the fun the group had had in the dining room.

They chatted about personal things, content simply to be in each other's company again as they crossed the road and strolled along a moonlit lakeside path in the crisp night air.

Jan told him about the odd "gift" that had been left on Virginia's pillow and those of several of her friends. No new insights came to her in the retelling.

Bob said, "That does sound strange. And you're sure they're not a part of some game?"

"Everyone's been asking that, and there's been no reaction at all from anyone in charge. You know, if it was something planned as part of the retreat, I'd have thought there might be some 'Wait and see's' or some amused winking. But nothing. I'm inclined to think it was not done as a part of the retreat program."

Before she could say more, her cell phone rang. Pulling it from her pocket, she absentmindedly thumbed it on to receive the call without checking the screen. "Hold on a sec," she said to Bob, assuming it was probably Elaine with a question of some sort. "Hello?"

"Jan, hello. How are you?"

To her consternation, she recognized the voice of Clifton Young, Rose's father and a man with whom she'd gone to lunch recently, purely on a platonic basis—at least on her part.

She cleared her throat, trying to unobtrusively lower the volume switch on her phone. It sounded to her like Clifton's voice was booming out of the little device. "I'm, uh, fine, thank you. How are you?"

"Good. I was hoping you could get away from your duties tomorrow afternoon. I thought maybe we could take a little stroll."

It was just too ironic that she was doing exactly that now with Bob. It had never occurred to her that she would be speaking with Clifton this weekend, but she realized she needed to let him know her heart was already spoken for.

And she hadn't even told Bob about Clifton yet. Granted, she and Clifton had only had a single lunch out together, but she felt she had to mention it at some point. Bob wouldn't mind, she was certain, but she would rather he knew she'd gone out with Clifton.

"That would probably work, but I'm a little tied up right now," she said to Clifton. "May I return your call in twenty or thirty minutes and we can discuss it?"

"Sure thing. I'll look forward to it," Clifton said in a warm tone. "Bye."

"Goodbye." Jan closed her eyes momentarily as she returned the phone to her pocket.

"It's an odd time for a business call. Vendor troubles?" Bob asked Jan.

"Not exactly," she said uncomfortably. She didn't want to lie, but she needed to formulate her thoughts carefully when she told Bob about Clifton. She'd be tempted to simply never tell him, but she was too afraid a chance comment from someone might alert him to the fact that she'd been seen with another man in his absence, and she wouldn't want there to be any misunderstanding between them. Especially now, when she sensed—or perhaps she only hoped—that they might be drawing closer to discussing their future together. Now that he was back in Lancaster to stay, she knew that if he asked her again to marry him, she'd say yes without a single reservation.

Stop daydreaming like a teenager, she admonished herself. Bob's words made her think of Elaine's tea problem, though, and she shifted the subject in that direction. "But we did have a major glitch this week that still hasn't been resolved."

"What happened?"

She explained the problem with Elaine's order of the Friendship and Memories tea that had yet to arrive. "So Archie's going to have to scrounge through our inventory and bring a variety of substitutes over here if we can't track down that shipment."

Bob made a face. "That's unfortunate."

The walk concluded a short time later. As they stood holding hands on the front porch, Bob said, "I find I'm reluctant to go a day without seeing you. Shall we do this again tomorrow evening?"

"That would be lovely. It'll get me through the day."

"So will this," Bob said, smiling as he drew her close and lowered his head.

After sharing one final kiss, Jan pulled open the lobby door, smiling at him over her shoulder. "See you tomorrow evening."

ELAINE SPENT A pleasant hour after the Jeopardy game chatting with her mother, her daughter, Eleanor, and several other women in a small library near the reception lounge. She envied Jan her time with Bob, but she hadn't wanted to take time away from Sasha this weekend, and Nathan hadn't suggested it. Spending this time with her daughter was a wonderful—and rare—treat.

Shortly before nine thirty, she and Sasha said good night and made their way upstairs, while Virginia remained behind for a while longer. Several of the women she was visiting with had traveled from some distance away, and she didn't see them regularly as she did many of her other friends.

Sasha went straight to her room to lay out her running clothes for the morning and get ready for bed, while Elaine headed into the room she shared with her mother. After changing into warm pajamas and a robe, she completed her bedtime ablutions and then took a seat in the overstuffed chair in one corner. She had promised to call Nathan this evening, and she was looking forward to hearing his voice.

Before making the call, she checked her e-mail from her phone and then quickly pulled up his number and hit the call button.

"Hello, pretty lady." Nathan's voice was tender and affectionate. "How's everything going there? I sure miss you."

"And I miss you." Elaine smiled. "Although Mom is so thrilled to have me, Sasha, and Jan here with her that I'm glad we all made time for it. And it's fantastic for me to have this time with them all. I wish I'd thought of it before."

"I can imagine. I've never stayed at the Whisperwood. Is it nice?"

"It's charming," Elaine said decisively. "Maybe a little faded around the edges and not quite as glamorous as it once was. But still lovely. The hotel doesn't get the tourist trade it used to. Everyone wants condos and cottages now."

"That's too bad. I always thought it would be a great place for a party."

"It would be. The dining room is a very nice space, as is the conference area."

"Where will you be holding your tea presentation?"

"In the dining room. Speaking of which, I told you about my missing tea, didn't I?"

"Yes. You mean it still hasn't shown up?" Nathan sounded surprised. "I figured there was a shipping delay or something, but I assumed it would get there on time."

"No," Elaine said. "I just read an e-mail update from the company. According to them, it was definitely delivered on time—but they may have delivered it to the wrong address. They said it could have been a zip code error, so heaven only knows where my tea is now."

"And that doesn't really help you, does it?"

"Not one little bit. They're trying to track it down now. Well," she amended, "probably not right now, but they assured me they would check into it first thing tomorrow morning. They're supposed to let me know immediately when they've found it."

Nathan chuckled. "I hope it's quickly fixed. When did you say you needed it? Sunday morning?"

"Yes. For a presentation Jan and I are doing on tea traditions in the Victorian era."

Chatting for a short while, she told him about the evening's events. "The Jeopardy game was amazing," she told him after she'd explained it. "Jan has it in her head that we should make one for the tearoom. I guess that means we would have to create a special event geared around the game."

"Maybe you could borrow the board your friend made," Nathan suggested. "I can't imagine that there's a pressing need for those."

"That's a good idea," Elaine said. "And Betty Lee doesn't live too far from my mother, so it would be easy to pick up and return it. I'll ask her about it in the morning. Tomorrow, we have a number of different workshops and presentations on Victorian life. I'm really looking forward to them."

"Maybe you'll find some new inspiration for the tearoom," Nathan suggested.

"I hope so," she said. "The customers always seem to love it when we give them more Victoriana."

"Speaking of Victoriana, I saw a lot of teacups and things at an estate sale outside of Waterville coming up next week. Is there anything you want me to look for?"

"Ooh." Elaine thought for a moment. "We could use some new cups and saucers if they don't go too high," she said. Nathan, she felt confident, could be trusted to know what might work for Tea for Two.

"How's Sasha? I bet it's wonderful to see her."

"She's doing great." Elaine related the report of Sasha's recent gold medal and her standings.

"It was nice seeing her at Christmas," Nathan said. "I knew this would be a girls' weekend, but I look forward to getting to know her better one of these days."

After another few minutes, Elaine blew him a kiss over the phone. "I'm sorry we couldn't get together this weekend."

"Me too. I decided that since I couldn't see you, I'd drive up to Presque Isle tomorrow and hit two estate sales that are going on."

"That's quite a hike," Elaine said. "Be careful."

"I may stay the night and drive back Sunday so I don't have to make an eight-hour round trip in one day," he told her.

"That would be exhausting," Elaine agreed, "and you'd probably be doing most of the drive back in the dark, so I am fully in favor of you spending the night. The last thing you need is a close encounter with a moose on a dark road."

Nathan chuckled. "True. Even a white-tail can total a car." There was a short silence. "Can I come by Sunday evening after you get back? I miss you."

"I miss you too. I'd like that very much." She was smiling. "Have a safe trip."

As they said their goodbyes and she ended the call, Elaine reflected on how very fortunate she was. She had been loved by a wonderful man with whom she'd had two lovely children, and now, after suffering one of the worst heartbreaks she could imagine, she had been lucky enough to find love again.

"Hey, Mom?"

Elaine glanced up to see Sasha hesitating in the doorway.

"Come on in," she said.

"I didn't want to interrupt your time with Nathan," Sasha said. "How's he doing?"

"Great. He's headed for a couple of estate sales this weekend." Elaine pointed to her bed, a short distance from the chair. "Feel free."

Sasha came into the room and flopped on her belly across Elaine's bed, her legs bent at the knees with her stockinged feet in the air. "Can I ask a question without upsetting you?"

Elaine was taken aback. "Of course." Was she easy to upset?

"I just didn't know…do you ever think of Dad anymore?"

Elaine softened immediately in the face of her daughter's melancholy question. Now she understood. "Oh, honey, probably more than you can imagine. We spent over three decades together, and because of the nature of his job and the way we moved around, we were each other's best friends. Sure, we made friends wherever we went, and we always had family connections, but he was my go-to for everything important. I was terribly lonely for a while."

"I've been thinking of him a lot recently," Sasha confessed. "I keep wondering if I'll ever meet a guy as wonderful as he was."

"I'm sure there's one out there for you," Elaine said. She shook a fierce finger at her daughter. "And don't you dare settle for less. Are you worrying about it?"

Sasha shrugged. "A little. I know I'm only twenty-six, but it seems like most of my high school and college friends are married or have found *the one*. Even some of my competitors are married, although it seems to me that would be incredibly stressful."

Elaine smiled. "With the right person, I imagine it can be done. But it would take a lot of compromise."

"I had a good laugh at myself," Sasha confessed, "when I realized I was comparing myself to you. I mean, you loved Dad, and now you seem to have found a second wonderful guy. How come there are none my age hanging around?"

The question was self-mocking, and Elaine had to laugh. "I certainly wasn't expecting a new man to enter my life," she said. "And actually, Nathan isn't really new. I've known him since I was a child."

"He seems like a great guy," Sasha said. "I really liked him the times I've met him. Maybe you could even bring him along if you come out to Colorado to visit."

"You wouldn't mind?" Elaine asked.

"Absolutely not," Sasha said.

After a few more minutes of chatting, Sasha slid off the bed and kissed Elaine's cheek. "See you in the morning, Mom. I'm going out for a run at five."

"Five," Elaine groaned. "I'll see you when you get back. I might be up by then." She grinned as her daughter left the room and then picked up the inspirational mystery she'd been reading before bed the past several evenings.

A short time later, she heard Jan come in from her walk with Bob. Her cousin stuck her head around the corner and said hello before taking herself off to get ready for bed.

Elaine continued to read for a few minutes more. Finally, she rose and set her book aside. She walked between the beds to plug in her phone before she would slide beneath the covers.

"Ouch!" Her exclamation echoed around the room.

"What happened?" The door of Jan and Sasha's room opened a moment later, and the pair peered through the connecting door at her.

"I stepped on something." Elaine leaned down and patted around on the carpet near the bed. A small, hard edge poked her hand, and she cautiously closed her fingers around the object. "It's a...it's a fingernail," she said, slightly disgusted. "A tip that someone lost, I guess."

Jan advanced into the room, peering at the fake nail that Elaine held up to the light. "It's a French tip. Does Aunt

58

Virginia wear French tips?" She referred to the natural color of the nail, tipped with a white half moon.

"Grandma doesn't wear polish," Sasha volunteered. "Me neither."

"I'm not wearing any right now either," Elaine murmured, "so all four of us are out. Maybe the last person to occupy the room left it."

"But they vacuum," Sasha objected. "Surely they'd have gotten something like a nail."

Elaine chuckled. "I imagine the vacuuming is more of 'a lick and a promise' than serious cleaning. Hotel cleaning staff are usually pressed for time."

"Still," Jan said. "What if it was left here *after* the house-keeper cleaned?"

Elaine got the point immediately. "Oh. You mean what if the person who left the gift on Mom's pillow is the one who lost the nail. That would be quite a windfall, wouldn't it? We might be able to figure out who did it."

"At least half the women at this retreat have beautifully manicured hands," Sasha said. She held up her own hands with the nails filed short and utilitarian for her skiing and shooting endeavors for the biathlon. "I've been feeling a little self-conscious, to tell the truth."

Jan and Elaine both chuckled, but then Elaine sighed. "You're right. There are a lot of women here with gorgeous nails."

"Still," Jan persisted, "they can't all have French tips."

"Oh, they don't," Sasha assured her. "A lot of them have polish or gel on, and I even saw two with those nail wraps that are becoming popular."

"How do you even know the difference between polish and gel?" Jan wondered.

Sasha laughed. "I've gotten my nails done to be in a couple of weddings. Trust me, I can spot them."

"So we should be able to narrow it down," Elaine said slowly. "How many do you think might be wearing French tips? We'd have to look to see who's missing one."

"I would think that's doable," Jan said. "There are what, eighty to ninety women here?"

"There were eleven dining tables, counting ours," Elaine said. "Remember? There were eleven Jeopardy teams. And eight seats around each table, so that's eighty-eight people, if all the tables are full."

"Surely there can't be more than a dozen women out of ninety-ish, if that many, wearing French tips."

"And maybe fewer than that," Sasha said. "Am I invited to help sleuth? I'm a little annoyed that someone put a damper on Grandma's weekend with that little mystery gift, if you want the truth. She seemed really bummed."

"She did seem upset, didn't she?" Elaine asked. "Thankfully, she appears to have put it behind her."

The other two nodded.

"That photo near the end of Jeopardy didn't help, though," Sasha said. "For some reason, Grandma was near tears after she saw that picture."

"Eleanor was disturbed too," Elaine noted.

Jan nodded. "I wonder who the fourth girl was," she said. "No one mentioned her name."

"What fourth girl?" Sasha asked.

CHAPTER SIX

"There was a girl in the background looking over their shoulders," Elaine said thoughtfully. "You're right. I almost forgot that. No one said a thing about her."

"Maybe she was incidental to the picture," Sasha said. "Seems like if she was important she'd have been included in the clue. Besides, have you ever seen a candid yearbook picture that didn't have extra people in the background?"

Jan and Elaine both chuckled.

"Back to this," Elaine said, holding the nail aloft. "It could be meaningless. But if there's a chance it was left behind by whoever delivered that gift, I'm all for tracking the person down."

"I'm in," Jan said. "I'll start checking manicures tomorrow."

"Me too." Sasha grinned. "I feel like a detective."

A key scraping in the lock made them all look up as Virginia entered the room.

"Are we having a slumber party?" she asked, her eyes twinkling.

"This whole weekend feels like a slumber party," Sasha told her.

"Hi, Mom," Elaine said. "Are you having fun seeing all your friends?"

Virginia looked a little less stressed than she had earlier. "It's nice to see everyone," she said, "especially those who don't live close anymore. Normally, we only get together with the out-of-the-area folks at class reunions, so this is a rare treat."

Elaine held up the nail tip she had found. "I stepped on this a few moments ago."

Virginia made a pained face. "I bet that hurt. It's a fake fingernail, right?"

Elaine glanced at her mother's hands. Virginia had long, elegant fingers, but she rarely painted her nails, and Elaine was certain she'd never had tips applied in her life. "It is."

"That's odd. I suppose the housekeeper missed it." Virginia did not appear to connect the tip with the gift that had been left on her pillow.

Elaine cleared her throat. "That's certainly possible. But we were thinking that there's an outside chance that the person who left the note and gift on your pillow could have lost this nail."

Virginia's elegantly filled-in eyebrows rose. "I suppose you could be right." She walked across the room to examine the nail more carefully. "It's a French tip." Her eyes sharpened. "There can't be many people here with French tips, and of that number, surely there can't be more than one or two with a broken one. Maybe we can figure out who came into this room."

"That's our hope," Elaine said.

"Are you going to join our little detective agency, Grandma?" Sasha asked. She grinned. "I can't wait for tomorrow so I can start checking out people's fingernails."

"I can't wait either," Virginia said, but her face was perfectly serious. "I'd really like to know who left these notes and what they're supposed to mean."

THE FOUR OF them were ready for breakfast at eight the next morning. As Sasha had indicated, she'd gotten up to run at five. By the time she returned, the others had arisen and were in the process of preparing for the day.

They were among the first people to enter the dining room. The sessions started at nine, and Virginia wanted to have plenty of time to linger over coffee beforehand.

The foursome set down their handbags at their assigned table and headed straight for the made-to-order omelet station as other retreat attendees began to trickle into the room. From the omelet station, the buffet line extended along both sides of a long set of white cloth-covered tables, upon which were set a number of double and triple stainless-steel server warmers.

In addition to the omelets, there was a plethora of offerings to suit every palate: crisp bacon and mini sausages, scrambled eggs, toast and English muffins with pressed-butter patties on ice, pancakes, french toast, fresh fruit, and even cold cereals for those who preferred a simpler meal. Guests who so chose could go to yet another station to toast their own bagels and spread them with cream cheese, butter, or a variety of jellies.

Jan and Elaine headed along the left branch of the buffet after they got their omelets, while Sasha and Virginia moved along the right side.

As the cousins browsed the offerings, Babette Parture hurried up behind them. Her lacquered hair did not appear to have moved a single inch since the night before. Jan's own hair usually looked like a wild bush first thing in the morning, and she was tempted to ask Babette how she managed to keep her hairstyle in place, but the woman forestalled her. "I fished that note I got out of the trash can," she told the cousins, extending a small pink piece of paper toward them. "You said you wanted to see it, so here you go."

Elaine took the note, reading it aloud to Jan. "*You're in too deep, but you can make it to safety.*"

"Ugh," Babette said. "That sounds unkind, doesn't it? I don't care if it is a game clue. I don't want it. You two can keep it." And she moved off to join the line for the omelet station.

As the blonde woman departed, Elaine looked at Jan. "So Mom's not the only one who feels these notes aren't particularly friendly."

From the other side of the buffet, Virginia asked, "What did hers say?"

Elaine read it again. Virginia made a grimace of distaste, and Sasha shook her head. "You're right. There's something...not very nice about it," she said.

Jan took another look at the wording on the note Babette had received. "It almost sounds like a veiled threat, doesn't it? But...a threat to get the recipient to do what? Or to keep her from doing something? Nobody who received these appears to have any idea what they're about."

Virginia moved forward as the person ahead of her left the line, effectively moving out of earshot, while Sasha followed.

"I'm not so sure about that," Elaine said quietly to Jan, watching her mother. "Did you notice Mom and Eleanor looking at each other last night? I think they may have some notion what these notes refer to."

"Although the 'gifts' seem to have all of us puzzled," Jan noted.

"And did you realize the all notes we've seen so far have to do with water?" Elaine folded the note and placed it in her bag with the one her mother had received. Using her fingers to tick them off, she said, "'Out of your depth,' 'in over your head,' and 'in too deep.'

"You're right." Jan stopped dead, looking back at Elaine. "We still need to find out what Kinley's note said," she reminded her cousin. "I can almost promise you it uses the same kind of water-themed expression."

"I thought the same thing." Elaine picked up her plate, veered around Jan, and headed for the hot drinks. "Since we're on vacation, I'm going to have a hit of the coffee," she said, leaving Jan smiling as she took her own plate and went to get orange juice. Although she was in the business of serving tea, Elaine did love her coffee, especially espresso.

After breakfast, the first morning session was conducted right there in the dining room, because it was literally a work session, and they needed the space.

One of the guild members owned a string of flower shops down in Boston. She had been tapped to present a workshop on the language of flowers, which they all knew was floriography, thanks to last night's Jeopardy.

As the cousins also knew, making little nosegays called tussie-mussies had been quite the thing in Victorian England.

And also thanks to last night's Jeopardy, everyone was game to learn.

"Meaning has been assigned to flowers for thousands of years," the presenter began. "There are records of flowers being used to send messages in Persia and the Middle East, but the practice really came into its own during Queen Victoria's reign in England between 1837 and 1901. One of the chief reasons for this was the strict etiquette that came into prominence during the Victorian period. Particularly in the upper classes, where young ladies were shielded from nearly every realistic aspect of life, social conventions and outright rules prohibited certain questions, comments, and flirtatious conversation between the sexes. As you can imagine, secret messages sent using flowers to convey the meaning became exceptionally popular."

The presenter went on to discuss some of the most popular sentiments. "The earliest flower dictionary I have been able to find dates back to 1819, and it includes not only the meanings of one hundred different plants and flowers but also stresses the etiquette involved in certain situations, governing what types of flowers were appropriate to send for what occasions."

After the brief history lesson, the presenter brought out several completed flower arrangements, towering things in tall, sometimes ornate vases using pearl or ribbon accents along with masses of flowers. "As you can see," she said, "the Victorians were not fond of subtlety. Gigantic arrangements even larger than these representations were a standard feature in most upper-class Victorian homes, varying to showcase the seasons, of course. The wealthiest of those had elaborate greenhouses in which a wide variety of plants were grown so that there would never be a paucity of fresh blooms." She pressed a hand to her heart. "Oh, how gauche one would be considered if one didn't have masses of fresh flowers for one's ballroom."

The group gave an appreciative chuckle.

At the conclusion of her remarks, the speaker gave each participant a copied sheet with the meanings of selected flowers and herbs on it. A large box at each table held silk flowers and leaves, wire cutters, floral tape, a variety of precut pretty ribbon, paper doilies, and other supplies.

"First," the woman told the group, "choose a message using the meanings of flowers on your sheet. Then select the flowers you want to convey that message. Two to four is all you want. Although the Victorians often got quite eloquent with their unspoken language, our goals are somewhat more modest. Cut each bloom to about a six-inch length. Then gather them together in one hand and bind them with floral tape. Once you've done that, move on to the second step, which is to surround your base blooms with filler plants like herbs and ivy. Then you're going to use your tape again to bind the nosegay together.

"The next step is to set your flowers aside and pick up your doily. Mark an X in the center, cut a hole, and insert your flowers through it, and secure the base with floral tape. Then tie ribbon around the stems and voilà! You've got a lovely tussie-mussie. Stick it in a bowl or vase in the middle of your table for a centerpiece or place it on your guest room vanity or dresser. I've even seen them used as curtain tiebacks for a lovely, Victorian-themed decorating look. Or you can always give it to a special someone. If you wish to do that, there are index cards and colored pencils in the baskets with hole punches. You can tie one of those to your ribbon with the meanings on it if you wish."

As everyone got to work, the noise level in the room rose by several decibels, making conversation difficult.

"What's yours going to say?" Jan asked Elaine, who was seated right beside her.

Elaine smiled. "I'm going to make one for Nathan with a yellow rose and forget-me-not. And maybe ivy for the surrounding plant matter. That would mean"—she consulted the list—"'I treasure our friendship and I love you truly,' basically."

"Very nice," Jan approved.

"Who's yours for?"

Jan grinned. "Bob, I guess. I'm using this purpley-red zinnia and white violets. It'll mean 'lasting affection' and 'let's take a chance on happiness.' And I'll use maidenhair fern for my filler, which indicates a secret bond of love."

Betty Lee was seated on Jan's other side. As they completed their tussie-mussies and began to write the information about their flowers on the index cards, the music director picked up her large handbag and began to rummage through it. "I'd rather use a pastel than those plain old white cards," she muttered.

Finally, she appeared to find what she was looking for. Withdrawing a small notepad from her handbag, she tore out a sheet of paper. Pink paper.

Jan was astonished. Surely this was one of the notepads the women had spoken of earlier. "Is that...?" She pointed at the small pad of paper.

Betty Lee followed the direction of her gaze. "Oh," she said. Her cheeks turned bright pink. "Yes, this is the notepad we were talking about earlier. Some of them had different images on the front, but they all were the same size, and they all had pink paper. I keep it in my 'spring' handbag, which is why it's lasted so long."

It was a plausible explanation. But Jan couldn't help wondering how many other people would still have those notepads and would have brought them to the retreat. If Betty Lee was the one who'd penned those notes, she was exceedingly clumsy about covering her tracks.

As the session concluded, everyone helped clear away the remnants of the project, and some of the women took advantage of the break to carry their tussie-mussies to their rooms.

Jan hurried to catch up with Elaine, Sasha, and Virginia. "Did you see that?" she hissed in her cousin's ear.

"See what?"

As they headed to their rooms to drop off the flowers, Jan caught Elaine's elbow, holding her back a pace while she explained what she'd just seen.

"I missed it entirely," Elaine said. "I can't believe if she was the one who wrote the notes that she'd yank that notepad right out of her purse in plain sight, especially after we'd just talked about it earlier."

"I know. On the other hand, it could be the perfect cover. 'We all have these, and here's mine.' Although she looked pretty chagrined when she realized what she'd done."

"Maybe." But Elaine sounded doubtful. "But Betty Lee seemed quite put out that she didn't receive one of those notes."

"Smoke screen?"

"Maybe." Elaine broke off the conversation as she moved to the door her mother was holding open. Jan realized that while Virginia seemed to be determined to find out who had left the notes, she might not be prepared to consider one of her nearest and dearest friends among the suspects, so she held her tongue for the time being. She entered her own room behind Sasha and laid her tussie-mussie on the dresser before following the rest of her family back downstairs.

ELAINE WAS HEADING to the drink station to refill her coffee when Kinley Devore caught at her elbow.

"Hey, did you want to see that note I got? I'm headed upstairs to drop this nosegay off. If you want to walk along, you can read it."

"I'd love to." Quickly topping off her coffee, Elaine then replaced the lid of her insulated drink tumbler and walked up the stairs with Kinley. So what if she'd just come back down? The exercise couldn't hurt.

Kinley's room was one floor up from Elaine's, and when they entered, she said, "I apologize in advance. I'm sort of messy. I don't have a roommate because I don't expect anyone to tolerate me getting up at 5 a.m. for my morning run, so I'm not as good as I should be about picking up."

"My daughter ran at five this morning too," Elaine said. "Maybe you two could run together tomorrow."

"No way," Kinley said. "I talked to her when I heard she was a runner. I'm a leisurely sort of girl, not a warrior. She'd have to drag me along at the pace I'm sure she sets."

Chuckling, Elaine walked into the room behind Kinley. Even with the warning, she was unprepared for the tornado that apparently had thrown all of the room's contents up in the air and let them fall where they would.

A running shoe lay on its side in the middle of a pillow. The rest of the bed was barely visible beneath a liberal layer of discarded clothing, and papers from the retreat packet and what looked to be the contents of an entire extra purse covered the top of the desk and dresser. Elaine shrugged mentally. It wasn't her style, but if it didn't bother Kinley, it didn't really matter.

"I know I laid it right here somewhere." Kinley tossed her tussie-mussie atop the clothing on the bed. She stepped over her empty suitcase, open in the middle of the floor, and surveyed the littered desk. "Ah, I knew it. Here you go." She snatched up a wadded piece of pink paper and tossed it to Elaine. "I found it mildly offensive or something," she said, waving a hand at the note. "I can't really tell you why, but it didn't give me warm fuzzies." She stopped and turned to face Elaine. "And I don't think it has anything to do with any party game either."

"Holding your breath and waiting for the right time is never productive." Elaine surveyed the note. "What could it mean?"

Kinley frowned. "I don't know. I sort of felt as if it was an insinuation that I'm not hardworking, which I find really insulting." She patted her svelte hip. "I mean, I run almost every day to keep this figure, you know? The whole thing is just really strange."

Elaine took out her phone. Smoothing the little note as flat as she could, she laid it on the bed. Before she could photograph it, though, Kinley waved her arm. "Oh, go ahead and take it. What am I going to do with it?"

She had a point. Elaine placed the note in her handbag with the others she had kept, and the pair headed back downstairs again for the second session.

As she descended the stairs, Elaine saw Jan waving to her from a corner of the lobby, where she stood with Virginia and Sasha.

"Hi," she said when Elaine joined them. "Did I see you with Kinley?"

"You did, and I got her note," Elaine said. Although she didn't pull the note out, aware that there were a lot of women in groups around them, she quietly related its contents to the others.

"Another water reference," Jan said immediately.

"They all were, right?" Sasha asked. "That's got to mean something."

Jan nodded. "Eleanor's note said something about being in over your head."

"Mine talked about being out of my depth," Virginia added.

"And finding your footing," Elaine reminded her.

"Babette was in too deep, and now Kinley has this one about holding your breath. Whoever is sending these must have some reason for including water sayings in the notes."

"But the gifts aren't water-themed," Jan said. "Don't you find that odd? I can't see any pattern in those gifts."

Elaine raised her eyebrows. "You're right. The postcard was a downtown scene. It had nothing to do with water. Nor did Mom's two-dollar bill."

"And Kinley got a race brochure and Babette's was that speed limit sign. Absolutely no way those had anything to do with water. It doesn't make any sense."

"What could they mean?" Virginia asked. Her expression was puzzled, but Elaine thought she seemed upset again as well.

"And more importantly," Sasha said, "what do they have to do with those notes that all mention water?"

"Are we certain no one else got one?" Elaine asked.

"No one else has said anything," Sasha said. "At least, not that I've overheard. And I would think after hearing Kinley and Babette talking about it at the reception last night, that if anyone else had received one, they'd have mentioned it."

"So four notes, all referencing water," Jan summarized. "Any idea what that could mean, Aunt Virginia?"

Elaine's mother shook her head slightly. "No," she said, but Elaine noticed that her mother averted her eyes when she spoke. She pressed her fingers nervously over her lips after she uttered the single quiet syllable. Was there something she wasn't saying?

A bell rang, signaling to the group that the second session would soon be starting. Everyone filed into the large conference room where they had held the reception last night. Today, the chairs were arranged in rows with an aisle down the center.

To Elaine's surprise, a familiar face sat at one side of the podium. The club's president stood and tapped the microphone, and the room quieted.

"Good morning again," she said. "I'm glad you all enjoyed making your tussie-mussies. Now I'd like to introduce Priscilla Gates, who will be talking to us about Victorian-era poetry. Priscilla is the librarian at the Lancaster Public Library. Welcome, Priscilla."

The cousins' hometown friend rose. She looked slim and attractive in a navy-blue pencil skirt and a rose twinset. "Good morning, everyone. Thank you for inviting me to speak. Victorian poetry is a self-defining literary form in one sense: all of it was written during the reign of Queen Victoria of England between 1837 and 1901. Tennyson, the Brontës and the Brownings, Lewis Carroll, Oscar Wilde, Charles Dickens…the Victorian era gave us some of our most beloved writers and poets. Before the reign of Victoria, there were very few well-known female poets. But during these years, a number of women joined the ranks of acclaimed British poets."

Elaine very much enjoyed the rest of Priscilla's talk, which focused on the female poets of the time.

In keeping with Priscilla's presentation, a woman in the room rose and recited a poem by Victorian poet Christina Rossetti, titled "One Sea-Side Grave."

At the conclusion of the reading, someone began vigorously clapping. A few more people sporadically joined in as everyone turned to see who had begun to applause. Heloise Invers, the hotel manager, stood in the doorway of the room, smacking her palms together for all she was worth. As the clapping died away, she finally stopped, laying a hand theatrically over her heart. "That is one of my very favorite pieces of poetry in the whole world!"

Elaine noticed one woman roll her eyes at the person sitting beside her. The friend appeared to agree with her, biting back a grin. While Elaine realized that Heloise's enthusiasm was a little overdone, she thought the other women could have been kinder. It didn't escape Elaine that Heloise was standing in the doorway rather than having taken a seat in the room. It was obvious that the woman desperately wanted to be a part of the group even now, so long after their high school years.

Clearing her throat, Priscilla took control of the room again, and went on to discuss the themes of mourning, death, remembrance, and love that populated many of the author's other poems. Then she moved on to share some information about the life of Elizabeth Barrett Browning, concluding the section with another guild member offering a reading of Browning's "A Musical Instrument," in which the poet used Pan, the Greek god of shepherds, to illustrate the duality of art.

If she was honest, Elaine felt that section of the talk was a little deep, and the audience appeared to be more befuddled than dazzled by the analysis. Fortunately, Priscilla seemed to realize she'd lost them and moved on quickly to the Brontë sisters: Anne, Emily, and Charlotte.

The trio had acquired the nickname "the Romantic Rebels" in the lexicon of literature for their continued use of Romanticism, which was passing out of fashion in favor of Classicism during the Victorian Age. The talk then moved on to a reading of Emily Brontë's "Often Rebuked, Yet Always Back Returning," a poem in five stanzas, and concluded with a final few thoughts from Priscilla. Elaine and Jan applauded enthusiastically, as did the rest of the attendees, when the librarian finished her presentation. Priscilla smiled and acknowledged the praise.

At the conclusion of the talk, Elaine and Jan made their way to Priscilla at the front of the room to congratulate her on a job well done. Afterward, they wandered toward the lobby.

"Shall we give Rose and Archie a call and make sure everything is going all right?" Jan asked.

Elaine chuckled. "You read my mind. I'm sure they have business under control, but I'll feel better if I know for sure."

Jan laughed, withdrawing her phone from her pocket. "Me too." The cousins moved to a quiet corner. Jan hit the button to dial the number and put her phone on speaker.

"Tea for Two, Archie speaking. How may I be of service?"

"Oh!" Jan exclaimed. "You should always answer our phone. Your accent alone invokes the idea of teatime."

"Hello, Jan," Archie said, laughing. "Having a good time?"

"We are!" she exclaimed. "Elaine's here too."

"Hi, Archie," Elaine said. "How's business today?"

"Brisk and happy," Archie said. "The patrons have loved Rose's macarons paired with that Marshmallow Macaron herbal tea you ordered."

"Wonderful," Elaine said, pleased by the report.

"Any news on your missing tea order?"

"Not yet," Elaine said. "I'm still working on it." Just then, she put a startled hand to her pocket, withdrew her own cell phone, and waved it at Jan. "I'm getting a call," she announced. "Perhaps it's about the tea. I'll talk to you soon, Archie. Thanks for holding down the fort." And leaving Jan to conclude the call, she withdrew.

CHAPTER SEVEN

Moving between groups of chattering women, Elaine stepped outside onto the front porch of the hotel. The air was brisk but fresh, and the sun shone, promising to warm it even more over the next few hours.

"Hello?" she said, raising the phone to her ear.

"Hello, Ms. Cook. This is Joanie from B&B Teas returning your call."

Elaine waited expectantly. B&B Teas was the company from whom she had ordered the Friendship and Memories tea she needed for tomorrow. She'd spoken several times with Joanie in their customer service department. "Hi, Joanie. Do you have good news for me?"

"We've located your shipment," the woman on the other end of the call said, a note of relief clearly evident.

"Wonderful," Elaine said. "Where is it?"

"It was mistakenly delivered to a tearoom in Bangor," Joanie told her.

"Oh. That's good, I guess. Bangor's only an hour away, more or less." Elaine felt her spirits rising.

"Yes. We can pick it up and get it delivered to you first thing on Monday, and we also will be happy to refund all shipping charges on this order."

Elaine was silent for a moment.

"Ms. Cook?"

"That doesn't help me," Elaine told her. "As I explained in my message, I specifically ordered that tea for an event that will occur tomorrow. Monday will be too late."

"I understand." Joanie sounded truly regretful. "Unfortunately, we simply don't have the ability to make delivery happen today. If you wish to cancel the order, we can refund your money in full. I apologize again for the mix-up."

"No one's perfect," Elaine said. "Mix-ups happen. I appreciate your offer of a refund." She exhaled heavily. Tea grew stale if it was left too long, and teas also tended to absorb odors, so she often tried hard to use most of her orders before placing too many new ones. Additionally, a major order had been delayed and now would be coming in Monday, so their stock was lower than normal. She knew she didn't have enough of a single brand of any one tea to offer eighty to ninety women. They'd simply have to grab whatever was available at Tea for Two. And beyond the appropriate name, she knew that the tea itself was delicious, and she could only guess at what the ingredients or proportions might be that gave it its unique flavor.

That would present a major problem, to her way of thinking. She had tailored much of her presentation to the ideas of friendship and memories found in the title of the tea. Her talk would lose a lot of impact and make much less sense if their audience was just drinking any old tea they happened to be able to serve. Unless…

"If I were able to find someone to pick it up, would you still forgo the shipping charges?" she asked Joanie.

"Absolutely. I hate for you to go to that trouble, but I understand that you need it quickly. And we still will offer you the refund, since the error was ours."

Elaine didn't point out that the order had been placed over two weeks ago. "All right," she said. "Let me see what I can do. Do you have the address and phone number of the place in Bangor?" Quickly, she put her phone on speaker and opened up her notes app so she could jot down the address.

"I'll call them and let them know they may be hearing from you," Joanie said. "Again, please accept my deepest apologies."

Returning to the lobby, Elaine found that everyone had already moved to the dining room for the lunch buffet. She quickly headed in that direction. Unfortunately, her table already had been called, she saw, and they were nearly at the buffet. She would have felt rude going to join them, so she simply tacked herself on to the end of the line.

"Hello," Kinley Devore said. Her table had just been called, and she walked up to join Elaine. "Your gang is all at the buffet now."

"I know," Elaine said, smiling, "but I had to take a call, so I came in a little late. I'll just sneak in here before the next table."

"I *am* the next table," Kinley said. "And Laurette too." She indicated the other woman. "Have you two met yet?"

Elaine smiled. "Yes. At the reception last night, just a quick hello."

Laurette gave her a short nod, withdrawing her hand from her purse where she'd apparently been fishing for something. She was unsmiling, as she'd been last night. "Hello again. I hope you're enjoying the retreat." She spoke slowly and deliberately, without any indication that she was finding the weekend a pleasure.

"It's lovely," Elaine said. "I've enjoyed all the sessions so far."

"I'll introduce you to the rest of my group when they get here." Kinley indicated a gaggle of women who were slowly making their way through the tables toward them. "Michelle Graham has two daughters with her, and Lara Page invited her daughter-in-law and her sister. Laurette and I are solo."

"No daughters," Laurette said in her slow, ponderous way. "No children, in my case."

"And one divorced son in mine," Kinley said, cheerfully ignoring Laurette's gloomy outlook.

Elaine had not considered how touchy an event like this might be for those who did not have female family members, and she felt sad for both women. Kinley did not appear to mind. She already was chatting away with one of the other guests from her table. Laurette, however, stolidly stood facing forward. Perhaps this weekend was more a trial than a pleasure.

Elaine cleared her throat. "Do you still live in Maine?"

"I never left Augusta," Laurette said. "I got married right out of high school. He died shortly after our twenty-fifth anniversary. I remarried again and spent ten years being cheated on before he replaced me with a younger, blonder model. Been single ever since."

Elaine was nonplussed at the woman's blunt recitation of her very personal trauma. "I'm sorry for the loss of your first husband," she finally said. "And for the disappointment in your second marriage. That sounds as if it was very difficult."

"It was, but I had a lot of support." Paradoxically, Laurette seemed happier now that she had succeeded in making Elaine a little less comfortable. "I go to church with your mother and Kinley and some of our other high school friends, and they were really there for me the whole time. And in the long run, I've found more happiness this way, I believe. My first husband was a very good man. I should have been satisfied with one good love."

Elaine wasn't so sure about that, although it startled her to realize that not much more than two years ago, she had felt much like Laurette. She would have been satisfied to have been Ben's widow, to have had "one good love," as Laurette put it. True, she'd been lonely, but she had expected that would subside in time as she adjusted to a single life.

One thing, though, was very different in Laurette's case, something Elaine had not had.

"It's wonderful to have such good friends. You're very fortunate to have all these gal pals close by." And truthfully, Elaine envied her mother those connections. True, she'd been close to Jan throughout her childhood, but Elaine had been far away from her during much of their adult lives. "I was married to a career army officer. We spent our married lives moving every few years."

"You're not still married?"

After living in Lancaster for over two years now, Elaine realized she had grown accustomed to most of the people around her knowing her marital status. She shook her head. "I'm a widow. It'll be three years later this year."

"I'm sorry for your loss." The words were formal, but Elaine heard the sincerity in Laurette's voice.

"Thank you. As I was saying, I spent my adult life moving around with my husband wherever the army sent us. I had good friends from school, but while I was globetrotting, they were getting their children together to play, doing volunteer work and managing careers in the area, socializing, and building lifelong bonds. Most of my shared memories with them are from many years ago, so even though I've come back to stay, it's not particularly easy to slide right back into the kind of friendship you have with my mother and your other friends."

"I'm sure it's not." Laurette pulled her purse strap up tighter across her shoulder. "I do realize how lucky I am to have these friendships. These women have saved my sanity on more than one occasion, I can tell you."

They continued to chat until they reached the buffet line, and Elaine felt that they had established a tentative rapport. But as soon as they stopped talking, Laurette's face fell back into its unsmiling mask.

"Don't pay her too much mind," Kinley whispered in Elaine's ear. "She really changed after her second husband left. It's been seven years now, but she can't seem to get past it."

Elaine wondered what Laurette had been like before. She certainly made it a challenge to be optimistic and sunny. How sad that the woman had allowed the experience to define the rest of her life, despite the fact that her friends had surrounded her with support.

AFTER LUNCH, THE group had about fifteen minutes before the afternoon's presentations began.

"Come over here, girls," Virginia said to her relatives. "Have you seen my high school yearbooks yet?"

"What? I didn't know they had yearbooks back in the day!" Sasha exclaimed in a teasing tone.

Virginia lightly punched her grandchild's bicep, then pretended to wring her hand. "Ouch."

Sasha grinned. "I know you're not that feeble, Grandma."

Virginia led them over to a table along the wall. Jan had seen people browsing there throughout the morning, but she hadn't realized they had gathered around the women's high school yearbooks.

"This is my senior yearbook," Virginia said. "Well, not mine. I believe this particular copy belongs to Betty Lee. But this was my senior year."

"Did all of you here graduate the same year?" Jan asked. In her high school, clubs had been for anyone of high school age, whether they were freshmen or seniors.

"Yes," Virginia said. "This particular guild forms a chapter each year. Our high school had grade ten, eleven, and twelve, so there were three chapters of the Delta group. We worked together on many things, but each class year was its own subset of the national group."

"I found you, Grandma!" Sasha pointed to her senior class photo. "It's like looking at me, almost."

"Sasha *does* look a lot like you," Jan said, a little surprised by the strong resemblance. She had known Virginia all her life, it was true, but time tended to blur her memories of the more youthful version of her aunt.

"People have often told me we resemble each other," Virginia said. "And here's Betty Lee." She pointed as she turned the page. "Oh, and Eleanor and Laurette too."

Jan and Elaine both leaned forward to scrutinize the double-page spread.

"Wow," Elaine murmured. "That was Betty Lee?"

"Wasn't she attractive?" Virginia asked softly. The photo showed a dark-haired girl with strong eyebrows and a lovely smile draped in the traditional velvet. Curls cascaded past one shoulder. "She was so happy then. She got engaged to her high school boyfriend, Mitch, right after graduation and he went off to college. But after a year, he decided college wasn't for him and he enlisted in the army. Once he finished boot camp, he was sent to paratrooper training. Our country wasn't at war; Korea had just ended and our presence in Vietnam hadn't started. He should have been safe. But he was killed in a Jeep rollover accident at the post."

"Oh, how sad," Elaine said.

"It was awful," Virginia said. "She never married. I often wonder if she'd had a family, whether she'd have turned out differently, been a little less focused on her music. She's quite a driving force in music education and in our church music program, you know. But sometimes I wonder if her life might have been very different if she'd had a family on which to focus that formidable energy."

Formidable energy, Jan thought, was a good way to describe Betty Lee.

All of them were silent for a moment as Virginia's finger traced Betty Lee's smile.

After a moment, Sasha cleared her throat and pointed to Eleanor's headshot. "I totally would have recognized Eleanor from this picture. She's still got the dimples and the twinkle in her eye."

"And the cute pixie cut," Virginia said. "She wore it longer for a while, but recently she cut it short again, and it really looks a lot like this picture, doesn't it?"

They looked through additional pages of the yearbook, seeing Virginia as a member of the homecoming court with a giant chrysanthemum pinned to her jacket, as a member of the Future Homemakers of America club, which made Sasha giggle, as a starter on the girls' softball team, and as a member of the student council.

Turning another page, Jan saw the photo Betty Lee had used in the Jeopardy game last night. The three friends were bent over a table filled with what appeared to be yearbook photos, rulers, and other accessories presumably needed to put a mock-up of the yearbook together before computer access became commonplace.

And hovering behind them was the fourth girl. She appeared to be trying to look over Betty Lee's shoulder. To Jan's eye, the girl seemed to have an uncertain smile on her face, as if she was not exactly part of the group but was trying hard to be. Rather like the smile Heloise Invers occasionally wore when her exuberant enthusiasm flagged for a moment.

Jan touched the girl's image with her index finger. "Is that girl at the retreat?" she asked her aunt.

"No," Virginia said, her smile fading. Abruptly, she closed the book. "I need to visit the powder room. Anyone want to come with me?"

"I will," Sasha volunteered.

Jan turned back to the table as the pair exited the room. "Was that curt or am I the only one who felt that way? I wonder what that girl's name is."

Elaine was staring after her mother and daughter. "Mom seemed upset again, didn't she? Do you think it's from looking at the yearbook?"

"Or something specific in it," Jan said. "You couldn't see your mother's face from where you were standing."

"I just wish we knew what it was," Elaine said, frowning.

"I don't know," Jan said, "but I'd like to learn more about the fourth girl in the photo."

"The one standing behind Mom, Eleanor, and Betty Lee?"

Jan nodded. "We should—"

"Excuse me." Another group had come to the table, and a woman deftly slid the yearbook over so that her guests could see it. "May I sneak this away to show my daughters a couple of pictures?"

Elaine smiled. "Sure. We were finished with it."

The cousins turned and headed for the double doors that led into the hotel proper.

Jan smiled at Elaine wryly. "I was about to say we should look at that photo and see what her name is."

"I'm curious about her too, but we'll have to check it later." Elaine pointed toward the hallway. "The line for the restroom is a mile long. I'm going up to the room for a minute."

"I'll come along."

As the cousins walked upstairs, Elaine told Jan about her lunchtime chat with Laurette Martel. "She doesn't seem anything like she looked in high school," Elaine said. "Kinley said she used to be a lot happier. It's a shame life turned out so poorly for her."

"Still, you said she spoke fondly of how helpful the guild members were," Jan said. "That kind of solidarity really helps people know they aren't alone."

A few minutes later, after they relocked the doors of their respective rooms and started along the hallway, they saw the pregnant housekeeper again.

"Good morning, Adrianna," Elaine said.

"Good morning," the younger woman replied with a smile as they passed.

Jan poked Elaine in the side as they descended the steps. "Her fingernails were short and unpainted. Did you notice?"

Elaine laughed. "I forgot, although I've been suspiciously scrutinizing all our fellow guests' hands this morning."

"It occurs to me that if someone noticed her nail was missing, she could have taken all of them off," Jan said. "So maybe we need to consider people with natural nails as well."

Elaine groaned. "I can't believe I didn't think of that. We'll have to tell Mom and Sasha to check natural nails too. But back to Adrianna...what reason could that young woman have for leaving weird little notes on guests' pillows?"

"I don't know anything about her, other than the fact that she's expecting," Jan said. She lowered her voice dramatically. "She could be hiding deep, dark secrets."

A chuckle burst out of her cousin. "She could," Elaine agreed, "although I suspect the only thing she's hiding right now is an almost-full-term baby."

"Oh, look," Jan said. "Heloise is behind the desk. I asked about the room keys last night, but there was a different clerk on duty, and she didn't know anything." She approached the desk with Elaine close behind her.

"Hello, Mrs. Invers," Jan said. "Can you tell me who might have been given access to guest rooms yesterday for the purpose of distributing little gifts?"

"It may only have been a few rooms," Elaine put in.

Heloise blinked, looking taken aback. Her eyelids moved so slowly that the motion reminded Jan of a doll she'd had as a young child whose eyes closed when she was laid in a horizontal position. "That," Heloise said, "would be against hotel policy. We occasionally have groups that want to give out little favors, and we ask them to place them over the doorknobs. We would *never* allow a guest into someone else's occupied room." She sounded quite firm, and Jan appreciated the hotel's desire to protect their guests' privacy.

"I understand," she said. "Thank you for the information."

Elaine cleared her throat as they moved across the room to wait for Virginia and Sasha. "She had no nail polish or tips on.

I suppose we have to add her to our suspect list of nefarious gift-givers."

Jan grinned. "I suppose we do. And did you notice how short her nails were cut? It seems to me that if someone broke off a tip and wanted all their nails to look alike, they might cut them all to the same length the broken one was. Could she have lied to us?"

"By omission, maybe," Elaine replied. "Did you notice she didn't say anything about *staff* entering the rooms?"

CHAPTER EIGHT

Y ou're right!" Jan exclaimed. "I didn't catch that."

"It's possible that Heloise might have misled us," Elaine said. "The question is, did she do it on purpose or not? She was quite vehement about guests not entering occupied guest rooms, but she omitted the obvious—that hotel staff could get in there when they need to."

"So it probably wasn't a guest, given her reaction," Jan said.

"And let's assume for a moment that it wasn't the hotel employees. Who else could have gotten into the guest rooms?" Elaine asked.

"Someone with lock-picking skills," Jan offered. "These old-fashioned locks would be very easy to pick, I bet. I can't speak from personal experience, though."

"That's not strictly true," Elaine teased. "Remember our crash course in lock picking from Greg Payson?"

Jan laughed. "In the age of the keycard, I doubt it would be very useful anymore."

"So the obvious choice is still a hotel employee."

"What if Heloise misled us on purpose? She might know that an employee entered those rooms."

"Or what if Heloise isn't lying, but she isn't aware that an employee let someone into guest rooms?"

"Oh boy. I feel sorry for the employee," Jan said. "I don't think I'd like having Heloise Invers mad at me."

"I wonder how many employees have access to those guest rooms," Elaine said, sobering. "Heloise and the clerk you spoke to last night would certainly be able to get the master at a moment's notice."

"And the housekeeper," Jan said. "I wonder if there are others. Surely Adrianna can't be the only person responsible for cleaning all these rooms."

"There might only be two cleaning staffers," Elaine said. "It's a relatively small hotel. And what about custodians? I bet they employ a handyman or jack-of-all-trades to deal with problems like faucets, lightbulbs, and all the little things that can go wrong in guest rooms."

Jan sighed. "I suppose the first thing we need to do is approach Adrianna and ask her directly if she entered those rooms. She probably was the only housekeeper on duty yesterday during dinner, since most of the room-cleaning work is most likely done earlier in the day. I don't think Heloise is going to appreciate us asking her more questions that imply her staff might not be following hotel policy."

The cousins were silent for a moment. Jan could almost hear the gears turning in Elaine's head as they were in hers, sifting through all the things that had happened since the retreat began.

"What could the gifts mean?" Elaine wondered aloud. "It's not as if they're really gifts at all."

"That's for sure," Jan agreed. "A two-dollar bill, a race brochure—a 1K race brochure at that. An old postcard and the picture of the street sign. What could they possibly have in common?"

"I have no idea," Elaine said. "Absolutely the only similarity I see is that they are each made of paper."

"But not even the same kind of paper," Jan pointed out. "Glossy paper, photo paper, currency paper, and that heavy old postcard paper, which is really more like cardboard. I just don't see anything cohesive."

The cousins fell silent again, stymied.

"Let's go check that yearbook again if no one's looking at it," Elaine said. "I can't stop thinking about how my mother teared up last night, and how unhappy she was today when she saw that picture. I have a feeling it's important somehow."

Quickly, they made their way into the now-deserted dining room, where the table along one wall held high school memorabilia and the yearbooks they'd been looking through earlier. There was a cheerleading uniform laid out along with a program from the senior prom, another from graduation, and a couple of laminated photos of the homecoming and prom courts and other noteworthy events.

"Let's see," Elaine said, drawing the book they wanted closer. "It was somewhere in the middle, right? Behind the senior class portraits?"

Jan nodded. "And after the section where all the clubs are listed."

It took a few moments, but eventually the cousins found what they were seeking. "Here we go," Elaine crowed. "Okay, the caption lists Mom, Eleanor, Betty Lee, and this must be Sally Manling." She tapped the caption underneath picture where all the names appeared.

"Sally Manling." Jan repeated the name. "There are copies of the retreat roster in those packets of papers we received. I wonder if she's on there."

"Mom said she wasn't here, remember?"

"But I believe all the guild members are listed, aren't they? The ones not attending were listed separately."

"You're right. But even if she is listed, she's probably married, so her last name might be different."

"And Sally is sometimes a nickname for Sarah."

"So we need to check for Sarahs and Sallys, spelled any old way just in case." Elaine sighed. "I don't feel like I can ask Mom any more about Sally. She seemed so upset, and this is supposed to be a fun, family-bonding weekend."

"I know." Jan agreed with Elaine. It was hard to see Aunt Virginia struggling to enjoy herself during what should have been a carefree weekend among friends. "If we run into dead ends, we may need to ask her, but let's try it this way first."

As Virginia and Sasha joined them, Sasha consulted the program that she had stuck in her shoulder bag. "The next workshop is about magic lanterns," she said. "Does that mean we're going to see a genie?"

The others laughed. "Not exactly," Jan told her. "Come on, we'll go see what a Victorian magic lantern is."

In the conference room, they found seats near the front. Elaine went into the row first, followed by Virginia, then Sasha and Jan. A large white screen stood at the front of the room, and a primitive-looking little wood-and-metal box with a lens sticking out of the front was prominently displayed.

A small man in front of the podium wore a nearly knee-length black cutaway coat over a high-collared dress shirt with a black patterned ascot and a paisley vest in shades of wine. Close-fitting black pinstripe trousers, white satin spats over black rounded-toe boots, and a black silk top hat completed the outfit.

"Welcome, ladies," he cried cheerfully in a distinct British accent. "Welcome to Masterson's Magic Lantern Show. I am Benjamin Masterson, the operator of this amazing invention." He gave them an exaggerated wink and set his hat aside, sliding into an easy British speech pattern with far less theatrical flair. "Image projection dates back thousands of years, to the days when humans discovered fire and were able to make shadow-plays on the walls of their caves. About a thousand years later, people realized they could intentionally produce a source of light to project images.

"So! What do you need for image projection? Four basic things, my friends." He flourished one hand with four fingers raised before them. "First, you need a strong source of light; second, some object you wish to project. Next you need a device or manner of forming the image of that object, and finally, you need a space, generally a screen, on which to project the image."

Jan leaned forward, the science nerd in her finding the presentation fascinating.

"Around 1650, the simple versions of the lantern you see here began to be made. Of course, I am skipping entire centuries of the development of this most marvelous invention, but I'm eager, as I'm sure you are, to get to the Victorian era."

There was a ripple of laughter from his audience.

Masterson went on. "The heyday, if you will, of the magic lantern show occurred in the late Victorian period, in the decade of the 1890s. During the two preceding decades, lanterns and slides were manufactured en masse for every conceivable occasion. By the year 1890, there were over thirty companies engaged in the production of lanterns and their accompanying slides in London alone."

"Wow," Sasha murmured beneath her breath.

"So, what, exactly is a magic lantern as the Victorians knew it?" Masterson asked. The audience understood that this was a rhetorical question, and he went on. "A lantern such as the mahogany-and-brass one I have here today utilized something called 'limelight' to produce a bright light. Hand-painted scenes on three-inch glass slides are changed about every thirty seconds, and the light projects those images onto a wall or screen."

Masterson went on to explain that limelight was produced by squirting liquid oxygen and hydrogen onto a piece of limestone. When the resulting gasses were ignited, the incandescent light produced was as bright as that in a modern movie projector. Then he proceeded to demonstrate the process.

Attentive as she was to the lecture, Jan took the time to note the women around her, checking their manicures to see who might have lost a French nail tip. Unfortunately, all the ones she could see appeared to be complete.

A nudge in her side made her turn to Sasha, who was inclining her head meaningfully toward the row in front of them.

Jan raised questioning eyebrows, and Sasha tapped an index finger against the back of her nails on the other hand. Getting it, Jan nodded. She stretched her neck slightly until she could see the object of Sasha's gaze. There was only one row of women seated ahead of them, and in that row, Jeanice Evanak sat with her hands neatly clasped in her lap. Although Jan could not see all of her fingertips, those she could see all were neatly polished with French tips.

Jan nodded slightly, grinning at Sasha. She could not tell whether the manicure used Jeanice's own nails, or whether they were tips like the one Elaine had stepped on.

Mr. Masterson turned out the lights a few minutes later and resumed his expansive personality from the beginning of the presentation, complete with British accent. He proceeded to regale the room with a humorous story which accompanied the slideshow. He sang and provided sound effects as a true magic lantern artist from the Victorian era would have done, and he encouraged the audience to clap, cheer, and boo in appropriate places.

When the program ended, there was enthusiastic applause. As women surged to the front of the room to inspect the magic lantern and slides and speak to Mr. Masterson, Elaine tugged Jan out of the way of the crowd, with Sasha and Virginia following close behind. The group quickly pooled their information.

"I saw one French manicure," Elaine volunteered, "but I was on the end and had a limited view. And a lady in the row in front of me had naked nails, but they were long and beautifully manicured, so I doubt she's our culprit."

"I saw what Elaine saw, plus Joan Clayton has plain nails," Virginia said. "But I think we can count her out because I have never seen her do anything to her nails in her whole life. She's a master gardener, and the only adornment she usually has is soil under her fingernails."

"I've seen four French manis and five sets of naked nails," Jan reported. "All the French manicures were perfect, though, with no tips missing. But Sasha—"

"Grandma's friend Jeanice has a French mani," Sasha said breathlessly. "But I couldn't tell if the nails are real or tips. Could you?" She turned to Jan.

"No. We'll have to try to get a closer look," Jan said.

Elaine sighed. "It's quite possible that French tip I stepped on came from a prior occupant of the room. Housekeeping may just have missed it."

"It's equally possible it's a valid clue," Jan insisted. "I'm not giving up on that angle just yet."

Sasha chuckled. "I feel so official, helping you figure this out! I'm taking a bathroom break and then I'll be right back."

"I'll go with you," Virginia said. "I shouldn't have had two cups of coffee at lunch."

As Elaine's mother and daughter walked away, Jan switched topics. "Have you spoken with Archie yet about pulling together a selection of teas?"

Elaine sighed. "No. I know I need to do that. I keep hoping some brilliant idea will occur to me. Nathan's gone out of town until tomorrow, so I can't ask him to do it. I considered asking

Rose or Archie to drive up to Bangor in the morning, but I hate to do that on their day off."

"Archie and his wife are going to a classical guitar concert at the Bar Harbor Community Church tomorrow," Jan said. "I believe they're going over for lunch first. So I doubt he could fit it in."

"And I just remembered Rose and Brent have plans too, so she's out," Elaine said. She sighed. Brent was Rose's boyfriend, and Jan knew Elaine would hate to put any barrier in the way of Rose's relationship with him and his little daughter, Emma.

"I can ask Bob when I see him tonight," Jan said. "I don't think he's got anything going on tomorrow, and I bet he'd be happy to do it. Even if he can't make the long drive, I'm sure he'd go over to the tearoom and pick up whatever Archie gets ready."

"I could run over to Tea for Two myself if I need to," Elaine said. "Why don't you check with Bob, and see if there's any way he could go to Bangor in the morning? I have the address, and I can let the woman know he'll be coming. In the meantime, just in case, I'll call Archie and ask him to pull together a selection of teas. Then if the Friendship and Memories doesn't get here, I can run over and get it."

"Sounds like a plan." Jan gave her a thumbs-up. Then she cleared her throat. "So...guess who called last night while Bob and I were out walking."

Elaine's eyebrows rose. "Who?"

"Clifton Young."

If Elaine's eyebrows rose any higher, they'd be in her hairline, Jan thought wryly. Her cousin's expression was priceless.

"You were talking on the phone to Clifton at the same time you were out walking with Bob?" She began to chuckle.

"It wasn't funny at the time," Jan said, although she couldn't prevent a smile at Elaine's amusement.

"Let me guess. He asked you out on a date again."

"How did you know?" Jan was genuinely perplexed.

Elaine shrugged. "He's had a certain look in his eye at times lately."

"Oh dear." Jan put her hands to her cheeks. "That is not good. Not good at all. He's coming by here at three thirty, because I felt as if I needed to explain to him in person that I'm seeing Bob exclusively. But how do I say that?"

Elaine thought for a moment. "You could tell him your heart is engaged elsewhere."

"Oh, that's good. I like that better than just hitting him with 'I'm in love with someone else.' And maybe I should say I've realized I need to pursue that relationship."

The magic lantern show had lasted nearly two hours, so there was a significant break from three to four. Sasha and Virginia both headed upstairs to freshen up, while Jan and Elaine opted to stay downstairs.

Elaine gestured toward the door. "Let's go sit on the porch for a while. It's chilly but the sun is shining and it's beautiful."

"It is," Jan agreed.

They settled into white-painted rocking chairs on the wide front porch that gave a gorgeous lake view across the road. It was easy to imagine that one might be relaxing in those chairs fifty years in the past, just enjoying one's summer at the hotel, Elaine thought.

"I have to get up early tomorrow morning," Jan reminded her. "I need to get that friendship bread made first thing before their kitchen gets busy."

"Could you do it tonight?"

Jan thought for a moment. "I could, I suppose. But I think I'd rather it be just-baked and very fresh. There are a lot of women here, and many of them are local. Our presentation could translate into some business if they like us enough."

"You're absolutely right," Elaine said. "I sure do hope Bob can pick up that tea in time."

"I'm sure he can," Jan said. But she had a mystery on her mind. "I can't stop thinking about those notes and gifts your mom and her friends got. We have to figure out what they mean, if only for the sake of my sanity."

Elaine smiled, tilting her face up to the afternoon sun that slanted across them, but she said, "And for my mother's peace of mind too. She's being very close-mouthed, but I know it upset her." She shifted to face Jan. "Just like the picture of the Sally Manling in the yearbook upset her. Do you think the two things are related?"

"It's possible, I suppose, but I don't see how. We need to learn more. And I keep going back to who left the things in the rooms in the first place. And who has keys and could have gotten into those rooms. If it was Heloise, and she misled us, why might she have done it?"

"Well," said Jan slowly, "those notes appear to be designed to unsettle people, rather than to welcome them, right?"

"I guess," Elaine said. "Mom certainly seemed unsettled by hers. Eleanor didn't look very happy either. And Kinley told me she thought it felt 'mildly offensive.' Those were her exact words."

"Babette just seemed puzzled by hers," Jan recalled. "So if Heloise did it and intended the note to remind them of something, it may have missed the mark."

"But why would she do something like that?" Elaine asked.

"Aunt Virginia told us Heloise wasn't in the guild because her family went to church every Wednesday. What if she resents the club members because she couldn't be a part of it?"

"But then why wouldn't everyone in the guild have received a note? And do people really hold grudges for that long?"

Jan laughed. "Some people certainly do. But you see the flaw in my logic. I find it very odd that Betty Lee didn't get a note, when her two closest friends did. It almost seems like that should be significant."

Slowly, Elaine said, "I suppose the significance would make sense if she was the one who planted the gifts."

Jan caught her breath. "Oh. It certainly would."

"But again, why would she do something like that?"

"We don't know enough about the dynamics of the friendships," Jan said. "I feel like we're wearing blindfolds and trying to pick out the one brown-eyed person in the room."

Elaine laughed. "That's one way to put it."

"So we need to find out more about why either Heloise or Betty Lee might have felt the need to write those notes."

"Don't forget about the housekeeper, Adrianna," Elaine said. "She would have had the ability to get into all those rooms."

"But why? She would have to have a connection we haven't discovered yet."

"Maybe someone else approached her and asked her to open the doors for them."

"Now there's a thought." Jan nodded. "There was no note on the pillow when we checked in. We unpacked, freshened up, and went down for dinner, and when we came back, the note was there."

"Ergo, someone had to enter the room during the dinner hour," Elaine said. "I wonder if any of the guests missed dinner."

"Or even if they came in late," Jan said. "Betty Lee came in late, remember?"

"So did Laurette Martel," Elaine said. "But what possible motive could she have? Greed doesn't really work unless she stands to gain something. Could it be revenge? Payback for something?"

"Possibly, but she would hardly tell you if it were," Jan pointed out.

Elaine pursed her lips. "True."

"I wonder if anyone left the dining room early after dinner last night," Jan said. "First thing in the morning, I want to find that housekeeper and talk to her again."

Sasha came through the front door then, interrupting their chat. "There you are. Grandma said she thought she saw you come outside." She turned in a circle. "Wow, it's nice out here."

Elaine nodded. "It is. You want to join us? We have three-quarters of an hour before the four o'clock session begins."

"Thanks," Sasha said. "I think I will." She dropped into a rocker on the other side of Elaine, setting down the large shoulder bag she carried.

Jan noticed a folder sticking out of it. "Oh," she said. "Is that your retreat information folder? May I look at it?"

Sasha nodded, retrieving the item and passing it over idly, before she leaned back and closed her eyes.

Jan flipped open the folder. In addition to the program and some information about the hotel, there was a printed list of all the retreat attendees. The guild members' addresses and e-mails were included. At the end, there was a short list of guild members who had not attended the retreat—again with address and e-mail contact information.

Elaine leaned over to inspect the roster that Jan drew from its place in the folder. "Looking for Sally?"

Jan nodded.

"Who's Sally?" Sasha sounded drowsy.

"The girl looking over your grandma's shoulder in the yearbook photo," Jan said.

"Oh, you figured out who that was. Why are you looking for her?"

"We were just curious if she was a member of the guild," Jan told her younger cousin.

Elaine rapidly skimmed the list. "No Sally," she said after a moment.

"No Sarahs either, not even among those who aren't attending," Jan pointed out. "So she isn't a guild member."

"Why don't you just ask Grandma?" Sasha asked.

"We may," Elaine said. "But she and Eleanor both seemed a little distressed when they saw that photo the first time, and we thought it would be easier if we could identify her without having to make your grandmother think about it again."

All three women were silent for a moment. Jan glanced at Elaine, seeing the wheels turning as she silently reviewed possibilities just as Jan was doing.

Finally, Elaine said, "We didn't look for her yearbook picture. I wonder if she was also a senior that year."

"I can't help thinking that there's something important about her," Jan said.

CHAPTER NINE

W e should definitely check Sally Manling's yearbook entry," Jan said, continuing her train of thought.

"Absolutely. A little later, perhaps." Elaine closed her eyes as her daughter had. It felt lovely to sit and do nothing. As she relaxed, she thought about all the people she'd met in the past day. It was fascinating to be getting this glimpse into her mother's past, to be meeting friends who had known her for so long.

Inexplicably, the memory of Laurette Martel's palpable air of unhappiness floated into her mind. The poor woman. Her high school picture had shown a vivacious, attractive young woman on the verge of adulthood. It was a far cry from the woman she'd become. When life disappointed you so badly that it showed on your face, how much must that change you? How bitter would you feel? Bitter enough to do something mean to people who'd once been your friends? It probably was an unworthy thought to have, but Elaine couldn't dismiss it.

"You know," she said slowly, "that conversation I had with Laurette Martel gave me a funny feeling."

"Funny how?"

Elaine grimaced, opening her eyes again. "Her worldview seems to be very pessimistic and dark. Kinley says she wasn't like that until she went through an awful second marriage that ultimately fell apart."

"Wasn't she one of the ones who came to dinner late?" Sasha opened her eyes and sat up straighter.

"You're right. She came in with Betty Lee. Were they together?"

Jan shook her head. "I don't think so. They were talking, but Betty Lee said she had come from that wedding rehearsal. I kind of assumed they just met in the lobby."

"We'll have to ask Betty Lee if she knows when Laurette arrived," Elaine said.

"And we still need to find out who else might have had access to the guest rooms while the group was dining last night," Jan reminded Elaine.

"Asking Heloise is not really an option," Elaine pointed out, "given how defensive she was when we tried to talk to her about it."

"That's the woman at the front desk?" Sasha's eyes were still closed, but she was following the conversation.

"Yes, the manager," Elaine told her.

"She's a little scary," Sasha said with a grin. "I wouldn't want to make her mad."

It so clearly echoed their earlier conversation that the cousins both chuckled.

"Plus," Jan went on, "if she really was the one to place the gifts on the pillows, she lied to us." She frowned. "Did you get any indication that she might be lying?"

Elaine shook her head. "No, but we don't know her well enough to know what to look for. I wish there was someone else we could ask."

"There might be," Jan said. "What about the woman who was working in the kitchen who helped us yesterday when we arrived. Carol? No, Crystal. Perhaps Crystal would know which hotel employees might have master keys to the rooms other than Heloise, the desk clerks on duty at any given time, and the housekeeper."

"I think whoever is on duty at check-in during the supper hour is probably in the clear," Sasha contributed. "She would have had to leave her post at the desk for some time in order to enter four guest rooms. And if that happened, and Heloise found out about it, I suspect that clerk's job would be history. She seems like she'd be a strict boss."

Jan nodded. "You're probably right about that." She glanced at the time and rose from her rocking chair. "Oh, no. Clifton will be here any minute. I told him to meet me in the parking lot. I'd better go grab my jacket. It won't be as warm out walking as it is here on the porch where we're protected from the breeze," she said. "I'll see you a little later."

IN HER ROOM, Jan changed into sneakers suitable for a walk. As she locked her door on the way out, she wondered where she might find Adrianna, the housekeeper. Quickly, she walked along her hallway to the intersection where the stair landing was. She glanced down the other hallway, but there was no housekeeper's cart there. Acting on impulse, she took the steps up to the next floor.

Immediately, she found she was in luck. The housekeeping cart was parked at the far end of the adjacent hallway. Jan strode down the hall, arriving just as Adrianna came through the doorway of an open room, a load of towels in hand. She dumped the towels into a bag and then spotted Jan.

"Hello," Adrianna said. "Can I get anything for you?"

"No, thank you," Jan said. "I was actually hoping to speak with you for a moment."

"Oh?" The young woman's eyes looked wary.

"Well, someone got into the rooms of several guests during the dinner hour yesterday and left little gifts," Jan said. "Heloise said she did not authorize anyone to enter, so you are the next logical person to check with. Did you happen to open rooms for anyone or give a master key out?"

Adrianna busied herself pulling spray cleaner and several cleaning rags from the cart. "That's not in my job description. I'm not authorized to let anyone into a guest room. Heloise is very firm about that."

Jan studied the young woman for a moment, noting that color had risen in her cheeks. Because she wasn't happy that Jan seemed to be accusing her of something? "All right," she said slowly. "Thank you for your time."

Descending the stairs, she reminded herself to tell Elaine that Adrianna had not, in fact, given her a direct answer to her question. It might not be in her job description, as she'd pointed out, but Jan felt certain the young woman knew something more.

Clifton already was waiting in the parking lot as Jan approached.

"Hello there," he said. "I'm glad you could get away."

"It's a gorgeous day for a walk," Jan said obliquely.

"Rose and Brent are taking Emma up to Acadia later today," Clifton said, mentioning the national park near Bar Harbor that boasted extraordinary views. "If you hadn't had this event planned, I'd have invited you along."

"I'm sure they'll have a wonderful time," Jan said, avoiding the latter part of his statement. "Our retreat has been delightful. Aunt Virginia is so pleased that Elaine, Sasha, and I all were able to attend."

They crossed the road and started along a path that led toward Penzance, the town at the opposite end of the lake from Lancaster. Jan kept her hands firmly in her pockets. She'd thought that Clifton understood that they were just friends, but now Jan worried that he might reach for her hand. That comment about inviting her on Rose's outing hadn't helped. She felt as silly and nervous as a high school girl.

They chatted about inconsequential things, while in the back of her mind she wondered how on earth to introduce the topic of her relationship with Bob.

A car coming toward the hotel on the lake road caught her attention as it slowed for a moment. Jan's heart leaped. It looked like a silver Acura MDX—the make and model of car that Bob drove. She nearly raised her hand to wave, but the driver, whom she couldn't see clearly, had not waved or appeared to notice them. Perhaps it hadn't been Bob after all.

A moment later, the car resumed its speed and moved along the road toward the hotel. It was only her wishful thinking that made her see Bob in every silver Acura that passed. They were supposed to meet tonight, so he wouldn't be out here during the day.

She and Clifton shared a pleasant conversation as they crossed the road, looped around and took a walking path through the woods back toward the hotel.

Crunching leaves on an intersecting footpath ahead jarred them out of their chatter. "Another hiker," Clifton proclaimed.

As they came around a bend in the trail, Jan saw Rae Burns, her friend from their meal table, pausing and waving.

Rae wore casual khaki pants and a T-shirt with sturdy hiking boots that indicated she used them frequently. On her head was a long-brimmed baseball-style cap with a hummingbird emblazoned above the visor, and around her neck she had looped a small pair of binoculars.

"Hi, Jan!" she called. "What an absolutely perfect day. I had to get out of the hotel for a little while."

Jan returned the greeting and performed introductions.

"Would you like to join us?" Clifton asked.

"Only if I wouldn't be intruding," Rae replied, her eyes twinkling.

"Not at all," Jan said hastily. "Clifton's daughter works for me, and he just dropped by for a little stroll today. By all means, join us."

"If we go this way," Clifton said, indicating a path that led up a hill, "it will loop around through the forest, and it will bring us out on the other side of the hotel."

"I need to be back by four," Jan told him.

"As do I," Rae added.

"It's only a ten- or fifteen-minute detour," he promised, consulting his watch. "You should still be back by then."

"Great," Rae said. "Let's do it."

Rae was warm and friendly, chattering with enthusiasm, and Clifton responded to her easily. Gradually, Jan dropped out of the conversation as the pair discovered they had a shared interest in ornithology. Both were particularly fascinated by waterfowl, and they spent much of the hike discussing birds they had seen, birds they would like to see, and places they would like to go birdwatching. Jan liked birds in a general "hey, isn't that a pretty bird in that tree" way, but she didn't know the difference between the red-throated loon and the common loon, nor did she particularly care.

Rae was a delightful person, lighthearted and funny. Jan had enjoyed her enormously, and it appeared Rae and Clifton quickly were becoming friends. They chatted the whole way back to the hotel, while Jan followed along, inserting a comment here and there as she reviewed her responsibilities for the rest of the weekend in her mind. Tomorrow morning she needed to bake the friendship bread. Then later she would assist Elaine with their tea presentation.

Unfortunately, as they approached the hotel, Jan realized that she had not been able to have the "we're just friends" talk with Clifton that she'd planned. She cleared her throat.

"Uh, Clifton, could I—"

"I'd love that," Rae said, and Jan realized she had missed something vital. "There's a four o'clock workshop, but I would much rather have a cup of coffee with you. I'm dying to hear about that pink-footed goose you saw near Rockland Island. Jan, are you going to the next workshop?"

"Yes—"

"Great! Would you mind letting my mom know where I am?"

"Not at all." Jan drew a deep breath. "Clifton, might I have a private word with you?"

Rae looked chagrined. "Oh, Clifton, why don't I meet you in the dining room? I've totally crashed your walk together, haven't I?"

"Not at all," Jan assured her. "Not at all."

As Rae hurried away, Jan stopped as they approached the back terrace behind the hotel. "Clifton...we need to talk, I think. I need to let you know—that is, I felt I should tell you that, well, that my affections are otherwise engaged. This may be unnecessary, as we have a wonderful friendship, but I felt—"

Clifton held up a hand. "Thank you for letting me know. I guess I tipped my hand a little today, didn't I?"

"A little," Jan said.

He chuckled. "And here I was afraid I might scare you off if I acted too hastily."

"I don't want to hurt your feelings." She practically wrung her hands in her distress. "But I still am seriously involved with Bob. He recently moved back to Maine from Baltimore. I wouldn't want you to think I was free to...to..." She felt herself blush as she floundered.

"I understand." Clifton smiled at her. "And I appreciate your care and concern. The truth is, I think I could have fallen for you, Jan. You're a kind and lovely lady, and I've been lonely for what seems a very long time. However, I did sort of sense that your heart wasn't free."

"Oh, Clifton," Jan said miserably, "I'm so sorry. Thank you for understanding. Will we still be friends?"

"Absolutely," he said, smiling at her. "Always. And now, if you'll excuse me, I am going to join your fascinating friend for coffee and conversation."

"She's a widow," Jan said.

Clifton grinned. "So I learned." After giving Jan a one-armed hug, he turned and walked away.

Jan felt incredibly relieved. Clifton and Rae, she thought, might really enjoy each other's company. They seemed to have a lot in common, and clearly there was a spark. Yes, she thought, it would be lovely if Clifton and Rae made each other happy.

To her surprise, Elaine was standing on the front porch. "Hello there," her cousin greeted her.

"Hi," Jan said. "Were you waiting for me?"

Elaine nodded. "Have you asked Bob about going to get the tea yet?"

"No." Jan shook her head. "He's coming over to walk tonight, so I thought I'd just ask him then. I can't imagine he won't be willing to do it."

Elaine nodded. "No problem. Let me know what he says."

"Why were you waiting for me?" Jan asked as they headed back into the lobby.

"I talked to Archie and narrowed down a list of what teas we still have the most of and what might be appropriate to serve tomorrow if we can't get the Friendship and Memories."

She consulted a slip of paper she held in her hand. "We still have some of the Top o' the Mornin' from St. Patrick's Day, and we have about thirty of the rose green tea and some of the Euphoria too. I believe that would be enough."

"Okay." Jan thought of something else. "Did Archie say if he'd heard back from the guy about the note in the painting?"

Elaine shook her head. "I asked him, and he said he's left several messages, but he has yet to hear from the fellow."

Jan was disappointed. "I bet he won't hear anything now until Monday."

They all were eager to hear what the note said. Archie had learned so much about his father, Henry, but he still had questions. Why had Archie's father never told him about his half sister? Or about his former life as a renowned painter? It wasn't until chance—or divine providence—had led Elaine to purchase a painting for the tearoom with the artist's signature in the bottom corner that Archie recognized as his father's mark. After a great deal of searching, Archie had found that his father had been uniquely talented and his paintings hung in several London museums. Along the way, Archie had found what he believed to be a long-lost sister, Geraldine, who had— she thought—been orphaned by the war. Every sign pointed toward the two being siblings. They were all hoping the note in the painting might offer him more answers.

"Mrs. Blake?" Heloise Invers called to Jan from the front desk, interrupting their exchange.

Jan looked over as the woman approached. She was carrying a vase with red roses in it. "These are for you," Heloise announced in delight, drawing the attention of everyone in the lobby. "A handsome fellow with dark hair dropped them off about thirty minutes ago."

There was a small card nestled among the babies' breath, velvety blooms, and greenery, Jan saw. She took the vase, her heart melting at the thoughtful gesture as she read the card written in a strong masculine hand she recognized: *I'm already missing you. Hope you enjoy your weekend. I love you. B.* The silver Acura she'd seen must have been Bob's, as he'd driven out to bring her these lovely flowers.

CHAPTER TEN

Elaine led the way up the wide flight of stairs as Jan clutched the vase of roses, beaming. "What a sweet gesture," Elaine commented.

"It was." Jan bent her head and inhaled deeply, but like most hothouse roses, the flowers had little scent. It didn't matter. She was thrilled anyway.

Elaine took the flowers while Jan dug out her room key and opened the door. She set the flowers on the large dresser in the room. "Are you ready for the next workshop?"

"Yes, but I want to thank Bob for the flowers," she said, smiling. "You go ahead. Save me a seat."

Elaine nodded as she headed for the door. "Will do."

As her cousin left the room, Jan pulled the card from the small white envelope nestled in the arrangement and read the words again.

She flopped down on the edge of the bed. Pulling out her phone, she quickly found Bob's number and hit the button to initiate the call. The phone rang. And rang several more times until his voice mail came on. Disappointed, she said, "Hey, it's

Jan. I just wanted to thank you for the roses. They really made my day. Can't wait to see you later. Love you."

Slowly, she pulled the phone from her ear and ended the call. She realized she'd been hoping Bob was screening his calls and would pick up the moment he heard her voice.

She wished she'd been able to touch base with Bob, but rather than lingering and hoping he'd call her back, she returned to the conference room. Virginia, Elaine, and Sasha already were there, and they had saved her a seat. Virginia threw up a hand and waved, smiling broadly as she beckoned to Jan.

"This should be fun," she said. "We're going to have a talk on Victorian entertainments, and then we're playing charades."

"I love charades," Elaine said.

"Sounds like fun," Jan added.

Betty Lee was sitting next to Jan, and Jan suddenly remembered the question she'd been hoping to ask the choir director. "Betty Lee?"

"Yes?" The older woman turned toward her with a smile.

"When you came in late to dinner last night, Laurette was with you. Did she help with your wedding reception?"

Betty Lee laughed. "Oh no. Weddings aren't really her thing. No, we just bumped into each other in the lobby as we were about to enter the dining room. Why?"

"I was just curious," Jan said.

Clapping silenced them, and everyone settled into their seats. One of the guild members was giving the presentation this time. An elementary school teacher by trade, she was used to being in front of groups of distractible students, and her style was vivacious and compelling, designed to keep wiggly children interested. It worked on wiggly adults too.

"Good afternoon," the presenter began after she had been introduced by the club president. "Before televisions and smart phones, people were forced to find ways to entertain themselves without electronic assistance. Imagine that!"

Everyone chuckled.

"Actually, though many of you grew up with radio and early televisions in your homes, you probably can imagine the non-digital existence of the Victorians far better than some of our younger guests. The moneyed classes in Victorian times had lots of leisure time. Most upper-class gentlemen were exceedingly well educated; women's education was far more hit-or-miss. In the absence of electronics, the Victorians' social activities included lots of organized entertainment. Performances included ventriloquists, theatre troupes, choirs, orchestras, poets, and comedians. Carnivals and circuses traveled regularly, and fairs were held annually.

"People received lessons in art, singing, dancing, and even cooking, depending on social status. Those who could afford the fee joined newly created libraries and read for pleasure. Ladies of leisure learned various needlework forms. They joined clubs, church groups, sporting groups, and committees to improve the lives of the working classes. In well-to-do homes, they frequently organized their own entertainments, such as piano sing-alongs, magic lantern shows, musical instrument performances, board games like chess and checkers, card games, recitations, games such as Twenty Questions, and dancing. But today, we are going to play one of the Victorians' favorite entertainment pastimes, the game of charades."

There were varying degrees of enthusiasm expressed by the audience. Jan thought there were as many groans as there were exclamations of delight.

"Of course, modern charades incorporate a few things the Victorians did not have in their repertoire," the speaker said. "In case there is anyone who is not familiar with the game, let's review the rules."

Quickly, she went over the six categories in classic modern charade games: Quotations, Movies, TV Shows, Books, Plays, and Songs, demonstrating the gestures for each, as well as other helpful hand motions like a hand cupping the ear for "sounds like," holding up fingers to illustrate the number of words in the answer and tapping certain numbers of fingers on the opposite forearm to show the number of syllables in a given word.

"I have created some fairly well-known answers within each of these topics. They have been divided into two groups and placed in these bags," she said, indicating a nearby table filled with paper gift bags. "The first person chosen from each team will draw a random selection from the bag to act out for her group." She explained a few more nonverbal cues—if a word was longer or shorter than the guess, and if a guess was "warmer" or "colder." Jan hadn't played charades in years and was thankful for the reminder as people were divided into teams of six or seven and play began.

Jan, Elaine, Virginia, and Sasha teamed up with Laurette and Betty Lee. Their opposing team was Eleanor, her daughter Roxanne, Kinley, Babette, and Joan Clayton, the master gardener.

Virginia pulled the first charade answer from the paper bag. Taking one look at it, she said, "Oh boy."

The rest of her team and the opposing team laughed.

"Um, four words," she said.

"You can't talk!" exclaimed at least three different people.

"Oh, I forgot." She glanced at her piece of paper again and then held up two fingers.

"Second word," Elaine said.

Virginia smiled and nodded. She held out her arms as if she was flying.

"Airplane?" guessed Jan.

Virginia shook her head.

"Jet. Helicopter," Sasha tried. "Goodyear blimp."

Virginia shot her granddaughter an incredulous look. She flapped her arms.

"Bird!" Betty Lee said.

Virginia nodded triumphantly. Dropping her arms, she looked expectant.

"A certain kind of bird?" Elaine asked.

Virginia nodded again.

"Robin."

Negative head shake.

"Wren."

Another negative shake.

More guesses, including loon, swan, duck, goose, crow, and hummingbird. All received negative head shakes.

Laurette appeared distracted, looking into her handbag for something, and Betty Lee elbowed her. "Pay attention!" Laurette straightened up, shooting her classmate a dirty look.

"Can you give us more of a hint?" Elaine asked.

Virginia looked blank. Then she brightened. She held up her hands before her, bent at the wrist, and hung out her tongue like a—

"Dog!" Jan said.

Virginia wilted, shaking her head.

"A type of dog?"

And so it went. They tried to think of two-word bird dogs, and then it devolved into naming every possible dog on the planet. Everyone was laughing, even Virginia.

The three-minute timer buzzed, and there was a chorus of disappointed groans.

"What was it?" Elaine asked.

"The Eagle Has Landed," Virginia said.

There was a moment of silence.

"But that's a book," Jan said. "You could have made the sign for book."

"It's also a movie," Betty Lee exclaimed, holding up her hands and cranking one as if she was showing a motion picture. "It's based on the book."

"I'm not much of a book or movie person," Virginia said apologetically. "I didn't realize that."

"All you had to do, Grandma," Sasha said, "was make the sign for bigger when we first guessed birds. If we'd gotten to eagle, we might have gotten the rest of it."

Virginia sighed. She crumpled up the note with the title written on it and tossed it at Sasha, shaking her head and grinning. "I've always been terrible at charades. Since you're so good at this, you can go next."

They ceded the floor to the other team. Roxanne took the first turn. Her clue was a one-word movie, and to everyone's amusement, the first pantomime she did was the same one Virginia had done, extending her arms wide. But when her team guessed, "Bird!" she shook her head, held her nose, and pantomimed drowning, gasping for air and finally lying on the floor.

"Titanic!" Babette shrieked.

"Yes." Roxanne leaped up off the floor and pointed at Babette. "She's got it."

Although most of the members of both teams were laughing at the spectacle, Jan noticed her aunt sitting almost frozen in her chair. She had a strained smile on her face, but it was clear she couldn't see much humor in the situation. Elbowing Elaine, Jan tilted her head in Aunt Virginia's direction.

Elaine, in turn, cut her eyes toward Eleanor, who also appeared less amused than the rest. The cousins exchanged a look. What was going on? It was fairly clear to them that the topic of drowning, introduced solely in jest, had a profound effect on Virginia and her friend. Betty Lee, the third member of their trio, appeared sublimely unaffected, as did Babette and Kinley.

"Nineteen seconds from start to finish," Betty Lee muttered. "We've got some work to do, girls."

Jan, Elaine, and the rest of their team laughed and agreed as Sasha rose to take a turn. Virginia appeared to regain her equilibrium and joined in the guessing. Their luck improved, and the opposing team had a difficult time with "The Lady and the Tramp." By the end of six rounds, the teams were neck and neck, tied at three wins each.

Elaine was the final person to act out a charade for the cousins' team. After pantomiming a quotation that was three words long, she immediately put her hands together with her wrists face to face.

"Handcuffs," Jan guessed.

Elaine nodded, but immediately she appeared to violently rip the cuffs off.

"Your hands are free?" Sasha suggested. "Free?"

Elaine nodded vigorously, holding up three fingers and pointing at Sasha.

"Free is the third word?" Virginia asked. She was catching on.

Elaine nodded vigorously, pointing to Virginia. Then she held up one finger.

"First word," Sasha guessed.

Elaine nodded. Then she used the gesture to indicate expanding a word or making it bigger.

"What word are we expanding?" Jan asked, puzzled.

Elaine pointed emphatically to Virginia.

"Free again?" Virginia asked, and Elaine nodded, beaming.

"Freedom," Betty Lee said instantly.

She got nodding and vigorous pointing in response.

Immediately, the teammates began shouting out every quotation they could think of that had the word "freedom" or "free" in it.

"'Freedom lies in being bold.' That's from Robert Frost," Sasha said. "American Lit 101."

"Give me liberty—oh, never mind." Virginia waved a hand as if to erase the phrase.

Elaine kept holding up one finger, and then three, trying to remind them, Jan realized, that both words were in the phrase.

"Freedom and justice for all." Betty Lee said. "No, that can't be right."

"The truth will set you free." That was Sasha.

"Freedom isn't free." Jan had sung a piece in her high school choir once with that phrase in it, and the melody danced through her head.

"Yes!" Elaine grinned, pointing at Jan. "That's it!"

"And you're at twenty-nine seconds," Rae said. She clapped her hand and looked at her team. "We've got to do better than that."

Kinley was the final team member to select a charade. The moment she opened the folded slip of paper and read it, she groaned.

"You're not supposed to talk," Betty Lee commanded. Her tone sounded more like that of a drill sergeant than a friend.

Kinley sighed. Signaling Betty Lee to flip over the timer, she made the sign for a song title and indicated it was five words. Then she just stood there, until her team shouted at her to move. In the end, she was unable to convey anything approaching the title, "The More We Get Together."

"That was a hard one," Virginia exclaimed. "Maybe we should give them a second chance."

"Are you crazy?" Betty Lee grinned fiercely. "We won fair and square."

As the session ended, everyone was flushed and laughing, having enjoyed the game. Jan noticed Sasha, seated beside

Laurette, point at Laurette's fingers. They were natural nails, and although they were not extremely short, Jan supposed it was possible she had removed French tips after losing one.

"Your nails are beautiful," she said. She held up her own short fingernails. "I can't stop biting mine."

Laurette shrugged, holding out one hand. "I've always had strong fingernails," she said. "I can't really help you with the biting problem, since that's never been a habit I picked up. Maybe you should get some of those rubber tips secretaries used to wear to flip through paper. If you wore those, you wouldn't be able to bite your nails."

Sasha attempted to look pleased. "Now there's an idea I hadn't thought of," she said as everyone rose and the charades broke up.

En masse, they headed toward the dining room, where the dinner buffet had been set up.

"That was a good observation," Jan said in an undertone to Sasha as they walked through the lobby.

Sasha grinned. "I figured I need to hold up my end of this investigation. She could have removed French tips, right?"

"It's possible, but I'm doubtful," Jan said honestly. "None look short or recently broken."

"True." Sasha looked disappointed. "This is hard."

Jan and Elaine both burst out laughing. "Very true," Elaine said. "Very true."

The table where Jan and Elaine sat with Virginia, Sasha, and the others would be called close to last, if Jan figured it right. Nudging Elaine, she said, "Let's go look at that yearbook again."

Splitting off to the side of the room, the cousins stopped at the table where the yearbooks were displayed. As they casually flipped through the pages, Elaine said, "What's up?"

"I wanted to get a better sense of Sally Manling," Jan said. "See if we can find out anything more about her."

They thumbed through the pages of the seniors' formal portraits, quickly locating Sally's photo. According to the brief blurb beneath it, she loved marching band, singing in the choir, and her puppy, Tipper. She was the captain of the swim team, and she planned to study elementary education at Gorham State Teachers College. Gorham, Jan knew was near Portland and was now part of the University of Southern Maine system.

Laurette Martel came to stand at Jan's elbow. "Ah, you're looking at Sally's picture. What a shame about Sally. She was a sweetheart."

Both cousins turned, startled.

"Pardon?" Elaine asked. "What was a shame?"

Laurette turned inquiring eyes on her. "Sally's death, I mean."

Elaine looked as stunned as Jan felt. "She's dead?"

CHAPTER ELEVEN

ally died the summer after we graduated," Laurette told the cousins. "I'd have thought your mother would have mentioned it to you. They were friends."

"What happened to her?" Jan asked impulsively.

The older woman's face was as somber as her voice. "She drowned at Damariscotta Lake." Damariscotta was a state park southeast of the cousins' hometown of Lancaster, closer to the coast.

Someone called Laurette's name then, and she waved and moved on. Jan and Elaine looked at each other in stunned silence.

"I wonder if she was in the guild," Jan said quietly.

"I wonder how it happened." Elaine's face reflected the deep sorrow Jan felt at the thought of that young, vibrant life cut short.

She'd wanted to be a teacher, Jan recalled. And she must have loved music and swimming, the activities mentioned in her yearbook summary. And she'd had a puppy. Jan swallowed hard, unable to prevent the thought that but for the grace of

God, that could have been one of her beautiful daughters. "That's tragic. If she was on the swim team, how on earth did she drown?"

"Who knows?" Elaine looked troubled. "Maybe Mom finds it difficult to talk about, and that's why she never said anything. But I suspect that's why she and Eleanor looked so distressed last night when that photo was shown during the Jeopardy game."

"And why the charade of 'Titanic' unnerved them." Jan suddenly was struck by a new—and awful—thought. "Elaine, all the notes that came with the anonymous gifts had water and swimming references in them. You don't suppose they could be related to Sally Manling's drowning, do you?"

Elaine's eyes were huge. "I certainly don't think we can discount it. We need to find out more about her death. I suppose it must have been accidental. Aren't drownings nearly always accidents?"

"Or murder," Jan said.

The cousins fell silent as the word dropped between them.

"Mom's avoided mentioning Sally on at least two occasions when she easily could have," Elaine finally said.

"And they were during the Jeopardy game when she was clearly upset, and when we were looking at the yearbook page where her photo was," Jan recalled.

"And you saw her face when Rae was pantomiming drowning." Elaine shuddered. "Now I understand what she must have been feeling."

"Eleanor was upset too," Jan recalled. "But Betty Lee didn't appear to be, not even last night when she showed that photo.

As close as Aunt Virginia, Eleanor, and Betty Lee were, surely Betty Lee would have known Sally too."

"I don't think I can ask Mom about Sally, if she hasn't mentioned her first. I don't want her to regret coming to this retreat." Elaine sighed. "But if there's a possibility these gifts are connected, we need to learn more about Sally Manling."

"Why don't we try an Internet search after dinner?" Jan suggested. "Maybe there's some mention of her online."

Their next step decided, the cousins joined Virginia and Sasha at the table. Betty Lee, Eleanor, and her daughters had yet to arrive.

"I have a question for all of you. Put on your thinking caps," Jan said, recalling something else she'd wanted to follow up on. "Does anyone remember who might have arrived late to supper yesterday evening?"

Virginia looked at her. "Well, Betty Lee came in late, remember? I knew she had that wedding rehearsal that might run over, and when she came in, that's exactly what she said."

"Laurette also came in late," Sasha said instantly. "Remember? She was talking to Betty Lee when they came through the door."

Virginia smiled. "That's right, she came in at the same time Betty Lee did."

"But I asked Betty Lee if she was at the wedding rehearsal, and she said they only met in the lobby," Jan put in.

"Didn't your friend Ida's daughter, Jeanice, come in late too?" Elaine asked. "She had her coat and her handbag with her, and she put her weekender against the wall, remember?"

"That's right," Virginia said. "And I'm almost positive that she was the last latecomer, so there only must have been those three."

"Did anyone leave early, do you recall?"

Sasha shook her head. "I don't think so. Everyone was paying attention because the president gave that brief overview of the weekend, remember? They would have had to pass right by our table to leave the room."

Which was a good point, Jan thought.

Virginia looked from Jan to Elaine. "You're asking about them because someone had to have put those notes on our pillows during dinner."

Elaine nodded. "Exactly."

"I can't imagine that Jeanice, Laurette, or Betty Lee would do something like that. It has to have been someone from the hotel, don't you think?"

"Heloise says staff are not permitted to enter rooms," Jan told her. "She says they encourage conference leaders to tie any gifts to the doorknobs."

"Oh, like at one of my races," Sasha put in. "We got bags of trail mix with rubber bands on them over our doorknobs."

But as Jan glanced at Elaine, she could see that Elaine didn't agree that the three people were entirely innocent. And, as she imagined Elaine was thinking, Betty Lee, Laurette, and Jeanice all would stay on their short list of suspects for the time being, if only because they appeared to be the only ones who would have had any opportunity to place the notes. That is, if the individual was a member of the guild. She still wasn't prepared to rule out Heloise or even the housekeeper, Adrianna.

After dinner, when Virginia, Elaine, and Sasha headed up to the soft-serve ice cream machine for dessert, Jan took the opportunity to ask the rest of their tablemates if they recalled anyone leaving dinner early on Friday evening. But no one had, and like Sasha, Betty Lee pointed out that anyone leaving would have had to walk right past their table.

"We have an hour to relax before we're supposed to meet in the lounge for a sing-along," Eleanor said. "What are you girls going to do?" She was looking at her daughters as she spoke.

"I'm going upstairs and call my family," Roxanne said. "Jenny said she was going to join us for breakfast and tomorrow's workshops, remember? I want to let her know she should be here by eight. Jenny's my daughter," she said to Jan. "She had plans for Friday and Saturday, but she's coming over tomorrow."

"It'll be delightful to meet her," Jan said sincerely. Eleanor and her daughters were lovely women, and she imagined this granddaughter would be too. "How far away does she live?"

"She's near Bangor," said Eleanor. "It's about an hour's drive."

"Near Bangor." Jan's eyebrows rose, as did her spirits. Maybe she could fix one problem, at least. "Do you think she would be willing to make a stop and pick up a package of tea for us?" Quickly, she explained their presentation in the morning as well as the zip code mix-up that had resulted in their tea being sent to the wrong place.

"Oh, I'm sure she'd be happy to do that," Roxanne said.

"Here comes Elaine," Jan said, indicating her cousin, who was approaching with a cone of chocolate soft-serve. "She can give you the name of the place and the person who is her contact there," Jan said. "Elaine, come listen to this," she called.

After she gave her cousin a quick summary of the plan, Elaine's face lit up. "Really? I wouldn't want to put your daughter out, but if she doesn't mind, that would be an enormous help."

Roxanne waved a hand. "I'm sure she'd be happy to help. I'll call her right now." Elaine shared the contact information with her, and then set off to make her own call to the other tea shop. It was sheer luck that the tearoom near Bangor was open on Sundays, Jan realized. If the company they'd ordered from had to deliver the tea to the wrong place, at least it was the right wrong delivery!

"I'm going to check out the library," Rae told her mother.

Jan and Elaine chose not to reveal their own plans: Elaine was going to research Sally Manling's drowning online, while Jan would go to the hotel library and see if there were any books of Maine state history that might mention it. Virginia and Sasha lingered over their ice cream.

"I'll meet you in the library," Jan said to Elaine, who had finished her call. "I want to check on something first." She had seen Crystal, the younger server who had helped them in the kitchen after their arrival yesterday.

Approaching her, she said, "Hi, Crystal. Do you have a moment to answer a question or two?"

The young woman grinned. "Sure. As long as you promise to save me a sliver of that bread you're planning to make tomorrow."

Jan laughed. "I'll leave enough for the whole staff, I promise."

"Awesome. So what's your question?"

"I'm curious about which people on staff would have a master key that opens all the guest rooms, or even would have access to one."

Crystal thought for a moment. "Well, the hotel manager, of course. I'm sure you met her. Mrs. Invers?"

Jan nodded. "I did."

"And Ralph, the maintenance man, has one, and Adrianna, our head housekeeper, has one. Ralph is off today. He'll be around after nine tomorrow morning, if you need to speak with him. As far as I know, those are the only masters. If none of them are around, there's a master in Heloise's office for whoever's on the desk or in case of emergencies. But other than maintenance and housekeeping, we have surprisingly few times that people lock themselves out of their rooms or anything like that. Those magnetic key cards that don't work half the time are a lot more troublesome than these good old metal keys."

"I'm sure that's true," Jan said with a smile. All the keys had been provided on little stretchy wrist bracelets, so if a guest didn't have a handbag or a pocket, they could even wear their key.

"Anything else?" Crystal didn't look particularly eager to get on with her tasks.

"Can you point out the kitchen manager, or whoever deals with arranging meals?"

"Sure thing," the girl said, pointing toward the buffet, where several servers were taking things down. "That would be Deanne. She's the tall blonde over there."

133

Jan thanked her, then approached the woman and introduced herself. "I have a quick question for you," she said. "Can you tell me if everyone who registered for the conference was here for the meal Friday evening?"

"Absolutely," Deanne said. "We had eighty-eight people signed up, and we served eighty-eight meals. Same for today. Eighty-eight meals every time."

"Thank you," Jan said. "You're a model of efficiency."

Deanne laughed. "I don't know about that, but I sure do hate to waste food."

Jan could agree with that sentiment. She and Elaine occasionally found it frustrating to decide how many pastries and assorted items they should make on a daily basis, as many of their clientele were walk-ins, except for special events like wedding receptions. "In any case," she said to the kitchen manager, "I really appreciate the information."

As she headed for the library, she saw Eleanor and Betty Lee standing in the lobby.

"But it just seems like I should have gotten a gift too," Betty Lee was saying. "Since you and Virginia did, I mean. Why would I have been left out?" She sounded distinctly disgruntled.

"It's not as if they were nice gifts," Eleanor said, her voice sharper than Jan had ever heard it. "The notes sound kind of mean, don't you think? And the gifts weren't really gifts at all, just weird little things that none of us understood..." Her voice trailed off, and Jan had to wonder if Eleanor believed her own words. She suspected both Virginia and Eleanor feared that the references to water and swimming in the notes pointed to Sally Manling.

"I just don't understand it," Betty Lee said. "I'm the only one of you who never married. All of you who got notes have husbands. Or had one."

"I can't believe that has anything to do with it," Eleanor said, sounding as if she was just about out of patience with her friend, who could not seem to get past the fact that she hadn't received one of the unwelcome gifts.

"It seems to me that there has to be some reason why I was left out, and that's the only one I can come up with," Betty Lee went on. "Especially since you and Virginia got them, and everybody knows we three did everything together. What else could it be?"

There was a pause. "I don't know," Eleanor said, "but I sincerely doubt that's it."

But it was an interesting point, Jan thought, and one that had been bothering her. Why wouldn't Betty Lee have gotten one of the notes? If she was one of Sally's closer friends, and if the notes related to Sally's drowning, it would be logical for her to receive one too. The picture of the three women with Sally hovering behind them was impossible to forget.

The other possibility, and one that she hated to even consider, was that Betty Lee herself had sent the notes. She'd had opportunity, coming in late to dinner as she had. And she certainly seemed fixated on the whole topic. Could it be that her interest was only to keep the pressure on the other women? Like when a murderer hovered around the crowd at the scene of a crime? Jan grinned at herself, thinking she'd been reading too many whodunits.

She made her way to the library, where Rae was talking animatedly on the phone to someone. As soon as she saw Jan enter, she smiled and nodded, and then she rose and politely left the room.

The library was small. It had an ancient armchair and a small loveseat along one wall. Between them sat a small table with a lamp perched on it. Floor-to-ceiling bookshelves lined the room, and a folding stool stood tucked behind the door so that people could reach volumes on the higher shelves. There was a surprising number of books crammed into the little room.

Jan wandered to the bookshelf closest to the door and began to peruse the titles. This section, top to bottom, appeared to hold a wide variety of mysteries and detective fiction, everything from Agatha Christie, Raymond Chandler, and Arthur Conan Doyle to works by current authors.

The next floor-to-ceiling section appeared to have science fiction and fantasy selections. She smiled as she trailed a finger over Tolkien's *Lord of the Rings*. Again, there was a wide variety of authors represented. "Oh, Pern, I love you," she said as she came to a collection of Anne McCaffrey novels, including a number from her popular Dragonriders of Pern series.

A third collection was romance, while a fourth on the back wall held selections of children's books, from those for the very young to those for young teens. She was amused and delighted to see several Nancy Drew mysteries there.

Another shelf on the wall opposite the door held a classical collection of fiction, plays, and poetry by Emily Dickinson, Henry Wadsworth Longfellow, Jack London, William Shakespeare, Herman Melville, Robert Frost, the Brontë sisters, and many others.

Moving on to the side of the room behind the seating arrangement, she found the top three shelves of the next section devoted to thrillers and true crime, while the bottom appeared to be autobiographies, biographies, and memoirs.

The next-to-last floor-to-ceiling arrangement was filled with different rows of reading materials: one row each of Christian nonfiction, humor, Westerns, and self-help manuals. There even were a few children's books on the bottom shelves, everything from books for early readers to middle grades fiction. Something, she thought, for a rainy day when there was little else to do with your vacation.

Finally, in the very last bookshelf, Jan found the local books she'd been hoping the little library would hold. Maine fiction authors, Maine memoirs, field guides for bird and plant lovers, haunted house stories, and lots and lots of tales of local Maine doings.

She blew out a breath. "Wow. Where might I even start?"

The door opened and Elaine walked in.

"Hey," Jan said. "Good timing. I just found a whole collection of Maine books. Did you have any luck?"

"Sort of. I'm glad I decided to bring along my laptop," Elaine said. "I Googled Sally Manling. There wasn't a lot of information, but she supposedly was mentioned in a book by a woman from Portland who wrote about drownings around the state."

"Ugh," Jan said. "Can you imagine doing the research for that? How depressing."

"I agree," Elaine said, "but since she mentioned Sally Manling in her book, I'm glad she did."

"What's the title?" Jan asked.

Elaine shot her a droll look. "*Drownings in Maine,* by Ellen Smathers."

Jan suppressed a smile as she turned back to the bookcase. She started with the top shelf, while Elaine knelt at her feet and took the bottom.

"Not up there," Jan reported as she began checking the titles on the next shelf down.

"Nor there." Elaine indicated the bottom and started on the next one up.

Finally, when Jan was nearly finished reading the titles on the third shelf from the top, she let out a whoop. "Found it!"

She pulled the slim volume from the shelf, then opened it and looked at the introduction. After a moment, she said, "Oh my, I guess I didn't realize drownings are the number-one cause of death in infants under a year. And this: they're the fourth leading cause of death for children under four."

Elaine shuddered. "I can't even imagine what it would be like to get there too late," she said in a low voice. "How do you get over losing a child?" She gestured toward the book in her cousin's hands. "Even a grown child like Sally. You'd never be the same."

"No. Never." Jan looked back down at the introduction, silent for a moment as she read. "This says the book does not cover every drowning death in Maine, merely the more widely publicized or spectacular ones. There are instances of people drowning in vehicular accidents, one from 1962 who drowned right in front of a lifeguard, and other things like that. Does it have an index?" She flipped to the back of the book and sighed with relief. "It does. Thank goodness. I was afraid we might have to read through it to find the pertinent information about Sally."

"That probably would give us both nightmares," Elaine added.

"Page 112," Jan muttered, flipping through the compilation. She stopped as a chill worked its way down her spine. "The title of the chapter is 'Out of Her Depth.'"

CHAPTER TWELVE

Elaine whistled silently. "'Out of Her Depth' is extraordinarily similar to the wording in Mom's note. Didn't hers start with 'You must have been out of your depth'?" Her shoulders drooped. "I was really hoping there was no connection. It just seems so cruel for someone to bring up a sad event in someone's past like this. I could tell how upset Mom and Eleanor felt."

"Oddly, Betty Lee doesn't seem nearly as upset," Jan said. "As we've noted. I mean, she saw the notes, and even if she didn't get one, it seems like she would find something that brought back the experience upsetting. But I just overheard a conversation between Eleanor and her a little while ago, and I would guess her biggest beef is that she didn't get a note. She thinks it's because she's the only one who didn't marry."

Elaine's eyebrows rose. "That's not an angle I'd thought of."

"Me neither," Jan said. "But I suppose it's possible that there's something to it."

"Then again," Elaine pointed out, "she was the one who enlarged the photo for Jeopardy. So if she'd had a sad moment, she may have gotten past it before this weekend."

"Hmm." Jan wasn't sure she agreed. "Maybe. Or maybe she's the one who planted the notes. If this all has something to do with Sally's death, could she really be hard-hearted enough to shove that photo at your mom and Eleanor with no warning just to shock or hurt them?"

"That's hard to imagine," Elaine agreed. "She's a little brusque and possibly demanding of her musicians, but she's friendly and fun. If indeed she is behind the notes, maybe she simply didn't realize how the water references would resonate."

Jan sighed. "I suppose that's possible. But that makes me doubt it's Betty Lee, because I can't imagine that she wouldn't realize the connection." Returning her attention to the book, she began to skim the paragraphs. As it turned out, Sally's story was only the beginning of that particular chapter. Even so, the spare facts were shocking.

"Elaine," Jan said in a low voice, "Sally was on an overnight camping trip at Damariscotta Lake State Park the night she died. It says here she was with three friends."

Her cousin looked horrified. "Was she with Mom, Eleanor, and Betty Lee? That certainly would explain Mom and Eleanor's reactions."

"It still wouldn't explain why anyone would send them threatening notes, though, or those weird little gifts that aren't really gifts. Who gives an old postcard as a gift?"

"There's got to be more significance to those things," Elaine said. "We just haven't figured it out yet."

Jan continued to read. "The friends are not named, but don't you think it almost had to be them? It just says she decided to go for a solo swim after dark. It doesn't say why none of the others went with her. They mention that she wasn't found missing until morning, and that she was on the swim team and should have been fine."

"I can't believe my mother has never mentioned a word about this." Elaine shook her head in disbelief. "The one thing I can say is that Mom always was almost rabid about making sure we could swim and that no one ever went into the water without a buddy."

"I remember that," Jan said.

"She made me that way too," Elaine confessed, "and now it makes sense. I bet this is why."

"Even if she wasn't one of the people on the camping trip, losing a friend like that would be difficult. But if she was right on the scene when they realized their friend was missing—and found in the lake—I can't even imagine how traumatizing that would be."

Jan closed the book and replaced it on the shelf. Checking the time on her phone, she said, "We're going to have to think about this. If the three friends with her were Betty Lee, Eleanor, and Aunt Virginia, then why *didn't* Betty Lee get one of the notes referencing swimming? And why did Kinley and Babette get them? It makes no sense, unless Betty Lee is the one behind the notes."

"That's possible," Elaine said. "Or maybe we're on the wrong track with this train."

The cousins exchanged a long look.

"You do realize," Jan said slowly, "that the only way to figure it out is to talk to them about it? If your mother says she was there the night Sally drowned, you can bet Eleanor and Betty Lee were too."

"So we should talk to all of them." Elaine clutched her head between both hands for a minute. "Okay, but can we do it after the entertainment? I wouldn't want to interfere with their enjoyment of the rest of the planned events."

"And the last thing we want to do is tip off whoever put those notes in the rooms," Jan said grimly. "I'm determined to figure it out."

ELAINE AND JAN were a little late to the beginning of the evening's entertainment. Fortunately, it began with music in the large conference room.

The tables and chairs had been rearranged, and an old upright piano had been uncovered and angled out from its customary space along one wall. Betty Lee sat at the piano, and one of the guild members stood near her singing a solo as Jan and Elaine slid into the seats Virginia and Sasha had saved for them.

"Where on earth have you been?" Virginia whispered. "We checked in the room and the lobby. Were you outside?"

"In the library," Elaine whispered back. "Sorry."

Aware of her mother searching her face, Elaine turned her attention to the music. The vocalist had a lovely alto voice. She was singing "Annabelle Lee," which Elaine knew was a poem by Edgar Allen Poe that had been set to music.

Polite clapping filled the room when the soloist finished the piece. Two more songs followed, one another solo and the other a duet. Next, Betty Lee announced, was a piano duet.

"It was considered quite genteel to be a skilled pianist during Victorian times, and many players were highly accomplished. Piano solos and duets were a staple at house parties. Although you may not know this, Queen Victoria and Prince Albert both were accomplished vocalists and pianists as well. In fact, their shared love of music was one of the things that drew them into courtship. And here's another tidbit you may not know: Victoria proposed to Albert, rather than the other way around."

"Why?" asked a woman in the front. "I wouldn't think that would be socially acceptable in that era."

"Normally, no," Betty Lee agreed. "But because she had already been crowned Queen, he could not propose to her, so she had to do the honors."

"Is it true they were cousins?" the same woman asked.

Betty Lee nodded. "Her mother and his father were siblings, so the pair were first cousins. Victoria confided to her diary that he was 'extremely handsome,' and later, in a letter to an uncle, she mentioned that Albert had all the qualities she desired to make her extremely happy. But I digress. Albert was a keen follower of Felix Mendelssohn's music. Albert himself was a composer, and when Mendelssohn was invited to Buckingham Palace to meet the Prince and the Queen, the story is that they were as starstruck as we might be meeting our own musical legends. With that in mind, I'm going to call on Terese Kofax to help me share with you a lovely piano duet by Herr Mendelssohn."

As another woman joined Betty Lee at the piano and the pair adjusted their seating, Virginia leaned over. "This should be quite a treat. Terese is the current choral music director in a nearby school system, and she's as amazingly gifted as Betty Lee." She paused. "What were you doing in the library?"

Elaine put a finger to her lips, thankful that the piano duet was about to begin. "I'll tell you later."

"Amazingly gifted," was quite an understatement, Elaine thought ten minutes later when the piece concluded. The entire room rose to offer a standing ovation to the two artists.

"Next," Betty Lee said when the clapping finally died away, "we're going to have a sing-along." She passed out sheets with the lyrics to several tunes on them before resuming. "I'm going to serenade you with 'Love's Old Sweet Song.' Many of you will recognize this song from your own childhoods. It was composed by an Irishman named James Malloy, and it was one of the best-known ballads of the first half of the twentieth century. When I get to the chorus, please feel free to sing along if you know it."

"I love this song," Jan said. "I catch myself humming for days every time I hear it."

As the first verse concluded, Elaine and Jan, and many others in the room, joined in singing the chorus:

Just a song at twilight, when the lights are low,
And the flickering shadows softly come and go,
Tho' the heart be weary, sad the day and long,
Still to us at twilight comes Love's old song,
Comes Love's old sweet song.

It really was a lovely song, Jan thought, heavy-laden with reminiscences from her childhood, when her grandmother had sung it. She imagined Elaine was recalling some of the same memories.

Sasha leaned over. "That would have made a great charades selection," she whispered, making Jan chuckle.

The sing-along continued with several more selections, all but one of which Jan knew. She was familiar with "The Lost Chord," which was one of her personal favorites, "Kathleen Mavourneen," and "Come into the Garden, Maud." But she had never heard "Ben Bolt," whose lyrics wept with the sorrow of aging and having lost most of one's friends and memories. They moved on to "Sally in Our Alley," "Cherry Ripe," and finally, to close out the singing, "Rule, Britannia." It was as wonderful in its way as the Jeopardy game had been the evening before. Betty Lee appeared to be a master at knowing how to please her guild members. But could she be a master at writing nasty notes as well?

The club president stood to thank Betty Lee and the others for giving of their talents to make the evening so memorable. "And now," she announced, "we're going to have another game night! It won't be exactly Victorian in nature, because we're including a number of contemporary board and card games. But the concept, that of social entertainment that doesn't depend on anything electronic, will mirror Victorian times." She clapped her hands. "Turn off those phones and let's play games!"

Women moved into different groups right away. There was a table of bridge players that included Virginia and Betty Lee, as well as another group playing mah-jongg. While Elaine and Sasha went to play Scrabble, Jan joined a table playing Clue. She always enjoyed the simple game, which required concentration, observation, and deduction. There were also tables playing Yahtzee and Parcheesi, while a few other people who apparently were not "into" games, took advantage of the colored pencils and adult coloring books that had been provided and were quietly chatting as they worked on their art.

Heloise Invers had pulled up a chair to that table, Jan noticed. Coloring furiously, she also appeared to be talking a mile a minute to Jeanice Evanak. Jan watched intently for a few moments, noticing that Jeanice rarely made eye contact with her. Her body language even discouraged conversation, as she had all but turned away. Her lack of attention seemed marked.

The other women at the table weren't much kinder. When directly addressed, one or another would respond, but it was clear that the coloring crowd either didn't know Heloise well and was somewhat taken aback by her familiarity, or they knew her too well and were trying not to encourage her. Whichever it was, it was sad.

Idly, Jan observed the group coloring at the table next to hers, taking the opportunity to check out everyone's manicures. Jeanice and one of the others had French manicures, but none of the nails was missing. Two had no polish at all, and one wore pale coral polish.

Then another thought occurred to her. Heloise had been at the desk when Jan and Elaine had checked in, and they'd seen her there for some time after that. But how long had Heloise stayed at the desk? Had she been there when the late-comers checked in?

The bridge players took a break just as the game of Clue ended. Jan approached Betty Lee, who was talking to Laurette. "Was Heloise at the desk when you arrived yesterday?"

Betty Lee nodded immediately. It looked as if she resisted the urge to roll her eyes. "Yes. One does not forget Heloise."

"I came in just after Betty Lee," Laurette said, "and she was there when I checked in too." So that answered one question—Betty Lee didn't contradict Laurette, which meant that she really must have arrived then.

Laurette had her handbag on her shoulder, but she had her hand inside the bag, and she looked into it occasionally. Jan wondered whimsically if she had brought a pocket pet to the retreat in her purse. She surely did seem concerned about whatever she had in that bag—Jan had noticed her doing a similar thing on several occasions.

As play resumed at the bridge table, Heloise was in the room still. She'd drifted over to another group and was watching play over someone's shoulder, offering suggestions that, from the look on the face of the woman seated in front of her, were not particularly appreciated. Knowing that the hotel manager had been at the desk then still didn't mean Heloise hadn't sneaked away after the latecomers had arrived, but it certainly shortened the window of time she would have had to get into all four rooms and leave the notes and gifts.

Then again, how long would it have taken? Jan realized that she needed to know where all the rooms were located. If they were all close, it could have taken mere minutes. If, however, they were at distant ends of hallways and not on the same floor, it would have taken a little more time. And there may have been more opportunity for someone to have seen the person slinking around. She made herself a mental note to talk to the housekeeper again.

As some of the games ended, some people drifted into knots to chat awhile, while others yawned and began saying good night to their friends. Seeing their opportunity to speak with the three friends about to vanish, Jan hurried to Elaine's side. "We need to catch your mom and her BFFs, remember? Maybe we should ask them to come to the library."

"Oh, good idea. You get Eleanor and I'll get Mom and Betty Lee when this bridge game ends. I believe they said they're going to play a short version because it would get too late. Hey, Sasha's going out for a run. Do you think it's safe?"

"Again?"

Elaine grinned. "Again."

Jan glanced at the deep velvety night outside the windows. "Yes, as long as she has reflective gear and wears a headlamp or something. The lake road is pretty quiet at night."

"Good. That's what I told her too."

Jan chuckled. "She's an adult. We're a little ridiculous."

Elaine grinned. "She may have mentioned something along those lines to me."

Glancing over at the card table, Jan saw that she had been just in time. The bridge players were laying down their final hands. "Okay. Meet you in the library."

Eleanor and both her daughters had joined the Parcheesi game, which also had ended. Approaching the group, Jan smiled at them all. "Who won?"

"None of us," Roxanne said glumly, but they all chuckled with good-natured humor. "I'm heading up to the room. I want to call home again before I hit the hay. See you in the morning, Jan."

"I'm, uh, going out for a walk," Rae said. Her cheeks blazed with red color. "Oh, Jan, I hope you don't mind," she burst out, "but Clifton Young asked me to meet him for a little stroll. He said you're just friends. Is that true?"

Jan smiled. Secretly, she was enormously relieved that she hadn't broken Clifton's heart. She suspected she hadn't even dented it since he appeared to be moving on with such speed. "That's absolutely true," she said, raising her hand to shoulder height in loose imitation of the Boy Scouts' three-fingered pledge. "Clifton is a lovely man. Go enjoy yourself."

Mentioning Clifton reminded Jan that Bob never had returned her call. Still, she would see him soon. Although she hadn't heard from him, he'd told her he wanted to take a walk again tonight. It was nearly eight now, and they'd met at eight thirty last night, so he probably assumed they would get together at the same time.

Unaware of Jan's preoccupation, Rae said, "Thank you so much. You're the best." She blew Jan a kiss before she turned and hurried off.

As Rae headed toward the lobby, Jan took Eleanor aside. "Would you join Virginia, Betty Lee, Elaine, and me in the library for a few minutes?" Eleanor looked surprised but agreed readily.

Just ahead of them, Jan saw Elaine, Aunt Virginia, and Betty Lee entering the library. Her stomach churned. What if they were wrong? What if the three friends mentioned on that camping trip had not been these three? They would be dredging up heartbreaking memories for the trio of friends unnecessarily.

Then again, those memories already had come up, she recalled, thinking of Virginia's face when she first had seen the photo of Sally during the Jeopardy game. Her aunt and Eleanor both had been upset.

Betty Lee, however, had not been. That was odd, to say the least. Was it simply because she'd already seen the photo and become desensitized to its impact? Or perhaps she wasn't a person to indulge in her feelings in public. Betty Lee struck Jan as an extremely capable and efficient person with a personal off-limits area about a mile wide. She might be very good at hiding emotion. Recalling Aunt Virginia's explanation about Betty Lee's fiancé being killed in an army accident, she wondered if such disappointment at a young age could have toughened the woman.

Jan followed Eleanor into the room and closed the door behind them. The small room felt cozy with five people in it. Virginia and Betty Lee had taken seats and Eleanor joined them. Elaine opened the folding stool and perched on the top step, while Jan leaned against one of the bookshelves.

"This feels like a secret meeting," Betty Lee said, grinning. "What's going on?"

Jan took a deep breath. "Elaine and I need to ask you some questions about Sally Manling," she said baldly.

Betty Lee's lighthearted smile died immediately. She looked as stricken as Virginia and Eleanor. "I knew I shouldn't have used that picture," she said quietly. She turned to her friends. "And I'm sorry I didn't warn you. I just sort of got used to it as I was working on the Jeopardy game questions, and I forgot how shocking it might be to you both—until I saw your faces when I unveiled the clue, and then it was too late."

Jan cleared her throat. It appeared that several of her questions about Betty Lee had just been answered. "We learned about Sally's accident. Were you the three who were camping with her at the time?"

There was a long pause. The three friends exchanged glances. Finally, Virginia nodded. Silent tears rolled down her cheeks. "Why are you asking?"

Elaine cleared her throat. "We noticed that all four of the notes received referenced water—expressions that refer to swimming and drowning. It made us wonder why someone would choose those words, and when we realized your friend had drowned, we couldn't help but consider that there could be a connection."

Betty Lee looked stunned. Neither Virginia nor Eleanor looked quite as thunderstruck. Jan suspected that both women had made the potential connection already.

"I have to confess that it crossed my mind," Eleanor said.

"Mine too." Virginia nodded. "But I can't imagine anyone being so cruel. What would be gained by dredging that up after all these years?"

"That's what we'd like to figure out," Elaine said.

"Can you tell us about Sally?" Jan asked. "Anything that comes to mind."

"She was smart," Betty Lee said immediately. "I mean, she was so intelligent that sometimes she didn't sound like a normal teenager when she talked. Does that make any sense?"

"We liked her, though," Virginia said quickly. "She spent a lot of time working with us on the yearbook."

"I think she always wished she could be as close to someone as the three of us were," Eleanor added. "She tried so hard to be…"

"To be our fourth," Betty Lee said flatly. "But we three had been tight since the beginning of junior high and we had a natural affinity for one another. I'm probably not explaining that very well."

"We were never unkind to her," Virginia put in. "But sometimes we would have sleepovers or activities with just the three of us, and we didn't include her."

"We did occasionally." Betty Lee still looked shaken.

"She really wanted to fit in." Eleanor spread her hands. "But she never seemed to get the joke at the same time, or she'd make a comment that didn't quite gel with the flow of the conversation…"

"It was like she was trying too hard sometimes." That was Betty Lee again. "I always thought it was because she was thinking so much faster than most of us that in her head she was about three conversational steps ahead."

"She was almost the class valedictorian." Virginia smiled. "I'll never forget how mad she was that Hazel Halterman beat her by some ridiculous half a percentage point."

Eleanor half-smiled. "That did make her mad, didn't it?"

"Was Sally in the guild?" Elaine asked.

Virginia shook her head. "No. She was in several clubs at school, and she worked at the YMCA as a lifeguard. I don't think she had time."

There was a silence in the library as the three older women traveled back through time.

"So what happened at the lake?" Elaine finally asked softly.

CHAPTER THIRTEEN

The mood in the room sobered further after Elaine asked about the drowning.

Eleanor swallowed a sob.

"It was all my fault." Betty Lee, usually so stoic, looked miserable.

"It wasn't," Virginia said vehemently. "It was a horrible accident that we all feel terrible about and will until the day we die. But it was not your fault."

Eleanor looked at the cousins. "We wanted to do something special together. We had just graduated and soon all of us would be going off to different futures. Sally was going to be a teacher, and Betty Lee wanted to study music. Virginia also was headed to college and I was getting married. So we decided to go on an overnight camping trip at Damariscotta Lake. It's a beautiful place," she told them, looking lost in the memory. "We roasted hot dogs over a fire—"

"Back when hot dogs weren't stuffed with icky additives," Betty Lee put in, a small smile appearing before it died.

"And then we made s'mores with roasted marshmallows," Virginia contributed.

"And we gabbed," Eleanor added. "Oh man, could we talk for hours about basically nothing."

"Sounds like most of the teenage girls we know." Elaine smiled.

The silence fell again, heavy and smothering, as the fleeting amusement died away.

Finally, Virginia sighed. "But then, something unfortunate happened."

"It wasn't 'unfortunate,'" Betty Lee said, her voice rising. "It was just plain mean, and I'm the one who said it." She turned to Jan and Elaine. "Sally never had a boyfriend that any of us knew of. My boyfriend, Mitch, was the quarterback of the football team. Half the girls in the school thought he was 'the bomb.'"

"Only back then we'd have said he was 'outta sight,'" Virginia interjected.

Betty Lee grinned briefly. "He sure was. Sally was one of the girls who liked him, and we all noticed her mooning over him at one time or another. So while we were talking about college and leaving each other and generally being really silly, I told Sally she'd have to keep an eye on Mitch for me, since she and he would be at the same school and I'd be going elsewhere. And then"—Betty Lee gulped—"I told her I knew she was sweet on him, and I told her she had to promise me she wouldn't steal him."

"It was supposed to be a joke," Eleanor said, her voice hollow. "What none of us understood at the time was that Sally had no idea how transparent her feelings were. She was mortified and so embarrassed, and she jumped up crying and ran away from the campsite."

"We were just a bunch of thoughtless, naive girls," Virginia said, clearly still castigating herself sixty years later. "We didn't know what to do, what to say." She spread her hands. "We just sat there staring at each other."

"We should have gone after her." Eleanor dropped her head into her hands and repeated it, scrubbing her hands hard across her face. "We should have gone after her."

"But then we heard a car door slam," Betty Lee said. She leaned over and put a hand on Eleanor's back. Her voice was a defeated monotone when she continued. "After a while, when she didn't come back, we assumed she had gone to sleep in the car. I felt stupid and horrified at what I'd said, and I couldn't face apologizing to Sally right that minute. So I told the others I'd apologize to her in the morning."

"And we all felt a little better after that, and we went to sleep," Virginia concluded.

"That's always haunted me," Betty Lee confessed. "If I had gone to find her right away, might I have realized she was going swimming? Maybe caught her before she did? Or at least gone with her?"

"You couldn't know," Jan said gently. She felt sick inside for the three women, mired in such a sad memory.

Silence fell, and again, Elaine was the one to break it after a short time. "When did you realize she had gone into the lake?"

Virginia exhaled heavily. "When we woke up, all three of us went to the car to apologize. But Sally wasn't there. We called and searched around the parking lot and the bathhouse. At first, we thought she had done something stupid like try to hitchhike home."

"But then we found her shoes, her shorts, and her towel by the edge of the lake," Eleanor said. "At that point, we were completely freaked out, because they were wet with dew, so we knew she'd left them there the night before."

"Virginia and I also were good swimmers, although we weren't as good as Sally, so we decided to stay and start searching the lake while Eleanor drove back to the closest town—"

"Jefferson," Eleanor supplied.

"But we never did find her. For a while we hoped she had swum across the lake to the far side, but there was no trace of her there."

"And then all these men came from Jefferson, policemen and firefighters and volunteers." Betty Lee stared into a distant past. "They didn't find her body until the next day."

The room went silent again. Elaine took a pack of tissues from her handbag and passed one out to everyone, then ostentatiously blew her own nose, giving the older women a chance to regain their composure.

"We were crushed by grief," Virginia said.

"And guilt." Betty Lee shoved her crumpled tissue into a pocket of the boxy jacket she wore.

"We were so young," Eleanor said. "We didn't know how to handle such an awful experience, so we really never spoke of the details again to each other or anyone else. At least I haven't."

Virginia shook her head, as did Betty Lee.

"That's probably why I was able to show that picture at Jeopardy," Betty Lee said. "I've never allowed myself to think much about it." She cleared her throat.

Jan could almost feel relief flowing from Betty Lee as she released the submerged guilt she'd lived with for so long.

After another long pause, Betty Lee said, "Sally always was passionate about swimming. And anything water-related, remember?" Turning to Jan and Elaine, she said, "She spent several summers as a lifeguard and camp counselor for at-risk city kids. She talked all the time about those kids and how much fun they had learning to canoe and swim."

"A lot of them came back summer after summer, so she really got to know them," Eleanor put in.

Virginia said, "The year after Sally died, I started sponsoring a child each summer. One child from the Sunshine Program gets to come to summer camp each year in memory of Sally."

"Oh, what a lovely idea." Betty Lee clapped her hands together. "We must be on the same wavelength. I make a monthly donation to a program that supports low-income girls with low self-esteem."

Eleanor was smiling. "And guess what? I donate a piece of my art each year to an auction at our old high school that benefits the Sally Manling Swim Scholarship."

Virginia made a small sound, reaching over to grab her friend's hand. "That's sweet."

"I think," Elaine said quietly, "your friend Sally would be very pleased at the way you've honored her memory."

"But that doesn't change that fact that something has brought her to our minds this weekend," Betty Lee said. "Do you really think those notes have something to do with Sally?"

"And if that's so, why didn't Betty Lee get one?" Virginia asked.

"Maybe," Elaine said, "someone went into the wrong room? Could that be why Kinley or Babette got one?"

But Virginia was already shaking her head. "No, my name was written on the envelope, remember?"

Elaine did remember, even as Eleanor nodded. "Mine too," she said. "So if it was in the wrong room with Betty Lee's name written on the envelope, wouldn't the person who found it have given it to Betty Lee?"

The five women fell silent.

"I have no idea," Virginia said. Slowly, she rose, and her two friends rose with her. "Whew! I'm exhausted. I'm going to bed."

After the three older women retired to their rooms, Jan and Elaine sat looking at each other in the library.

"Wow," Jan said. "My heart hurts for them. I can't imagine going through the loss of a friend in such traumatic fashion at the age of seventeen or eighteen."

"I don't believe Betty Lee is behind the notes and gifts anymore. Her reaction was too genuine, I think," Elaine said.

"Agreed. So that leaves us with Heloise, the housekeeper Adrianna, and the other two people who came in late, who might have had the time to place those in the rooms."

"If they were able to get their hands on a key," Elaine reminded her.

"But I continue to be baffled and befuddled by one glaring problem in our search for the person who left those strange gifts and notes." Jan pursed her lips.

"Betty Lee didn't get one."

"Exactly. Seems like she should have, if this really is about Sally's death."

"It doesn't make sense," Elaine said in agreement. "And I also don't understand why Babette and Kinley received the notes. Did they know Sally particularly well, or was there some other reason they received them?"

"We could be on the wrong track altogether," Jan reminded her.

"So what next?" Elaine looked thoughtful.

"Maybe we need to think more about those gifts that came with the notes. Could the fact that all of them have something to do with paper be significant?"

"Maybe." But Elaine sounded doubtful. "They don't seem to mean anything."

"They must be significant," Jan said.

"But how? The only similarity is the paper angle," Elaine said. "They have nothing to do with water, and they don't appear to be related to the clues in any other way either." She began to count on her fingers as she listed the four gifts. "A two-dollar bill, a brochure for a race, an old postcard from Augusta and... what was the other one?"

"A picture of a street sign," Jan said. "How on earth could all those things be connected?"

Elaine shook her head, spreading her hands helplessly. "I just don't see any commonalities. And I think if Mom and her friends had, they'd have mentioned it."

"We need to speak with Babette and Kinley next," Jan said. "If we split them up and each take one, we can ask them what they remember about Sally. There has to be some reason they were targeted."

They left the library and headed back to the game area to see if either of the other women was still there.

As luck would have it, Kinley came striding toward them as they walked along the hall. No need to split up.

"Kinley," Jan said, "may I ask you a question?"

"Of course."

"I was wondering how well you knew Sally Manling."

Kinley's eyes widened, and then a shadow crossed her face. "Dear Sally. I haven't thought of her in years. Whatever makes you ask?"

Jan shrugged. "I saw her picture in the yearbook and heard the story about her accident."

"She was a sweetie." Kinley smiled with obvious fondness. "She was my lab partner junior year, and I got to know her a little better than just as an acquaintance. She had a dry sense of humor and was always making hilarious little comments about whatever project our chemistry teacher had us doing. He was sort of a dry stick who liked to lecture, and Sally and I had a pretty good time at his expense." She smiled in rueful remembrance.

"Would you say you were friends?"

Kinley's smile faded. "Only in a very superficial way because of forced proximity, I suppose. We never socialized together outside of school, although we were friendly if we saw each other in class or the hallways, and sometimes she ate lunch at my table."

"And she wasn't a guild member, right?"

Kinley shook her head. "She worked at the Y as a lifeguard almost every day after school, so she couldn't have attended meetings. You had to attend at least seventy-five percent of the meetings to be eligible for the other activities we did. We met every week, so that meant we had to attend about three out of four meetings every month. The advisor was strict about it too." She cocked her head, eyeing the cousins. "This isn't just idle curiosity, is it?"

Caught, the cousins shook their heads.

"We are wondering if those notes and gifts you received had something to do with Sally's death," Jan told her.

Kinley looked thoughtful, but her expression morphed into confusion. "I can't imagine how. Although my note did mention something about water."

"They all did," Elaine said. "But we're only guessing. We could be wrong."

"Well, good luck figuring it out. You must like puzzles a lot more than I do." And she swung off down the hallway, her long legs eating up the distance to the lobby.

"Well." Elaine looked after the older woman. "That doesn't advance our theory, does it?"

Jan shook her head, troubled by the lack of a reason for Kinley to have received the note.

The cousins continued into the conference room, where those who hadn't headed for bed were still chatting, and one table of die-hard mah-jongg players was still completing a final round. To their surprise, Heloise was still there, watching the game and offering advice which by all appearances was largely ignored.

"She has more energy than I do," Elaine asked. "She's worked all day, presumably she has to work tomorrow, and yet she's still here."

"Maybe she's lonely," Jan said. "She certainly seems thrilled to see all these high school friends."

"Or maybe," Elaine said, "she's the one who put the notes and gifts in the rooms, and she's watching to see what happens."

Babette, they saw, was one of the mah-jongg players.

The cousins chatted with several new friends they had made throughout the weekend until the mah-jongg game broke up. Then as Babette headed for the doorway, both of them moved to intercept her.

"Babette, could we have a word?" Elaine asked.

The short blonde nodded. Her heavy blue eyeshadow looked somewhat the worse for wear by the end of the day, but her lacquered hairdo still had not moved the tiniest fraction. She smiled sweetly. "Sure thing. Did your mother go to bed already?"

Elaine nodded. "Yes. I'm ready to head that way myself shortly, and Jan is too."

"All this socializing is hard work," Babette agreed. "I'm exhausted."

By mutual accord, the three of them moved into the hallway that led to the lobby and the stairs.

"We'd like to ask you a quick question or two about Sally Manling," Elaine said.

Babette stopped dead, and a group behind them was forced to stop suddenly as well. "Sally Manling? Oh, that poor dear girl. I haven't thought of her in years. Does that make me a terrible person?"

Shaking her head, Elaine drew Babette aside so the others could pass. "We all move on. And she passed away a very long time ago."

Babette sighed. "That was the most tragic thing ever. I didn't even know her well, and I was devastated. I can't imagine how your mother and her friends who were closer to Sally must have felt."

"So you weren't well acquainted?"

Babette shook her head. "We were in concert choir together, but I was an alto and she was a soprano. I'm not sure if we ever exchanged more words than 'Hello.' Why are you interested in Sally?"

Elaine shrugged. "All the notes you and the others got referred to water, and we thought maybe they had something to do with Sally."

"*Hmm.*" Babette didn't look convinced. "I can't imagine why I'd have gotten one then."

"Do you know anyone besides Virginia, Eleanor, and Betty Lee who was close to Sally?" It was a shot in the dark, but Jan figured it couldn't hurt to ask.

"She wasn't in the guild," Babette said, "and we were a pretty tight bunch." She shook her head. "But I still can't imagine how those notes could have anything to do with Sally—oh, here's a thought. You know who might be able to tell you more about her? Heloise Invers, the manager here. They lived on the same street, and I remember they walked to school together."

CHAPTER FOURTEEN

The information about Heloise surprised Jan, and she suspected Elaine felt the same way. There was something a little different, too intense, about Heloise, and she itched to understand the woman better. Could her behavior possibly have something to do with those notes?

After bidding Babette good night, the cousins looked at each other.

"Let's talk to Heloise in the morning," Elaine said. "I don't know about you, but I'm exhausted."

"Good idea. I'm tired too." In her handbag, Jan felt her phone buzz. She pulled it out, seeing that Bob had left a text message earlier, apparently while she'd been busy talking in the game room, and she hadn't noticed it. "Oh no," she half-whispered as she read the brief message.

"What's wrong?" Elaine stopped with her foot on the first step and looked back over her shoulder.

"Bob and I were going to meet to take a walk tonight," Jan said. "But he just texted me and said he can't make it."

"Why not?" Elaine frowned.

"He doesn't say," Jan said. She held out the phone, too disappointed to speak.

Elaine read the message aloud: *"Can't make it this evening. Will talk after you get home."* She looked at Jan. "That seems kind of abrupt."

"It does," Jan agreed. An unpleasant thought crossed her mind. "When I was out walking with Clifton this afternoon, I thought I saw his car. When I arrived back here and found the flowers, I knew the car I'd seen must have been his. But— you don't think he'd be upset at seeing me taking a walk with a friend, do you?" Her brow furrowed. "Even if that friend is male?"

"Surely not," Elaine said. "That wouldn't be very reasonable. Bob's not the jealous type."

"No," Jan agreed. "He's not. But…after I texted him this morning, I didn't hear back from him all day. Until this."

"Try not to read too much into it," Elaine counseled. "It could simply be that he was distracted by something that came up. I'm sure you'll hear from him tomorrow."

"Thank goodness I don't need to ask him to pick up the tea," Jan said.

Elaine smiled. "It's really lucky that Eleanor's granddaughter is coming for breakfast tomorrow. She's a very good sport to stop by that tearoom and pick up our shipment."

"I wish I could talk to Bob," Jan said, her tone more than a little forlorn. "But I'm feeling pretty insecure at the moment. What if I call him and he doesn't pick up?"

"This retreat ends tomorrow," Elaine said. "And he did say you'd talk after you get home. It's quite likely that you're reading more into it than there really is. Try not to worry too much about it until then."

But she did. In fact, Jan thought of little else as she took the phone back and stuffed it in her bag before following Elaine up the steps. Bob wasn't an unreasonable man. Surely he'd never be upset with her for taking a walk with a friend who just happened to be male. But she certainly couldn't come up with any other explanation for their canceled date and his sudden silence.

BACK IN THEIR rooms, Elaine and Jan found Sasha and Virginia already in their night clothes. Sasha was sprawled across Virginia's bed much as she had Elaine's last evening, and Virginia was regaling Sasha with stories of her high school days.

"You know," Sasha was saying as the cousins entered through the door to Elaine's room, "it's funny. I grew up in the last age group not to have cell phones commonly available until I was out of high school. We used a forerunner to Facebook called MySpace and thought it was the coolest thing ever. Now, everyone can access pretty much everything through their phones, and you can't really even take a vacation because your ability to communicate is with you at all times."

Virginia shook her head. "A lot of that is beyond me. Or maybe I just don't care enough to want to be connected to everyone all the time that way. The telephone is still good enough for my needs most of the time." She grinned. "Although I do use e-mail regularly. That's how we deal with most of our guild stuff now."

Elaine noticed that Jan went straight through the connecting door into her own room. Her cousin was really upset by that text, she thought, wishing there was something she could do. At least Bob had said they would talk after Jan got home from the retreat. Surely that didn't mean by telephone. If he was upset by what he thought he'd seen, at least he should do Jan the courtesy of letting her explain exactly what she'd really being doing.

"You look a little fierce," Sasha said, making Elaine smile. "I hope you weren't thinking about me just now."

"Not at all." Elaine dismissed the problem from her mind. She couldn't fix it, nor was there anything she could do to help right now.

Jan stuck her head through the connecting door again. "I'm going to hit the hay soon," she said. "I just remembered I have to get up at five to get that friendship bread made."

"Ugh," said Virginia. "Sasha got up this morning and ran at five. It's a positively uncivilized hour."

Everyone chuckled, and even Jan smiled. "It is," she agreed. "'Night, all. See you before breakfast."

Virginia looked puzzled. "Is there something wrong?" she asked Elaine quietly.

Elaine nodded. She didn't want to take a chance on Jan overhearing them discussing her, so she went to the desk and grabbed a piece of paper from a notepad she had placed there.

I think she's missing Bob, she wrote. *She can't talk to him until after we get home.*

Virginia nodded. "That's understandable," she whispered.

Elaine shrugged, not knowing what else to say. She didn't want to make too big a deal out of what might be nothing at all.

Sasha took the pad and pencil. *Is there anything we can do?* she scrawled.

Elaine shook her head. Then an idea struck her, and she held up a finger as her eyes lit up. Sasha looked at her expectantly, passing her the writing implements.

What if we... When she had finished writing, Sasha looked at her with a devilish smile and nodded her head enthusiastically.

Looking mystified, Virginia took the pad and read what Elaine had written. Then she too began to smile, but she shook her head. Taking the pencil, she wrote: *I'll leave you two early birds to it!*

At 4:55 a.m., Elaine's phone alarm buzzed. She was awake instantly, and she quickly turned it off. Even though she'd set it to silent so it only would buzz, she still didn't want to wake Jan if she could avoid it.

Quietly, she sneaked out of bed and walked to the open doorway between their two rooms. Tiptoeing across the floor, she laid a hand on Sasha's shoulder without speaking.

Instantly, Sasha sat up, scrubbing her hands over her face. Nodding, she climbed out of bed and followed Elaine back to her room, where she had laid out her clothes the night before after turning off Jan's phone alarm for the early morning bread-making.

When both of them were dressed, they carefully eased open the door of Elaine's room and sneaked into the hallway. Closing the door quietly, they didn't speak until they were half-way down the stairs.

"We may have managed it," Elaine said. "I left a note in case she awakes before we get back."

"Before *you* get back. I'm going for a run after this." Sasha was grinning. "She's going to be so surprised when she wakes up."

"If she doesn't have a heart attack first when she realizes she overslept." But Elaine was smiling too.

They hurried down through the lobby with its low night lighting, through the still darkened hallway and dining room and into the kitchen. Elaine reached for a switch on the wall, and the room was flooded with bright lights that made them both blink and wince.

"Oh, how thoughtful of them." Elaine looked at the stain-less counter in the middle of the room where all Jan's baking supplies had been set, along with a number of items that someone—probably Crystal the helpful server—had thought they might need.

"This was a great idea," Sasha said. "Let's get to it."

Elaine read over the recipe in its plastic sleeve that Jan had brought along.

"First, preheat that oven to 325 degrees," Elaine told her daughter. "The starter is in the red-lidded container in the refrigerator, and we also need the eggs and milk that are right beside it." Quickly, she lined up all the nonperishable ingredients in the order they would be adding them. When Sasha returned with the cold items, Elaine placed them in order as well.

"Here," she said, handing over Jan's recipe. "You read and I'll add."

Working together, they poured the friendship bread starter into a giant plastic mixing bowl Jan had brought along, then added eggs, oil, milk, sugar, vanilla, cinnamon, baking powder, salt, flour, boxes of instant pudding, nuts, and raisins. While Elaine began to slowly stir, combining the mass of ingredients, Sasha lined up the large loaf pans Jan had packed.

Efficiently, she greased them and then dusted each one with a mixture of cinnamon and sugar. Just as she finished, Elaine completed her mixing. After bringing the large bowl over, she used a ladle to spoon out scoops of the batter until each loaf pan was evenly filled. As she finished, Sasha came along and sprinkled more of the cinnamon-sugar mix atop each one.

"Done!" she announced. "Now off to the oven we go."

After transferring the loaf pans to the large industrial oven, the pair turned their attention to cleanup.

"While I'm at it," Elaine said, "I'm going to lay out all the items for our tea so that we'll be able to set up quickly after breakfast is over. I know you want to run, so you go ahead. This will only take a few minutes."

"All right," Sasha said. "I'm just going for a short jaunt."

"What's a short jaunt?" Elaine asked, her eyes twinkling. "Ten miles?"

"Maybe just five." Sasha winked at her mother. "I'll see you back in the room later."

"Thanks for your help, honey." Elaine kissed her daughter's cheek before she turned back to unpacking the cups and saucers from the first box she opened.

JAN AWOKE SLOWLY. She felt groggy and discomfited, as if she hadn't slept at all. She'd tossed and turned half the night, probably subconsciously worrying about Bob's text message from the night before. He had seen nothing but two friends taking a walk though, and she couldn't imagine that he'd be upset about that. But what else could there be?

Sasha's bed was empty. She must have gotten up early to run again as she had the day before. Jan couldn't believe she hadn't heard her younger cousin.

Reaching over to the nightstand, she picked up her phone, assuming she was awake before the alarm. When she saw that the display read 6:15, she was stunned. Oh no! This was terrible. Somehow, she must have turned off her alarm, and now the kitchen would be in full swing and she couldn't possibly barge in there and make the friendship bread—

A sound in the adjoining room caught her attention, and she saw a dark shadow pass the door.

"Psst!"

"Oh, good morning." Elaine peeked into the room. "You're awake. Did you read my note?"

"What note? I'm late. I must have turned off my alarm." Jan threw back the covers.

"Wait," Elaine said. "Everything's okay. Look at the note on your nightstand. Sasha and I got up early and made the friendship bread for you. It's in the oven now. We need to get it out about seven."

Jan was stunned. "You...really?"

Elaine shrugged, grinning. "We thought it would be a nice surprise."

Jan shook her head with a smile. "Wow. I'm speechless. Thank you so much."

By the time Sasha returned, Jan had showered and dressed. She could hear Elaine and her mother moving around in their room. When Sasha headed for the shower, Jan poked her head into the adjoining room and said, "Good morning. I'm going down to the kitchen to make sure we have everything organized for our tea presentation."

Elaine smiled. "I already laid out everything we need, so it'll be ready to set the tables once breakfast is done."

"You are too efficient," Jan said. "You're leaving me nothing to do."

"You can go check on the bread," Elaine said. "I left a note for the kitchen staff just in case, but it should be about ready to come out."

"Sounds good. I'll meet you in the conference room for the service." The husband of one of the guild members was a retired minister who had offered to conduct a short, non-denominational worship service before breakfast on Sunday morning for those interested.

"See you then."

Jan turned and headed down the stairs. The lobby was still deserted. Finding a quiet corner, she drew out her phone and pulled up Bob's number. After a brief hesitation, she hit the Call button. *Ring... ring... ring... ring... ring.* After the fifth ring, Bob's voice mail kicked in. "Hello, this is Bob Claybrook. Please leave a message and I'll return your call as soon as I'm able."

Jan opened her mouth. Then she closed it again and ended the call without saying anything. What was there to say? She needed to talk to him in person. She would have to wait until she got home and hope that he had meant what he'd said in his text about talking to her tomorrow.

Replacing her phone in her handbag, she walked into the dining room, still deserted except for two servers setting up the buffet. Before she could move toward the kitchen door, she realized there was a third person in the room.

Heloise Invers was at the table that held the photo albums and yearbooks. She appeared to be idly flipping through pages, stopping every now and then to study something.

Jan crossed the room and stepped to her side.

Heloise said, "Good morning," but it sounded distracted, and she kept her attention on the yearbook she was leafing through. It was a different one than the senior year version Jan had seen.

"Good morning," Jan said quietly. As Heloise paused on a new spread, Jan saw that there was a photo of Sally Manling on the page. It was the swim team page, and Sally appeared to be accepting an award of some kind. "I understand you two were friends," she said, touching the photo of Sally gently.

Heloise nodded. "Friends and neighbors. We walked to school almost every morning from the first day of kindergarten through the end of junior year. Not home, of course, because Sally had to work a lot."

"You must have been terribly upset by her death."

Heloise nodded, still looking down. "She was so kind. I think if she had lived, she would have made a big difference in the lives of a lot of children. She wanted to be a teacher."

"So I heard." Jan's brain was racing now as she tried to think of some way to introduce the subject of the three friends who'd been with Sally when she died. This could be an opportunity to see if Heloise harbored anger toward them. "You weren't with her the night she died?"

Heloise shook her head. "She had gone camping with Virginia and her two closest friends. We were really excited about that trip, but then I couldn't go."

"What happened?"

Heloise shot Jan a wry smile. "If you had known my parents, you'd know I would never have been allowed to go on an unchaperoned camping trip." The smile faded. "I've always wondered if I had been there, if something might have been different. Would Sally still be alive today?"

Jan shook her head. "You can't think that way. It wasn't your fault."

"I resented those three, you know," Heloise said in a conversational tone, as if she'd just commented on the weather.

"Because of Sally's death?"

"No, before that." Heloise shook her head. "I didn't have many close friends. I didn't have many chances to do anything outside of school hours. I guess I felt like Sally was mine, and when we got to high school and she started branching out and hanging out with other people, I was crushed. You could say I withdrew from our friendship. We even stopped walking to school together our senior year, mostly because I stopped waiting outside her house for her." She looked down at her friend's smiling picture in the yearbook. "It seems so petty, doesn't it?"

"Not at all." Jan was moved to compassion. "Adolescence can be difficult to negotiate, and it's even worse if you're unable to be as social as everyone else. I would have felt left out and rejected too, I imagine."

"That was it in a nutshell," Heloise said. "Our friendship cooled and it was my fault. And then she died before I could fix it. Living with myself for doing that to her has been difficult."

"You were a teenager," Jan said. "I suspect everyone who ever lived has some regret that they'd like to fix from their teen years. The only difference is, most of us get a chance to make amends if we choose, and you didn't get that chance. I imagine if Sally were alive, you would have rekindled your friendship."

"I'd like to think that. I donate to the school scholarship they started for her every year," Heloise said tentatively. Then she drew her shoulders back, dashed a tear from her cheek, and was once again the cheery hotel manager. "Thank you for your kind words. I know you have your tea ceremony this morning. If there's anything you need from us, please don't hesitate to ask."

"I think we're in pretty good shape," Jan said, noting Heloise's ever-present professionalism. She might have been somewhat socially awkward, but she did an excellent job at managing the hotel. "Thank you."

She stared thoughtfully at the yearbook pages as Heloise left the dining room. She must remember to tell Aunt Virginia about this conversation. Perhaps it would help her to share her memories of Sally with Heloise. And it might help Heloise too. This was certainly the most genuine Jan had ever seen the woman act.

"Hey there." Elaine had come up behind her. "I saw you talking with Heloise. Anything useful?"

Jan beckoned to Elaine to walk with her. "I still need to check on the bread." She cocked her head. "I just don't feel like Heloise is the bad guy here, to be honest. She freely admits she was terribly jealous when Sally developed a closer friendship with Eleanor, Betty Lee, and Aunt Virginia. So in that respect, she makes a likely villain in our piece. But…" She explained about Heloise's restricted social life and the blame she had shouldered for abandoning the friendship. "This is beginning to reinforce my doubts about Sally's drowning being the motive for these notes and gifts," Jan said.

Elaine nodded. "We've learned to trust our intuition. I think we should listen to it in this instance too."

"Betty Lee didn't get a note," Jan reviewed. "Plus there's the fact that while Kinley did admit to a relationship of sorts with Sally, Babette certainly doesn't seem to have had any close contact."

"And as we've noted, the gifts appear to have nothing to do with the water references in the notes."

"True." Jan nodded.

"There's one other odd thing," Elaine said. "The three campers said that none of them ever talked with anyone else about the reason Sally went for that midnight swim. And I doubt that they would have had reason to discuss it in the years since. So my mom is the only one who would have known to blame them for Sally's death."

"That's probably an over-simplification," Jan objected. "Maybe they didn't talk about it, and their names might not have been in the news if they were minors, but I imagine some of their mutual friends knew who was on that camping trip. And Sally herself, or her family, may have told people, even if Aunt Virginia, Eleanor, and Betty Lee never spoke of it."

Elaine sighed. "You're right. But I still think there's something off about the whole thing. I'm just not convinced that Sally's death has anything to do with these notes at all anymore."

CHAPTER FIFTEEN

The cousins looked at each other as Elaine's response echoed in the air.

"You're right," Jan said. "I think we very well may be on the wrong track. All the notes refer to swimming or water, but perhaps there's some other reason for that."

"I agree. I think we have to look at it with a fresh eye," Elaine said. "But perhaps not just this minute. It's almost time for the service to start. Let's check on that bread and head to the conference room."

The timer was just beginning to ding as they entered the kitchen. Quickly, they removed the loaves from the oven and set them to cool. The loaves were golden brown, crusted with the cinnamon-sugar mix, and they smelled amazing.

Crystal groaned as she passed them carrying the large metal electric coffee urn. "You're torturing us with that scent."

The cousins grinned and skedaddled out of the way of the bustling kitchen staff that was preparing the breakfast buffet.

"We'll save you some," Jan promised as they headed off to the church service.

The service was as brief as expected, but the retired minister's thoughtful message was uplifting, focused on the power of friendship that had bound the group of women together for so many years, and the strength of those bonds that had seen many of them through life-altering experiences, such as marrying, childbearing, career challenges, and losing spouses and other family members. There was an opportunity for silent prayer before the benediction, and then everyone sang "Blest Be the Tie That Binds" together before the group dispersed to head for the dining room.

As they walked back through the lobby toward the dining room, a slender young woman with auburn curls cascading down her back came through the front doors. She carried a box beneath one arm.

"Jenny!" Roxanne, who'd been chatting with Betty Lee just ahead of the cousins, rushed over to embrace her. "Thanks for coming to join us."

The young woman smiled, hugging her mother, and then her aunt Rae and her grandmother, Eleanor. "I'm sorry I couldn't be here for the whole weekend, but I'm glad I could break free for today."

She held up the box. "Here's the tea I picked up."

Roxanne plucked the box from her hand and turned to Jan and Elaine. "Here you go," she said.

Elaine extended her palm to Jenny and introduced herself, Jan, Sasha, and Virginia. "Thank you so very much for getting that for us."

"No problem," Jenny said. "It smells divine. I can't wait to taste it."

Jan took the box containing the tea order and left the group. She made her way to the kitchen. Even though Elaine had said she'd set out everything they needed for their tea presentation, she couldn't prevent herself from double-checking. The teapots were assembled on a large tray. Organized groups of plates, cups and saucers, spoons, infusers, creamers, sugar, and napkins all had been placed so that she and Elaine would be able to quickly prepare the tables for service. They intended to leave the preceding workshop a little early so they could get everything set up, and she knew she would have some time to do the last-minute things while Elaine was making an initial presentation to the retreat-goers.

But she felt better once she had seen for herself that things were organized. She could recheck to be sure nothing had been missed later. They had brought their own bottled water to boil, which she would do while Elaine was speaking.

By the time she reentered the dining room, women were assembling for breakfast. As with the day before, the buffet groaned beneath the assortment of breakfast offerings. The meal was uneventful. They had squeezed an extra chair at their table to accommodate Jenny, who was cheerful and friendly.

Jan looked around the room, trying unobtrusively to observe the women she thought could be among those who had left the notes and gifts. Betty Lee, at their table, was her usual large-and-in-charge self, but she seemed to be having a good time. And since their talk last evening, Jan seriously doubted Betty Lee was the culprit.

Two tables away, Jeanice Evanak was ticking something off on her fingers as she spoke to the woman next to her, whose eyes had glazed over a little bit. Probably something to do with numbers, which Jeanice seemed to find a lot more compelling than most of the rest of the world, Jan decided with a smile. Laurette Martel, at the table in front of Jeanice's, was eating stolidly, eyes on her plate, while Kinley talked at her. Recalling Elaine's comments about Laurette's change of personality following her second marriage, Jan felt sad for the woman. She didn't appear to be enjoying herself very much.

As Jan watched, Laurette fumbled for her handbag on the back of the chair and slipped her hand inside. She appeared to feel around for something, and then her whole body relaxed a little and she withdrew her hand. What on earth was in that purse that was so valuable that she had to keep checking it? She'd been doing variations on that all weekend.

When the meal concluded, everyone headed into the conference room. The morning's presentation was a lecture on Victorian dress.

"We'll start from the skin out," the speaker said. She was the owner and chief designer of a business that made one-of-a-kind, period-authentic costumes for the Victorian era, particularly for Civil War reenactors, but also for museums, historical displays, and other purposes. Indicating a mannequin that stood beside her, she said, "Victorian ladies, particularly those of the upper classes, wore an extraordinary number of undergarments. These protected the corset and the dress from the skin and of course, vice versa."

She pointed at the mannequin. "Ermengarde here is wearing a chemise and drawers from the early part of the era." She went on to describe the evolution from the rather plain-looking corset and "bloomers" to, eventually, a garment called a "combination" by the 1870s, when a fashionable silhouette required extremely tight-fitting garments that precluded lots of under layers. She fitted a corset-cover over the mannequin next, explaining that it was the forerunner of the modern camisole and was created to give women the required silhouette, featuring a small waist and a lengthened waistline during the early Victorian era.

Bustles appeared, disappeared, and reappeared during the era, although the height of their fame occurred during the 1870s and 1880s. Multiple crinolines worn to add volume beneath skirts became "cage crinolines" with steel in their frames. In the Old South, hoop skirts became highly fashionable. But in the decades following the Civil War, crinolines slimmed down and eventually petticoats became narrower.

Then the speaker gave a nod to a side door, and a woman dressed in an old-fashioned costume entered. Jan recognized her as one of the guild members. She strolled up and down the aisle dressed in a costume representing the early years of the Victorian era while the speaker detailed the clements of the day dress and pelerine she wore.

Jan glanced at the time. It was 9:30, and the group would be breaking for tea in thirty minutes. Elaine met her gaze, and together they rose and slipped out of the room.

"As soon as we get the water on, we can zip through the dining room and set the tables, then run upstairs and change," Jan said. "While you give your talk, I'll get the teapots and friendship bread ready and begin serving."

"Jenny was such a good sport for helping retrieve that tea," Elaine said.

"Amen," Jan added fervently. "I'll thank her again when I serve her. In fact, why don't we get her address and send her a little gift certificate to Tea for Two?"

"Brilliant idea," Elaine pronounced. "I'll take care of it."

When they reached the kitchen, they were surprised to find two members of the kitchen staff ready and willing to help with whatever was needed. One put the water on to boil while the other helped the cousins set up the dining room.

Next, the cousins sprinted to their rooms and changed into their Victorian costumes.

"This is timely," Elaine said, laughing as they rushed toward the stairs. "Here we are, in Victorian dress right in the middle of the costume workshop. Whoa!"

As they rounded the corner to the steps, Elaine nearly knocked into the cleaning cart which was placed against the wall out of sight.

"Oh, I'm sorry." It was the housekeeper, Adrianna. "I'd better move that before someone falls."

Jan, stepping to the side, froze as her gaze caught on the pocket of Adrianna's capacious apron, where a pink-and-green-striped ribbon dangled. But before she could speak, Elaine was off down the stairs. "No problem," she called over her shoulder. "Come on, Jan."

Her brain a seething mass of excitement, Jan headed down the stairs behind her cousin. "Did you see that?" she hissed in Elaine's ear as they hurried into the dining room.

"See what?" Elaine's eyebrows rose.

"Adrianna had a piece of ribbon in her pocket. It was the ribbon used to tie the notes."

"You're kidding." Elaine stopped dead, but only for a moment. "We don't have time to check it out now. We'll have to do it later."

By the time the first women began to trickle in for the tea presentation, they had things well in hand and already were prepared to serve.

Elaine stepped to the podium while Jan stood near the kitchen door.

"Good morning," Elaine began. "While many of you know me as Virginia's daughter and my cousin Jan as her niece, we also are the owners and operators of Tea for Two, a tearoom in Lancaster at the other end of the lake. Tea for Two occupies the first floor of our lovely old Victorian home, and we are steeped in the atmosphere and the rituals of teatime every day. 'Steeped,' get it?" She grinned, eliciting chuckles from around the room.

"I'm going to tell you a little bit about teatime in the Victorian era while Jan serves a select blend called Friendship and Memories that we thought you might enjoy, since this is a very special weekend to renew and celebrate the bonds of friendship forged through precious memories from your past together. Friendship and Memories is a caffeine-free herbal tea, for those of you who are concerned about your caffeine intake. It's made of fragrant, yellow-white linden flowers and the leaves of the linden tree, which also is commonly known as the lime or basswood tree." She held up a small bag of the light-colored blend.

"Along with the tea, we'll be serving friendship bread made from a starter which is similar to sourdough, except it uses milk. We're also providing you with the recipe for the friendship bread." She indicated quarter-sheets of letter-size paper on which she had printed out the recipe. Jan had glued a small yellow-white silk flower blossom to one corner of each and trimmed the top edge with scalloped scissors to give each recipe a pretty, feminine effect.

Nodding to Jan, who headed back to the kitchen to fill the teapots, Elaine then launched into a brief summary of Victorian tea customs. The tea would be steeped just about perfectly when she finished speaking.

"The drinking of tea dates back as far as the Shang dynasty in China, and it was popularized in England under the reign of King Charles the Second and his Portuguese wife. But the custom of afternoon tea as a ritual event actually began in 1840 when the seventh Duchess of Bedford began serving tea and sandwiches every day around four o'clock. Dinner, of course, was served at the fashionably late hour of eight in the evening, and the lady became too hungry to wait that long. At first, she had her tea served in her room, but then her friends found out her secret, and she began inviting them to join her. The custom spread, and by the 1880s, tea became quite the event, with ladies donning long gowns, gloves, and hats for elegant teas."

As Jan and Crystal began to bring pots of tea and plates of friendship bread to each table, Elaine went on to talk more specifically about the food served at Victorian high teas, some of the popular types of tea sold today, and the resurgence of interest in traditional tearooms.

There was hearty applause as Elaine concluded her remarks. The cousins joined their own table for the remainder of the break, where Eleanor and her daughters peppered them with questions about Tea for Two.

"It sounds like so much fun," Rae said. "I bet you meet a lot of interesting people."

"We do," Jan said. "While winter has allowed us to enjoy repeat customers from the local area, I'm looking forward to the start of tourist season Memorial Day weekend when we'll begin to get a big surge of summer people again."

"Our first summer," Elaine said, "we were still just finding our rhythm and figuring out the business. I feel as if we have a much stronger handle on all that now, and we'll be able to enjoy it a little more."

When the retreat attendees returned to the conference room for the second half of the costume workshop, Jan and Elaine stayed behind to help clean up the remains of the tea and pack away the things they had brought along. The kitchen staff was delighted when the cousins left a tray of friendship bread for them.

"I'm going to come by your tearoom one of these days," said Crystal. "I think my mother would really enjoy a visit." She winked, taking a box from Jan's hands and starting for the door. Elaine had brought the car around so they could pack their things into it, and Crystal was happy to help them finish up.

"Quick," Elaine said as the cousins left the dining room, "let's see if we can find Adrianna. We need to talk to her."

Deciding that speed trumped discretion, Jan stopped at the front desk, where Heloise was tapping away at a computer keyboard.

"Can you tell us where the housekeeper is cleaning right now?" Jan asked her.

"Which one?" Heloise asked.

"Adrianna," Jan said. "I wanted to speak with her before we leave."

Heloise looked up at the large, ornate clock on the wall. "Probably on the third floor in the east wing with Lydia, who's also on day shift," she said, pointing to one end of the building. "Oh, wait—I forgot. Adrianna's on break. She'll be back in a bit. Is there something I can help you with?"

Jan shook her head. "Nothing important. Thank you."

"We'll have to try to talk to her after lunch if we don't get a chance earlier," Elaine said as they walked away. "I was hoping we could figure out who planted those notes and gifts before we left today. I'm finding Adrianna more and more interesting."

"But why would Adrianna have done it?" Jan asked. Something didn't feel right.

Elaine deflated slightly. "I honestly don't know."

Jan sighed. "Let's go back to the costume workshop. We'll figure it out later."

After quickly changing out of their costumes, the cousins rejoined the group in the conference room, where the final half hour was taken up with a display of the fashions of the last decade of the Victorian period, showing how the bustle grew smaller and eventually disappeared, giving way to soft pleats down the backs of gowns. The emphasis on a tiny waist above full skirts continued, and leg-of-mutton sleeves grew larger and larger, ballooning to giant puffs above the shoulders. As the speaker explained, the Victorian influence largely had waned by the end of Queen Victoria's long reign.

As Jan rose at the session's end, her cell phone buzzed silently in her pocket as she exited the conference room. Jan's heart leaped. Bob! Glancing at the readout, she saw that Clifton was the caller. Despite the fact that she'd really been hoping the caller was Bob, she smiled to herself, thinking of the conversation she'd had with Rae Burns. "Hello, Clifton."

"Hi, Jan." The lilt in his voice made her smile. "I just wanted to thank you again for introducing me to Rae. We have our first official date next Saturday."

"That's wonderful, Clifton." She was genuinely pleased for him. "I wish you well."

"And I wish you the same. Your fellow is a lucky guy."

They chatted for a moment longer, and she ended the call. Passing the library, she impulsively turned the knob of the library door and entered, considering whether or not she should try to contact Bob one more time.

"Oh!" Laurette Martel was sitting in the chair that was almost behind the door, unseen by a casual observer unless one entered the room. Few people, of course, would be doing so on Sunday morning, the last day of the retreat.

Laurette was holding a tissue, and the ragged, uneven breaths she took led Jan to believe the woman had been crying. Or, at the very least, struggling not to give in to sobs.

Jan stopped short. "Laurette, is everything all right?"

Laurette sprang to her feet and grabbed her handbag. "Of course. I'm fine, just fine. I just needed... breakfast didn't agree with me." And she pushed past Jan and rushed out the door.

Dumbfounded by the abrupt exit, Jan's eyebrows rose. What on earth...?

Automatically, she glanced at the chair in which Laurette had been seated. On the little table between the chair and the loveseat was a book that the woman must have forgotten. And sticking up from the book was a bookmark. A pink bookmark.

CHAPTER SIXTEEN

Suddenly alert, Jan crossed the room in three steps and picked up the book Laurette had been clutching. It was a Bible. Inside the flyleaf was an inscription to Laurette, thanking her for her service as a Sunday school superintendent for twenty years. Jan turned to the bookmarked page. It was in Psalms, but the bookmark itself was what drew Jan's attention.

It was the same notepaper as the four notes received by Virginia and the other guild members. It had been folded lengthwise, and Jan carefully pressed out the crease down the middle of the piece of paper. There was a message written on it.

If you've come up for air, you can still save yourself by doing the right thing.

Jan plopped into the chair. Laurette had received a note too. And presumably a gift. And it was another water reference. Swimming. Drowning. Once again, the clue pointed to the Sally Manling tragedy.

Or did it?

Jan rushed out of the library. She was certain Laurette had headed to the right toward the lobby. If the woman had gone to her room, Jan wouldn't be able to talk to her. But perhaps—yes! Jan caught sight of Laurette's short gray hair above the back of one of the rockers on the porch.

Slipping out the front door, Jan approached her. Laurette was sitting in the rocking chair, not rocking, just staring listlessly out over the view of the lake. Extending the Bible with the note securely back in its place between the pages of Psalms, Jan said, "You forgot your Bible."

Slowly, Laurette's head turned. She reached out and took the Bible, laying it in her lap. She sighed, fingering the pink bookmark that Jan had replaced in the book. "So you know I got a note too."

"Yes." Jan nodded.

"I guess you have questions."

Jan took a seat beside her. "Why didn't you tell anyone you'd also gotten one of those strange notes? And I guess you got a gift too?"

Laurette nodded in answer to the second question. To the first, she said, "I don't really know why I didn't want to share it. It felt...like a threat or something, I guess. It made me feel like hunkering down and hiding, if you want the truth."

That was a very disturbing statement. "Have you felt unsafe here?" Jan asked.

"No..." Laurette shook her head. "I couldn't say that. It was more of just a vague feeling." She sighed. "I'm glad it's Sunday. I'm ready to go home."

Acting on impulse, Jan asked, "Laurette, how well did you know Sally Manling?"

Laurette looked startled. "Sally Manling. That poor girl. I haven't thought of her in a long time. I didn't know her well at all—only to say hello to. Why do you ask?"

Jan shrugged. "I saw her photos in the yearbook and I was just curious."

Now Jan felt certain they had been following the wrong thread. As the weekend had worn on, she had felt that they were missing something important. She still didn't know what it was, but now she felt certain that those gifts and notes had nothing to do with Sally Manling.

And if they had nothing to do with Sally, that might mean Heloise Invers had nothing to do with them either, as Jan had suspected.

"I've been thinking a lot about those notes," Jan said. "It's bugging me that they seem to have taken some of the shine off the weekend for several of you. Can you think of any reason—any reason at all—that someone might have targeted you, Virginia, Eleanor, Babette, and Kinley?"

Laurette half-lifted her hands and let them fall back into her lap. "No. We don't have anything in common other than this guild and church."

"You all go to Cushnoc Community Chapel?" Of course they did. There had been mentions of the church throughout the weekend, but Jan hadn't given it a second thought. Elaine must not have either, or she'd have mentioned it.

Laurette nodded. She looked down at the Bible beneath her hands. "Thank you for bringing me my Bible."

It was a clear dismissal, but Jan barely noticed. "You're welcome." Turning, she hurried back inside to find Elaine.

Her cousin was with Sasha and Virginia in the lobby, chatting with several other people before lunch began. Quickly, she pulled Elaine aside and told her about the encounter with Laurette.

"Another note?" Elaine looked stunned. "A water reference, right? But why did she hide it?"

"She seemed to feel that talking about it might be more problematic than ignoring it," Jan summarized. "But I think it ruined her enjoyment of the weekend."

"It certainly didn't make my mother very happy," Elaine said.

"She said one thing that I think is really important," Jan went on. "Did you realize that everyone who received the notes and gifts goes to your mother's church?"

Elaine looked dumbfounded. "I guess they do," she said slowly. "Oh my. That could be significant."

"I think it might be," Jan said, "especially since we are not coming up with solid proof that those notes have anything to do with Sally Manling's drowning."

"Could we get Mom, Eleanor, Kinley, and Babette to come to the library?" Elaine asked. "With Laurette, of course."

"I think we must. There has to be some commonality among them that would cause someone to write those notes. It's especially weird that Betty Lee didn't receive a note. She's also a member of that church, remember?"

"Unless she's the one sending the notes," Elaine reminded Jan.

"Unless she's the one," Jan agreed. "But if she is, she's an excellent actress. I was sure she was genuinely sad last night when we sat in the library with those three talking about Sally."

Elaine nodded. "Me too, although being sad that her friend drowned doesn't necessarily absolve her of what's going on with the notes and gifts now."

"I suppose it doesn't," Jan agreed. "We really need to talk with those other five women together."

"We have about an hour until lunch," Elaine said. "Let me see if I can round them up. Sasha too, since she's invested in helping solve this."

"All right. I'll go get Laurette." Jan reversed her steps and headed back out to the porch.

Five minutes later, all eight women met in the tiny library.

"So what is it now?" Eleanor asked with good humor. "I see we've added Kinley, Babette, and Laurette to our secret group."

"And Betty Lee isn't here," Virginia said. "Should I get her?"

"We don't think she needs to be here right at the moment," Jan said.

"Laurette received a note like the rest of you," Elaine told the assembled women.

"Was it as unsettling as the others?" Kinley asked.

"What? Why didn't you tell us?" Virginia asked, looking bewildered.

Laurette shrugged slowly. "I don't really know. I guess I just wanted to pretend it hadn't happened. It felt mean-spirited."

Eleanor's smile faded, and she turned to Laurette. "Oh my. I'm so sorry."

"And you got a little gift, if we can call them that, too?" Virginia sat forward.

Laurette nodded.

"Do you mind showing them to us?" Eleanor asked.

Laurette reached into her handbag and pulled out a small item. Holding it up, she said, "It's a playing card with the jack of spades on it. I've been carrying it around with me all week-end, trying to figure out what it means."

Realization struck Jan, and her gaze met Elaine's. That must have been why Laurette was so obsessed with the contents of her handbag.

"What's on the back?" Sasha asked from her position leaning against the bookshelves in a back corner.

Laurette flipped it over. "An emblem that says 'Indianapolis 500.' Is that significant?"

"Who knows?" Jan asked. "Elaine and I thought bringing you all together might help to shed some light on why you five received these."

"What do you have in common?" Elaine asked. "You're all in the guild, of course, and you all attend the same church, I believe."

There were nods of agreement.

"But there are two other people at this event who also attend our church," Virginia said, "who didn't get these things."

"Unless they just didn't mention it," Laurette said.

There was a short silence.

"We know Betty Lee didn't get a gift," Jan said, smiling slightly, "but we should ask Jeanice if she received a note with a gift."

"Is there anything else that connects you?" Elaine asked. "Any volunteer work, anything all of you might have done even if not at the same time?"

Each of the five guild members looked blank.

"I don't think so," Virginia said. "We don't even all live in the same community anymore, although we all go to the same church."

"True," Eleanor said. "I drive half an hour to get to church, but Laurette lives just a few minutes away."

"And I moved even further away last year," Kinley added. "I only go to church about once a month now, anyway."

"I need to apologize to all of you," Laurette interjected. She looked at the floor rather than her friends. "I should have shown you mine on Friday night. It might have helped us figure out who sent them and why before the retreat ended. As it is, we have to go home in just a few hours."

"A few hours could change a lot of things," Jan assured her.

"Well, Betty Lee's nose was out of joint," Eleanor said with a chuckle.

"I don't think we can be certain that these were the only ones," Elaine said, "but no one else mentioned it, and surely everyone has heard about them now."

"You mean after we trumpeted it all over the room Friday evening," Kinley said, attempting a grin that quickly died.

"Why don't we lay all the gifts and notes out," Jan suggested, "and see if that brings anything to mind?"

They pulled the little table forward and placed all the gifts in a row on it, with each note above the gift it corresponded to. As they had realized earlier, every single note had a water theme.

*Out of your depth…in over your head…in too deep…holding your breath…*and Laurette's: *come up for air.*

And yet the language appeared to be the only potential link to Sally Manling.

"I can see why you thought maybe these were connected to Sally," Babette said. "But I can't imagine why I'd have gotten one. If that was true, Betty Lee should have gotten one, and Heloise probably should have received one too. I think they were close until near the end of high school."

"Maybe. Although Heloise isn't a guest, nor was she in guild with us," Virginia said. "And she doesn't go to Cushnoc Community Chapel, either."

Refocusing, Jan looked at the five items lying on the little table. Virginia had received a two-dollar bill; Eleanor, an old Augusta postcard featuring the five-and-dime. Kinley had gotten the 1K brochure, which was weird enough to make Jan think it could be an important clue, if only they could figure out what it was. Babette had received the speed limit sign, and Laurette had gotten the jack of spades with the Indy 500 emblem on the reverse—

"They're all numbers," Jan blurted.

"What?" Sasha and Elaine spoke together.

Everyone was looking at her.

"All these little items have something to do with numbers," Jan explained. "I was just looking at Laurette's and thinking of the Indy 500 emblem on the back."

"Hers also could have to do with the jack of spades," Virginia pointed out. "In some card games, that's worth a certain number of points. So the picture on the flip side could be coincidental."

"Let's assume, for a moment, that the reason these notes were written does have something to do with numbers." Jan looked around. "Does that jog any memories? Any ideas? I don't care how far out there it is, feel free to say it."

There was silence in the room. Virginia and her friends looked blank.

Elaine leaned forward, perusing the five items on display. "So here," she said, picking up the paper money, "we have two dollars. And the five-and-dime could potentially be added together to indicate fifteen. The thirty-five and the one speak for themselves, I guess."

"But does the 1K mean one or one thousand?" Kinley asked.

Elaine smiled. "I have no idea. I'm just—hey! Mom, did you notice there's writing on this bill?"

Virginia craned her neck. "No. What does it say?"

Elaine looked across at Jan. "It's got '$2,000' written right beneath the two at the top."

"Let me see that." Jan extended her hand. Sure enough, there it was in what appeared to be fine-point black indelible marker. As she lifted her head, preparing to pass the bill around the room so the others could look at it, she surprised an odd expression on Virginia's face. Almost one of horrified surprise.

"Aunt Virginia?" she asked. "Does this make you think of something?"

"Oh, it's probably nothing but a coincidence." But Virginia's voice shook.

"Mom? What's wrong?" Elaine pressed.

Virginia took a deep breath. "You mentioned my church, and with that $2,000, I remembered something." She took a deep breath. "This is embarrassing, but I may as well share it. Years ago, right before your father died, we made a pledge to a special building fund drive for the church to replace the roof, which was in bad shape. I believe they intended to upgrade the electrical wiring and the air-conditioning ductwork in the ceiling at the same time. Our pledge was $2,000." Tears filled her eyes and spilled over. "After he died, I was so worried about money that I asked to be released from my pledge."

Babette gasped loudly and pressed both hands to her mouth.

There was a silence in the room so heavy that Jan could almost feel it pressing down on her, a weight burdened with concerns. It felt as though they all were frozen, and a tiny shiver of knowing ran up Jan's spine. Something was about to break, she could feel it.

Then Babette's hands dropped. "I didn't connect that stupid speed limit sign, but Chip and I pledged $3,500 to that same campaign. And like you, Virginia, we had to ask to be released from our pledge. That was when we had to put Chip's mother in the Alzheimer's unit at the nursing home." She shuddered. "The cost was astronomical, but we felt certain that she would get excellent care there. We had heard so many horror stories about nursing homes..." She began to cry, and Virginia put an arm around her shoulders.

Jan looked at Laurette, Kinley, and Eleanor, all of whom had similar shocked expressions of comprehension on their faces. "Have we found our common link?"

CHAPTER SEVENTEEN

All three women nodded in response to the question. Kinley cleared her throat. "My grandson and his wife found out they were expecting triplets, and she had to be on bedrest and couldn't work for the last third of her pregnancy. We asked to be released from our pledge so we could help them out financially."

"You probably all know what happened with me," Laurette said quietly. "That was right after my husband left. I had to default on my pledge because he took a lot of our joint savings and left me with barely enough to get by."

Eleanor laid a hand over Laurette's. "And mine went instead to help pay for an experimental treatment for my granddaughter, who was diagnosed with leukemia. Pastor James was so kind about it."

"He was very kind to me too," Laurette said. "He told me not to worry about it, that people's lives and circumstances are fluid and always changing. He just asked that someday when I'm in a position to do so, to try to assist the church or someone in need. And I have. I made a large donation to the youth pro-gram's summer camp last year."

The others were nodding, and Kinley cleared her throat. "We purchased the new pew cushions after the pews were refinished two years ago." She looked at Virginia, Babette, and Eleanor. "And I bet each of you have done something to pay it forward when you've been able to as well, haven't you?"

The other three women nodded, slowly. They all looked shell-shocked.

Jan cleared her throat. "Can each of you confirm that in some way, the amount that you pledged is represented by the 'gift' you got?" She made air quotes and a wry face to show what she thought of the gifts.

All five women nodded.

"I would never have thought of it, although it makes sense," Kinley said. "But I don't get it. Who would have known about those pledges? Pastor James has been gone for almost seven years."

"He's not still your pastor?" Elaine asked, frowning.

"He wasn't with us more than a few months after I spoke with him," Virginia told her. "He received an offer of a senior pastorate at a church near Bar Harbor, and he left very shortly after that. I believe their pastor passed away unexpectedly, so that was why it happened so fast."

"He's the one I spoke with also," Laurette said.

"And me," Virginia said, and Kinley and Babette nodded in agreement.

Silence again.

"Thank you," Laurette said to Jan and Elaine, "for pursuing this. It's a nasty little puzzle. I still can't imagine who would have done it, but it does help to have figured out why the five of us were the recipients." She stood, and the rest of the guild members did likewise. Within seconds, the room had emptied, except for Jan, Sasha, Virginia, and Elaine.

"Don't they want to know who's behind this?" Jan asked. "I sure do."

"Me too," Sasha said.

"Maybe," Virginia said hesitantly, "it's too difficult for them to face the fact that someone we might know—and might know well—harbors that much enmity toward us. It's hard for me to imagine it. This was really a mean thing to do."

"It was," Elaine agreed. "Do you think your pastor who moved away could be involved?"

Jan shook her head, as did Virginia. "I don't see how. Do you?" Elaine's mother asked.

Elaine shook her head. "I agree. I can't imagine that. Especially when he made such a point to absolve each of you of any guilt for having to back off those pledges. I mean, financial situations change all the time. I would imagine any time an organization asks for pledges, that there are a certain number that aren't honored for a multitude of very good reasons."

"So who could have done it?" Sasha asked. "It almost has to be a fellow guild sister, or someone who works here at the hotel."

"Like Heloise Invers." Jan hated to say it, but the possibility existed.

"Like Heloise," Elaine said, "although I don't see a reason she would do this, particularly since we know now that it had nothing to do with Sally. And Heloise doesn't attend your church either. Right, Mom?"

"That's correct," Virginia said. She rose. "I'm going to bring down my luggage from upstairs. We can think some more about this over lunch."

"I'll come with you, Grandma," Sasha said. The pair left the library.

"We still need to talk to Adrianna about that ribbon," Jan said to Elaine. "Maybe she just found it."

"Or maybe," Elaine said, "it has something to do with the gifts. I wonder if she's ever attended Mom's church, even if she doesn't go there now. We should ask at lunch."

Jan took a deep breath, feeling adrenaline surge through her. "So let's assume it had something to do with the church. It almost has to, I think, now that we know it had nothing to do with Sally Manling. Why might someone send those notes and gifts?"

"Clearly, someone must have found out about the defaults and been upset by them." Elaine spread her hands as if to explain her logic. "It's the only thing that makes sense."

"I agree. But who would be upset about it? Every single one of these people had a very good reason to back away from their pledges. And the pastor didn't sound as if he were upset by them in the least."

"But I wonder..." Elaine tapped a finger against her lips. "The pastor left very shortly after that. I'm sure he had a thousand and one loose ends to tie up. What if he forgot to tell anyone else about the reasons these pledges weren't honored?"

"Oh." Jan pondered that. "Excellent thought. If our mean-note-sender is a church member who knew the pledges didn't get paid but did not know they had been forgiven by the pastor, then they might feel angry."

"Not that it would be their place to judge, but I agree that it's very possible," Elaine said.

"We need to talk more to Aunt Virginia." Jan headed for the door.

Virginia and Sasha still were both upstairs, using their time to finish packing up their things. Although there was an additional session after lunch, checkout was at noon, so everyone was scrambling to get their things organized and stowed back in their vehicles.

Both Jan and Elaine carried down their own luggage, then helped Virginia and Sasha. As they walked through the lobby and out to the parking lot, Elaine said, "Mom, how many other people here attend Cushnoc Community Chapel?"

Virginia cast her a sidelong glance. "Because you think it had to be someone from my church who left those notes?"

Elaine nodded. "It was in response to your pledges, so I'd say it's a definite conclusion now."

Virginia shrugged. "Betty Lee and Jeanice Evanak are the only other ones. I just can't imagine either of them doing that."

"How about the hotel staff? Did you happen to see anyone here that you know from church? Or who might have visited?"

Virginia shook her head slowly. "No, not that I can think of, although it's possible someone from our congregation works here."

"Do you remember anything else," Jan asked, "anything at all that happened regarding your pledge and the pastor forgiving it?"

Virginia looked mystified. "Not really. I think we told you everything—wait. There is something else. Although I doubt it's significant."

"What is it?"

"I got a call from that pastor a few weeks after we'd first spoken, and he told me another church member was donating money to cover several people who couldn't meet their pledges. He said that I should not worry about it but consider it a gift from heaven. And as I believe I mentioned, he simply asked me to be the agent of grace for someone else in the future. So you can see why I really didn't give it another thought. In fact, I recalled that request just a few weeks ago, and I gave Jeanice a donation to help pay for a youth mission trip this coming summer."

"Why did you give it to Jeanice?" Jan asked.

"She became our church's financial secretary in January."

A sudden *zing* of excitement surged through Jan. Involuntarily, she glanced at Elaine. Her cousin's eyes were wide and bright, and Jan knew Elaine was thinking along the same lines as she was.

Virginia looked at Jan and Elaine's expressions, and Jan could see the moment she realized what they were thinking. "Oh, no. I had forgotten she took over that job. Someone else did it for years and years." She looked troubled. "Surely Jeanice would never—"

"But she might know something that would help us." Elaine smiled, putting an arm around her mother's shoulders.

Virginia seemed to accept that, although Jan suspected that if they were right, the truth was going to be a hard pill to swallow.

As Virginia headed back into the hotel with Sasha, who had put her duffel into the rental car she'd driven, Jan and Elaine lingered on the far end of the front porch, away from the bustle of women coming and going with luggage.

"Jeanice is the financial secretary," Elaine said.

"Since January."

"But she doesn't have a broken nail, so either the tip I found isn't connected to the notes, or she managed to repair it somehow."

A memory teased the edge of Jan's mind... "What if she repaired a broken nail herself, rather than removing all her tips?"

Elaine's lips pursed as she considered that. "We've been looking for someone with short, bare nails or a broken tip. If we go back to looking at all the French manicures, that opens up a lot of people."

"But not a lot of people who attend Cushnoc Community Chapel. Only one, other than our 'victims' and Betty Lee, in fact."

"You're right." Elaine sighed. "Jeanice only has been handling the church's finances since January. Those pledges are seven years old."

"Still..." Jan's eyes narrowed in thought. "What if she only learned about the defaults when she took over as financial secretary?"

Elaine's eyes lit up. "That's possible. It seems more and more likely that in the rush of preparing to move on to his new position, the pastor may have forgotten to pass on the information about those five people's predicaments."

Jan nodded. "Which might make it appear that they just decided not to pay up."

Elaine shook her head. "Which still doesn't explain why she would choose to do something as mean-spirited as this to five of her friends. I'm sure the church leadership would be appalled."

"It had to be Jeanice," Jan said. "But how do we confirm it?"

Elaine nodded. "We can't just accuse her without proof. She might simply deny it."

"We still have to talk to that housekeeper again." Jan had already related to Elaine her encounter with Adrianna from the afternoon before. "And I saw that ribbon we should ask her about. How do you suppose that's connected?"

Elaine snorted. "I have no idea. But you said she avoided telling you directly that she didn't let anyone into the rooms."

Jan nodded. "She got defensive and said Heloise didn't allow it. But she never said she didn't do it."

Elaine started for the door. "We need to find her right now. We don't have a lot of time left. People will be leaving today."

Adrianna was on the second floor when they ascended the stairs, placing fresh towels in a cleaning closet just down the hallway from the landing. Jan and Elaine stopped right beside the door.

"We'd like to talk to you for a moment," Jan said.

Adrianna's face grew red, the same telltale sign Jan had noted the day before. "I already told you we're not allowed to let anyone into guest rooms," she blurted.

Jan smiled. "I know you did. May I ask where you got the ribbon in your pocket?"

Adrianna looked confused by the change of subject. "What?"

"The striped ribbon that was sticking out of your pocket earlier. Where did you get it?"

Adrianna reached into her pocket and pulled out a length of ribbon. "This? It was in the trash can in a guest room. My nursery is pink and green, and I thought I could use it somehow." She held it out. "Does it belong to you?"

"No," Jan said. "I'm sure you can keep it. I was just curious."

Then Elaine cleared her throat. "You didn't answer our question," she said gently. "We are asking if you let anyone into five guest rooms on Friday during the supper hour."

"No," the girl said, and her tone was almost defiant. "I did not."

But Elaine wasn't finished. "Did you loan a master key to someone else who might have entered those rooms?"

Adrianna's face grew redder, and she burst into tears. "Oh, please," she said, "you can't tell Heloise. She'll fire me if she finds out, and I can't afford to lose this job. My husband's laid off and this is all we have. Please don't tell."

"We're not going to tell anyone," Jan reassured her. "Can you share what happened?"

Elaine pulled a tissue from her handbag and gave it to the sobbing housekeeper.

"A lady came up to me on Friday," Adrianna said, after taking a deep breath. "She said she left her handbag with her key in it in the dining room, and she didn't want to disturb the prayer and could she borrow my master. I offered to let her in, but she said her room was on the next floor all the way at the end, and she didn't want to make me walk that far. So I gave her my key. I don't know anything about five rooms or gifts on pillows, and I know Heloise will fire me if—"

"We're not going to tell Heloise," Elaine said. She patted Adrianna's arm.

"I wouldn't have done it if I'd known she was going into other people's rooms," the young woman declared. "When she came back, she gave me twenty dollars as a thank-you. I told her she didn't need to do that, but she insisted."

"Do you know her name?" Elaine asked.

Adrianna shook her head. "But I've seen her a time or two since."

"Can you describe her for us?" Jan asked.

"Dark hair that's showing lighter roots," Adrianna said. "Shorter than I am."

Jan glanced at Elaine. That could be Jeanice.

"And she was wearing her coat like she'd just arrived," Adrianna said, "but I saw her come out of her room so I know she had been in there already. She took her suitcase back downstairs with her."

"On Friday?" Jan pretended puzzlement. "Why would she take her suitcase back downstairs?"

Adrianna shrugged. "You wouldn't believe the weird things guests do. I don't even try to guess what people are up to anymore."

Jeanice had entered the dining room with her suitcase, Jan recalled, still wearing her coat and claiming to have just arrived.

"Thank you for telling us the truth," Jan said.

"Please—"

"It'll be our secret," Elaine said. "We promise we won't tell."

The cousins turned and headed back downstairs. At the foot of the stairs, they stopped near the wall, staying out of the flow of traffic.

"So what now?" Elaine asked. "It was Jeanice who put those notes and gifts in the rooms. We know it. We can prove it if necessary."

"Because she found out about those failed pledges," Jan said. "And I guess she decided to take matters into her own hands. Somehow, we have to get her to tell us."

The cousins stared at each other for a moment.

"We already have Adrianna's statement," Elaine said, "but what if she just denies it? It would be good to force her to admit to losing that nail."

Then Jan snapped her fingers. "I have an idea." Quickly, she outlined her plan for Elaine.

"It's worth a try," Elaine said. "I'm nearly certain she's the one in the lobby at check-in who was talking about bringing her nail repair kit with her. On a different topic, do you think there is any way we could help out Adrianna?"

Jan laughed. "I was about to ask you the same thing. She's obviously worried about finances, and if her husband is laid off, the expenses that come with a new baby sure aren't going to help the situation."

"What if we had a baby shower theme next week or the week after at Tea for Two?" Elaine suggested. "We could let all the customers know we are collecting items for a mom-to-be."

"That's a great idea. And what if we involved Heloise?" Jan couldn't help but think of the loneliness in the woman's voice. "She could be in on the secret and bring Adrianna for tea on Friday or Saturday, and anyone who wanted to attend could come for a little baby shower."

"Yes! I know Rue and Macy would come," Elaine said.

As if they had conjured her up, Heloise appeared, passing them on her way to the desk.

"Heloise!" Jan grabbed the manager's elbow. "We had an idea, and we need your help."

"Oh?" Without even knowing what they wanted, Heloise looked delighted to have been asked.

Quickly, the cousins explained the baby shower plan.

"That's a lovely idea," Heloise enthused. "She's been so worried about money. Her husband was laid off a few months ago, and I know they're on a tight budget. I've been stockpiling packages of disposable diapers to give her when the baby arrives, and we were going to go together as a staff to get a gift, but a shower would be wonderful."

"Do you know anyone who might like to be invited to the shower?" Elaine asked. "We'll extend a blanket invitation to our customers. They love to be involved in special projects, and I suspect this will really appeal to some of them."

"I know some of her friends," Heloise said. "Here's an idea. Why don't I make up a little notice right now to give out to all the guild members at lunch? Many of them still live around the area and might like to attend or contribute."

"Excellent idea," Jan said. "Thank you."

Without further ado, Heloise scurried off, excited by her opportunity to contribute.

"Now," Jan said, "for the next step." Looking around the room, the cousins spotted Jeanice standing on the fringes of a group in the lobby as everyone waited to go in to lunch.

Making her way in that direction, Jan said, "Hello, Jeanice. Wasn't that costume workshop wonderful?"

"Good morning, Jan. I enjoyed it."

Her mother, Ida, beside her, said, "I thought that woman could have done a better job. She didn't tell us much about the fabrics. I would have liked to hear about how the fabrics were acquired, what dyes they used, that kind of thing."

Jan only nodded. She thought the presentation had been fascinating. The woman clearly had a wealth of knowledge about the fashions of the past.

Then Jan thought of the way Sasha had complimented someone earlier in the weekend. As if she had just noticed Jeanice's French manicure, prominently featured by the way she had splayed her hand over the strap of her bag without curling the fingers under, Jan channeled the same compliment. "Your nails are lovely." She held up her own short, unpainted fingernails. "I can never get mine long enough without tearing them up. And even if I do, I mess up my polish."

"You should get tips," Jeanice said. "My nails have gotten softer as I've aged, and I get tips applied every couple of weeks. They're pretty much indestructible."

"I have a feeling I could even break a tip," Jan said.

"It's a rarity, although it does happen. I always carry a little manicure repair kit with me just in case. In fact, I broke one Friday and had to replace it myself, but you'd never know." Proudly, she held up her perfect French tips for Jan to admire.

"That's amazing," Jan said. *Gotcha.* "I can't even tell which one you replaced. I may have to try tips sometime. Although I draw the line at repairing my own nails. I have a vision of accidentally gluing my fingers together."

Jeanice laughed. "Oh no, it's a breeze once you get the hang of it. Really."

"I'll take your word for it." Jan grinned, changing the topic before eventually moving on.

As soon as she could, Jan circled back to where Elaine stood with her mother and daughter and several other friends. Catching her cousin's eye, the pair moved a short distance away from the group.

"Bingo," Jan said. "She has a manicure repair kit, and she even told me she lost a tip and had to make a repair."

Elaine grinned. "Was it really that easy?"

Jan shrugged. "I didn't even have to fish for it. She volunteered that she had broken one on Friday and fixed it herself."

"Okay. That seems to clinch it. Now we just have to figure out— Oh. Hi, Bob."

Following the direction of her cousin's gaze, Jan whirled around. Standing right behind her was Bob!

"Hi," Jan blurted. "I didn't expect to see you here today." Immediately, she grimaced. "I mean, it's a wonderful surprise. I just wasn't—"

"Can we talk?" Bob interrupted.

CHAPTER EIGHTEEN

Bob's brown hair, tipped with silver, was ruffled, and there was strain in his brown eyes. He was an attorney who normally liked to be neat, orderly, and well groomed. Something was seriously wrong.

"Of course we can talk," Jan said. She reached for his hand and gave it a reassuring squeeze. "We can have a little more privacy on the porch."

The far end of the porch was still deserted, so Jan led him in that direction. When she reached the railing, she turned, clasping her hands tightly together in front of her. "What—"

"Jan." Bob reached for her hands, squeezing them tightly in his own larger fingers. "I...I'm sorry I broke our walking date last night."

Jan felt perilously close to tears. "You also didn't answer my calls. When I was out walking with a friend yesterday, I thought I saw your car pass. After I got back to the hotel and received the lovely roses you had dropped off, I was sure it was you. I assume you saw me?"

Bob nodded, releasing her hands and making a helpless gesture. "I was really taken aback when I saw you walking with Clifton Young yesterday. It looked intimate, and jealousy got the better of me."

Jan looked up into his face. "He's just a friend. In fact, he asked one of my new acquaintances out after I introduced them this weekend."

"Oh boy." Bob sighed, running a hand through his hair. "Now I really feel like an idiot." He cleared his throat. "I'm sorry. I'm really not one of those men who will mind you having friends of the opposite sex. I don't even know why I leaped to the wrong conclusion."

"Clifton really is just a friend." Jan reached for Bob's hand again, needing the contact. "I think that he may have been interested in something more at one time, but I made it clear that I was committed to you."

Bob squeezed her fingers. "Can you forgive me? I'm not normally this stupid."

Jan laughed. When he opened his arms, she went into them. "Of course."

"Any chance we could get together this evening after you get home?"

"That would be lovely." Jan sighed, resting her head against his shoulder. "Thank you again for the roses."

Bob took his leave a few minutes later, and Jan walked back inside the lobby.

Elaine was sitting in a wing chair waiting for her. "All's right with your world again," she observed, surveying Jan's face. "You're glowing."

Jan grinned, pressing her hands to her cheeks. "Am I? And yes, it is. Bob got jealous when he saw me walking with Clifton, if you can imagine that."

"Of course I can. You're a treasure and he knows it," Elaine said staunchly. She cleared her throat. "I've been trying to think of the best way to approach our gift-giver."

"I have a glimmer of an idea, but I don't know if it will work." Jan frowned. "The next session is about to start, and then it'll be time for the farewell luncheon."

As the cousins turned, they saw Virginia coming toward them. Sasha was just coming down the stairs, having done a final check of her room to make sure she had gotten everything.

The four family members headed for the conference room, where the final workshop of the weekend was being held. Jan saw Jeanice and her mother, Ida, filing into the room just ahead of them, and she poked Elaine in the side. "Let's try to sit beside them," she said, indicating the pair.

With Jan leading the way, their little group followed Ida and Jeanice along a side aisle until they were about four rows from the front. Fortunately, the room appeared to be filling from front to back, so when Jan entered the same row and took a seat beside Jeanice, it didn't appear unusual.

"Hello again," she said brightly. "Can you believe the weekend is almost over?"

Jeanice shook her head. "It went too fast."

"Welcome to the last session of our fabulous Victorian retreat," warbled the president of the club. The group of women quieted immediately. "We've had a great deal of fun learning about clothing styles, entertainment, and leisure activities in

Victorian times this weekend. Our final workshop will give you an overview of what being a Victorian woman really entailed. Here is Everything You Wanted to Know about the Victorian Era but Were Afraid to Ask."

A ripple of laughter rolled through the room.

"With us for this final look at Victorian England is Dr. Sharon Bodin, author of *Women's Professions in the Nineteenth Century*. Dr. Bodin has a wealth of knowledge about many aspects of the time. She joins us today from Bar Harbor, where she is spending several months working on a companion volume to *Women's Professions*."

The woman who took the podium was tall and thin, with piercing blue eyes that held a twinkle of humor. "Hello, ladies," she said. "Today I'm going to talk about the ways in which a Victorian woman's life differed from ours as women in a more modern era. First, if you voted in the last election, you should thank the many women who worked hard to give you that privilege. In Victorian times, women could not vote. The Victorian woman, regardless of her class, was essentially considered to be her husband's property. When she married, everything she brought to the marriage became her husband's unless her father had put a trust in place to prevent her husband from spending her money. Likewise, she did not receive her husband's property upon his death unless a will specifically stated she should; in most cases, it went to the closest surviving male heir, and the widow had better hope he was charitable enough to continue to support her. A woman could be disposed of through divorce if she was found to have strayed, although she could not rid herself of a straying husband. Her children were her husband's property, and he could prevent her from seeing them if he chose."

There were several shocked sounds from around the room.

"Oh yes," the professor went on. "Be very glad, my friends, that we live in America in the twenty-first century."

As she continued to speak in that vein, Jan's gaze strayed to the quietly folded hands of Jeanice, sitting next to her. How was Jan to get the woman to admit to what Jan and Elaine believed she had done?

Then her gaze fell on the capacious handbag Jeanice had tucked beneath the seat in front of her. It did not have a top zipper, merely a clasp that depended on a magnet to hold it closed. The clasp was currently hanging down, unused, and the bag gaped open. There, lying tangled in a mass of other items, was a miniature craft spool of pink-and-green-striped ribbon.

Jan couldn't believe how easy it was. There in Jeanice's bag lay the perfect way to introduce the topic of those gifts.

Dr. Bodin said, "Now let's discuss some of the things that were not to be spoken of by a Victorian woman. Back in that era, the ideal woman was supposed to be chaste, modest, and very, very refined. Much like all of us."

Another round of chuckles filled the air.

"How many of you are wearing underwear today?" She glanced out over the crowd of attendees. "May I see a show of hands?"

There were murmurs and a few more hints of laughter as every woman in the room raised her hand.

"Uh-uh-uh!" the speaker said. "You have just committed a grave offense in Victorian times. Ladies *never* spoke of nor alluded to undergarments. And of course, on those rare occasions when it may be unavoidable, one would refer to them only as 'unmentionables.'"

"But you asked us," came a plaintive voice from the back, making everyone, including the presenter, laugh again. She went on to read a passage from an 1859 account of an incident in which the Duchess of Manchester tripped over her hoop skirts while attempting to step over a stile. The lady, apparently quite limber, did a complete somersault and sprang to her feet, which might have been the end of the matter had not the cage of the hoop skirt and all her petticoats stayed upside down over her head. At that point, her companions, including the Duc de Malakoff, the Marshall of France, were treated to the sight of a pair of scarlet tartan knickers.

By this time, every woman in the room was in stitches, envisioning all too well the embarrassing incident.

"Moving on," the woman said, "childbirth was another taboo subject. Women hid pregnancies as long as possible, using modified corsets. How would you like to be laced into a corset simply to try to keep your waist looking trim and tiny while you're incubating a baby? Once one's condition became impossible to hide, one entered 'confinement' and was discouraged from leaving one's home, and in some cases, even one's bed. Of course, the mere act of giving birth was quite hazardous, given that midwives and doctors rarely washed their hands. Additionally, there was no such thing as prenatal vitamins, so pregnant women often were severely anemic, raising their risk for a number of complications. And doctors routinely discouraged women from eating things which might make a child's disposition sour, so heaven help the mother with a craving for pickles."

That provoked a slight swell of laughter, despite the somber turn the topic had taken.

Dr. Bodin was fascinating, ranging from the professions women routinely were permitted to hold, to less conventional ones. "Governesses, housekeepers, and ladies' maids were, of course, among the professions most sought after. Less educated women became cooks, laundresses, and kitchen and house maids if they were fortunate enough to find a position working for their 'betters.'" She made air quotes with her fingers.

"Then there were those who worked in manufacturing. The Industrial Revolution created many opportunities for women to work outside the home in industries such as textiles, metals, and pottery. Sadly, most of these jobs were hideously ill-paying. Teachers were not required since education was private and reserved for the upper classes until 1876, when a formal act of parliament required compulsory education for all children. Although it was done primarily to end child labor, it was still an enormous step in the right direction."

There was a burst of clapping from a retired teacher in the front row, and everyone smiled.

"I'd like to leave you with the fascinating story of Dr. James Barry," the speaker said. "Dr. Barry practiced medicine from 1812—well before Queen Victoria took the throne in 1837—until Barry's sudden death in July of 1865 of dysentery. When a woman came in to wash and lay out the body, she discovered that Dr. Barry was actually a woman, who all that time had been masquerading as a man."

The women in the room hushed.

"Wow," said Betty Lee, also seated near the front. "I bet that was a shock."

"I bet it was," Dr. Bodin said, grinning. She went on to enumerate Barry's early life as a girl in Ireland, and her metamorphosis, probably helped along by her mother and a few friends of her uncle, the Irish artist James Barry, who taught painting at the Royal Academy of London.

"Dr. Barry was a skilled surgeon," the speaker went on, "and in 1826, she performed one of the first successful Caesarian sections, saving the lives of both a mother and infant."

It was a fascinating tale of a woman who could ordinarily never have achieved such heights at a time when only men could attend medical college, and all the more so for being true.

But as the presentation drew to a close and the women began clapping, Jan found herself eyeing Jeanice's bag again. She had to act or—

People around them began to rise and Jan quickly did the same, pretending to stumble. She lurched to the side, kicking over Jeanice's handbag as she grabbed at the woman for support.

"Oh, I'm so sorry!" Before Jeanice could react, Jan knelt and in the process of attempting to pick up the bag and its contents, managed to completely upend it over her own lap, spilling things every which way.

As items rolled hither and yon, she tracked the progress of the tiny spool of ribbon. It rolled very satisfactorily across the floor and fetched up against Elaine's shoe. Elaine reached down, saw what she was about to pick up, and froze. The cousins' eyes met, and Elaine quickly slipped the ribbon beneath her shoe and instead picked up a lipstick close by.

"Here you go," she said, handing the lipstick to Jeanice over Jan's head and drawing the woman's attention away from the floor momentarily. "I'm sure you wouldn't want to be without this."

Jan set the bag upright and began scrambling to pick up everything that had spilled. "I'm so, so sorry," she gushed. "Sometimes I am just the clumsiest person on the planet. Let me pick all this up for you."

"It's all right," Jeanice said. "Accidents happen." But her lips pressed tightly together immediately, as if she had to hold herself back from saying more.

"I've told you and told you to stop carrying that gigantic thing around," Jeanice's mother said. "Now see what's happened? If you had a proper handbag, you could just slide the strap over the back of your chair and things like this wouldn't happen."

Jeanice sighed. "Not now, Mom."

"There." Jan dumped the last load of items, sans the ribbon, which was still beneath Elaine's foot, back into the large bag and placed it in Jeanice's lap. "Please accept my apologies again."

"Forget about it." Jeanice turned abruptly and followed her mother, who was exiting the row from the far end.

As they left, Jan turned to see Elaine bending and picking up her own handbag from the floor beside her chair. One hand was sliding back out of her purse, and as she caught Jan's eye, she nodded and smiled. Jan held up one thumb in response, and the cousins exchanged a satisfied look.

"Now what?" Elaine whispered over her shoulder to Jan as they proceeded along the hallway.

"The library."

Jan watched as Elaine muttered something to her mother, just in front of her.

Virginia nodded. "We'll meet you in the lobby then. I want to show Sasha something else in those old yearbooks. I think there are some prom pictures that will make her giggle."

Elaine grinned before slipping into the library behind Jan. Immediately, she pulled the ribbon from her handbag. "I can't believe she just had this in plain sight." She ran a thumb over the gaily striped pink-and-green ribbon, while Jan dug through her own bag and pulled an identical strand of ribbon out that she'd kept from one of the other gifts.

"It's absolutely the same." Jan sighed. "I think we need to ask her about the notes."

Elaine nodded. "It just seems so mean. I can't imagine her doing this to her mother's friends. They've been close since high school, after all."

Jan exhaled. "I know. There has to be some reason."

"Maybe she just found the ribbon somewhere."

Jan's eyebrows rose. "And she just happened to break and repair a nail on Friday like she told me? And she just happens to be the financial chair at the same church all of these victimized women belong to? That's a stretch."

"I know." It was almost a whisper.

"I can't imagine why she'd do that either," Jan said.

Elaine put a hand on the doorknob. "Let me see if I can find her. I'll ask her to come in here for a moment."

"What will you say?"

"I don't know." Elaine shrugged as she opened the door. "I don't even know."

Jan paced. She took the notes and gifts from her handbag and placed them where she wanted them. She examined every title on the biography shelf. She checked her phone three times in five minutes. Just as she decided Elaine must not have been able to convince Jeanice to come to the library, the door-knob rattled and turned. Quickly, Jan stepped to the spot she had selected.

Elaine stepped into the library, and Jeanice Evanak stepped in behind her.

Jeanice paused in the doorway. "I thought you said you needed help with something," she said to Elaine.

"I do."

"Hi, Jeanice," Jan said. "Come on in."

Jeanice's eyes flicked to Jan and back to Elaine, but she entered the room. Elaine slipped in behind her and quietly closed the door.

Jan stepped to one side, revealing the five notes and five small "gifts" that she had arranged on the small table. "We thought," she said carefully, "that you might know something about these, Jeanice. Can you help us?"

Jeanice's face drained of color and then furiously flared to a deep, dark red. "I have no idea what you're talking about," she said in an icy tone.

Jan turned and indicated the notes she had displayed on the table. "Did you write these notes?"

"Of course not." Jeanice's tone was sullen. "I've never seen them before in my life."

For a moment—just a moment—Jan allowed herself to fear that she and Elaine had come to a wrong conclusion. But then she reminded herself of the string of "coincidences" that she had cited to Elaine moments earlier. Without another word, she took the spool of ribbon from her pocket, where she had placed it moments earlier.

Picking up the length of ribbon she'd laid on the table, she closed the small space between Jeanice and herself and held up both items. "The first one came off one of the gifts. The spool of additional ribbon was in your handbag before I knocked it over today."

CHAPTER NINETEEN

Jeanice's gaze appeared to be glued to the two items of ribbon that Jan had produced. There was a long silence, and Jan almost relaxed, feeling that they might get somewhere.

"This proves nothing," Jeanice said. "Mom bought that ribbon at a craft store for a guild project. There's probably a dozen women at this retreat that have the exact same thing."

"Why don't I bring your mother in here, and we'll ask her about buying it," Elaine said. She turned as if she intended to walk out the door.

"Wait." Jeanice held out a hand. "I . . . I'm not sure she'll remember it. You can't involve my mother in whatever crazy agenda you have going on here."

"You're not leaving us much choice," Jan said.

Elaine turned and picked up her handbag, which she'd laid on one of the chairs. Jeanice and Jan both watched silently. Finally, Elaine found what she was looking for inside it. Approaching Jeanice, she opened her palm. "I found this beside my mother's bed Friday evening—right near her pillow where her gift and note were waiting for her return after dinner. It's an awfully big coincidence that it happens to match your manicure, which you told Jan you had repaired yourself after breaking a tip on Friday."

"And I saw the nail repair kit when I spilled your belongings," Jan said. "The housekeeper, Adrianna, described you quite well when we got her to tell us about you borrowing her key."

"She also told us you went to your room, but then took your coat and suitcase with you when you returned to the main floor," Elaine added.

Jan took a seat in one of the chairs, setting Elaine's purse on the floor, and indicated the other. "Jeanice, we'd like to understand why you did this," she said.

There was a moment of electric silence. Jeanice's eyes darted toward the door, and Jan's heart sank. She felt certain the woman was going to lie and walk out that door. And then what? She hadn't really done anything illegal. Unless they were willing to call the police and try to have her threatened with intimidation or harassment—and Jan doubted Elaine or any of the five guild members Jeanice had harmed were any more interested in such an extreme notion than she was—they had come to the end of the road.

Then Jeanice sighed. "All right," she said, crossing to the other chair and perching on the edge. "I left the messages."

"Why?" Elaine asked softly.

"When I took over as financial secretary at Cushnoc Community Chapel in January, I discovered seven pledges from the ceiling campaign, as it was called, that had never been paid."

"Seven?" Jan asked, startled.

229

"In two of the cases, there were notes explaining why the individuals had to renege on their pledges." Jeanice recited the facts in a flat, colorless tone. "The other five—well, I was shocked to see that all these good members of my mother's guild had decided not to honor their pledges."

Elaine stirred, but Jan held out a warning hand, silently asking her to wait.

"So you decided to give them a little reminder of sorts?"

"Yes. The pastor came to my husband and me seven years ago and said they had learned they were going to be short approximately $13,000 for the fund. He said several people had unavoidable expenses and would be unable to honor their pledges." Her face twisted. "We agreed to cover an additional $8,000 and another church member gave $5,000 more to cover the shortfall."

"That was extremely generous of you," Elaine told her.

The comment did not appear to soothe. "Too generous, as it turns out," Jeanice spat. "My husband lost his job the year after that, and we've been struggling financially ever since. Do you have any idea how often I've thought about that $8,000? Not to mention," she added, "the $6,000 that we pledged and donated. How is it fair that other people got to default without penalty when we didn't?"

Jan chose not to point out that their pledge was completed before her husband was out of work. If everyone who gave money to a charitable cause and found out later that they needed it could simply recall the donations, the world would be a very different place. Instead, Jan said, "So once you became financial secretary, you looked to see who the people were whose pledges you had covered."

Jeanice nodded defiantly. "As I said, two had a reason listed for why they were struck from the pledge list. The other five, apparently, just decided not to pay. I thought those awful people deserved to sweat a little."

One of those "awful people," Jan remembered, was her aunt, who had defaulted for a very good reason.

"I decided to give them a little reminder at the retreat," Jeanice said, "when I saw the roster and realized they all would be here."

"But your notes and gifts were so cryptic," Elaine protested. "None of the women had any idea what they meant."

"In fact," Jan said, "some of them were reminded of a high school friend who drowned because of the wording."

Jeanice looked shocked. "Oh no," she said. "I didn't mean to make anyone think that. I just went with the water theme after I wrote the first one because it sort of felt to me like I was going under after covering all those pledges."

And what anguish she had caused because of that decision, Jan thought.

Then Jeanice's face hardened again. "Before I got here, I planned to hand a note to each person and ask her why she hadn't bothered to fulfill her pledge. The little reminders were supposed to clue them in to how much they had pledged, in case they had forgotten."

"So why didn't you?" Elaine voiced the question, but Jan was equally curious.

"I arrived a tiny bit late, and when I was at the check-in desk, I saw the room reservation chart right there on the counter."

"So you saw where all their rooms were and decided to leave them there."

"I took a picture of it when the clerk turned away to get my key," Jeanice corrected, clearly proud of this piece of spy work. "I was going to slip them under the door or something. I didn't really have a clear plan. But then when I found the housekeeper—well, you know the rest."

"Are you hoping they'll pay you back?"

"Oh no." Jeanice looked taken aback by the question. "I just thought they should understand that defaulting on a pledge is not okay so they never do it again."

Jan thought that sounded disingenuous. She suspected Jeanice had liked the idea of the five women squirming and feeling bad. Still, she chose not to air that thought. "As Elaine said, it was very generous of you to cover those pledges when you were asked. But isn't it true that Christ Himself asked Christians not to give grudgingly?"

She thought for a moment, a few verses from 2 Corinthians arranging themselves in her mind. "'But this I say, He which soweth sparingly shall reap also sparingly; and he which soweth bountifully shall reap also bountifully. Every man according as he purposeth in his heart, so let him give; not grudgingly, or of necessity: for God loveth a cheerful giver. And God is able to make all grace abound toward you; that ye, always having all sufficiency in all things, may abound to every good work.'"

Jeanice stared at her, mouth slightly open, her eyes growing moist. "But it's so unfair," she said plaintively.

"Perhaps," Jan said. "But sometimes we just don't have all the facts when we make a judgment. All of those families had very good reasons for not honoring their pledges. They're personal, so I won't share them, but the pastor at your church seven years ago told every single one of them not to worry about it, just to do good at some future date when they were more able."

"Oh no."

"I'm wondering if the two additional ones you found spoke to someone else, and that's why their requests were recorded," Elaine said. "All five of these women spoke to the same man, who apparently was in his final days at Cushnoc and preparing to become the senior pastor at another congregation in dire need of a shepherd. I can't help but think he simply may have forgotten to write down the conversations."

Jeanice covered her face with her hands. "I was wrong. I'm so sorry."

Jan looked at Elaine as Jeanice's muffled sobs filled the small room. She clearly was a very unhappy person. Rising from the chair, Jan fished a tissue from her handbag and knelt beside Jeanice's chair.

"Thank you for being honest with us," she said. She put a tentative hand on the other woman's back. "Is there any way we can help you? Would you like us to get your mother?"

Jeanice shook her head, blotting her eyes with the tissue. "No. I don't want her to see me like this. I suppose... I suppose, if it isn't too much trouble, you should ask the five ladies I hurt to come in here." She sighed. "If I don't apologize now, I may chicken out and never do it."

Elaine said, "I'll go get them," and promptly exited the library.

Silence fell. Jan busied herself picking up the notes and other items and replacing them in her handbag.

Finally, Jeanice said, "I promise I'm not an awful person. I guess I just was so focused on what seemed unfair..."

"I never thought you were," Jan said. "We have all made mistakes in life, and sometimes we don't get to rectify them. It's hard to live with a wrong you should have righted and didn't. I'm glad you're choosing to fix this one."

The doorknob turned and Virginia came into the room. "Elaine asked me to come to the library," she said. Her gaze sharpened when it fell on the younger woman, but all she said was. "Hi, Jeanice. Jan, do you know what Elaine wanted?"

Jan nodded. "She's getting a few other people to join us. Let's wait for them so we don't have to repeat and explain things."

Virginia smiled. "Good idea."

Jan had stood when her aunt entered, and Virginia took the chair she had vacated beside Jeanice.

Virginia had left the door ajar, and Kinley came in. On her heels were the others, with Elaine behind them. Elaine closed the door as everyone crowded into the small room.

Kinley looked around and grinned. "If we invite many more people into this room, we're going to have to start climbing the shelves to make more room." She looked at Jeanice. "Don't tell me you got one of these notes too."

Jeanice cleared her throat. "No. I, uh..." She swallowed visibly. "I'm the one who sent them to you," she said.

Silence fell. Jan could not even hear anyone breathing.

"What?" Babette looked as if she was sure she had misheard something.

Jeanice's cheeks were blazing with shame, but she bit her lip and looked steadily around the room at each of the five women who were her mother's fellow guild members, women who had known her, Jan realized, since the day she was born. "I'm the one who sent each of you those notes and reminders."

Still, none of the five spoke. Virginia's face was ashen; Eleanor's eyes filled with tears.

Finally, Laurette broke the silence. "Why would you do that? Do you have any idea how hurtful that was? Don't you think we already feel bad enough about being unable to honor pledges we made to our church?" Her voice rose at the end, and Jeanice flinched.

To her credit, she nodded. "I made a mistake. A bad one."

"Tell us," demanded Kinley. "Explain why you would do this. It has something to do with you being the financial secretary now, I presume?"

Jan and Elaine stood quietly as Jeanice explained her faulty reasoning and her actions again. She patiently answered every question put to her. She cried when Virginia said, "I can't take this in. How could you do something so callous to your mother's friends?"

Finally, when all the questions had been answered, silence fell in the room again.

Kinley was the first to break it. "I don't know if I can forgive you," she said bluntly. "I—" She stopped and shook her head. "I'll be talking with the pastor about it. I'm not sure that I can, in good conscience, keep quiet knowing you have the ability to be so unethical with other people's personal financial information."

"I understand," Jeanice said.

Kinley studied her for a long moment. "I'll work on forgiveness," she said, before turning on her heel and walking out the door.

Jeanice took a deep breath. Then she turned and looked at the others. "Can you forgive me?"

"I can," Elaine's mother said. Then more firmly, "I can. It took a lot of fortitude for you to tell all of us what you've done."

"I think," Eleanor said hesitantly, "it would be good for you to share what you did this weekend with the pastor."

"I agree," Laurette said, and Jan could see that forgiveness was going to be a tougher sell with her too.

"I will," Jeanice said. "I will offer to step down if he sees fit, but if not, I promise this will never happen again. And one more thing." She indicated Jan and Elaine, standing well back from the conversation. "These two deserve your thanks. I was angry. I didn't know what had motivated each of you to step away from your pledges, and I was judgmental. They helped me see that I was wrong."

Slowly she rose. Extending her hand to first Jan and then Elaine, she gave each of them a firm handshake and then walked slowly toward the door. "I'm going to tell my mother now."

CHAPTER TWENTY

The final luncheon was a pleasant wrap-up of the weekend. The president thanked them all for coming and recognized the speakers who had come from the group again, including Jan and Elaine.

Heloise gave a speech thanking them for choosing the Whisperwood. Then she made an announcement about the baby shower Jan and Elaine intended to throw for Adrianna and invited everyone, handing out small paper invitations she had made as reminders.

Seeing how pleased Heloise looked to be participating in the little surprise gave Jan a warm glow. She was glad they had thought to include her mother's classmate in that way.

Very quickly, it seemed they were saying goodbye to friends old and new. Jan received a warm hug from Rae Burns, with whom she had exchanged contact information.

"I promise I'll come by the tearoom one of these days," Rae said. "Or maybe we could go to lunch somewhere that you wouldn't have to bake."

Jan laughed. "That would be nice. Let's plan it."

"Jan." Rae looked serious. "I'm fairly smitten with your friend Clifton."

Jan smiled. "If my heart wasn't already Bob's, I might be too. He's a lovely man."

"I'd like to meet your Bob someday," Rae said. "Maybe, if I continue seeing Clifton, we could go on a double date to dinner sometime."

"That would be fun." Jan thought of Bob's reaction to such a date. He was a pretty good sport, and now that they'd worked through his concern, she doubted he'd have a problem with it. Particularly if Clifton was as enamored of her pretty, vivacious new friend as Rae appeared to be with him.

She and Elaine said farewell to the rest of the guild members and their guests. Eleanor, Babette, Kinley, and Laurette all thanked them for their persistence in figuring out Jeanice's role in sending the notes and "gifts."

As they turned to their own family, Adrianna came waddling over, her very pregnant belly leading the way. "It looks like I'll be seeing you again soon," she said. "Heloise has invited me to have tea with her at Tea for Two on Friday."

"That's wonderful," Jan said sincerely, trying to restrain herself from grinning too much. "We'll look forward to seeing you then."

"Did you, um, straighten out that thing you were asking about?" Adrianna asked anxiously.

"We did. You don't have to give it another thought," Elaine said.

"Thank you for your help," Jan added.

Virginia was hugging Heloise when Jan turned in her direction. "Maybe we can meet at Tea for Two one day and share our memories of Sally," Virginia was saying. "I am sure you two shared some good times that I'd enjoy hearing more about."

Jan smiled to herself. Sally Manling may have passed away many years ago, but her spirit was very much in evidence, doing good works in a way Jan imagined the young woman would have been pleased to see.

The four family members walked out of the Whisperwood.

"What a great weekend," Sasha said. "Thanks for inviting me, Grandma. I had a great time. I even got to help sleuth a little bit." Her smile faded slightly. "Although I know that part wasn't a lot of fun for you."

"But it was a lovely weekend overall," Virginia said, smiling and nodding. "I am so glad all of you were able to join me."

"We learned lots of new things about the Victorian era that I hope we can use at the tearoom," Elaine said.

"Although not corsets," Jan added. "We will not be adding genuine Victorian corsets to our costume collection."

Everyone chuckled.

Sasha dug her keys out of her handbag. "Well," she said, "my flight leaves in three hours, so I guess this is it." She held out her arms to her grandmother, and they exchanged an affectionate goodbye, before she turned to Jan and did the same.

Then she turned to Elaine. "I'll be in touch, Mom," she said. "We'll plan a Colorado visit for you and Nathan, okay?"

Elaine hugged her daughter. "Love you, my baby girl. Travel safely."

"Love you more." Sasha kissed her quickly and pretended not to see the tear Elaine brushed away.

Then Jan hugged Virginia. "Thank you," she said. "It meant a lot to me that you included me in this family event."

"You are family, sweet girl," her aunt said, laying a gentle hand on her cheek. She laid her forehead against Jan's for a tender moment, then turned to hug her daughter.

Jan climbed into the car, waving to Sasha, who was beginning to pull out of the lot. A moment later, Elaine joined her, waving to her mother, who crossed the parking lot to her own car.

As Elaine clipped her seat belt into place, she sighed contentedly. "What a nice weekend. I am so glad we did this."

Fifteen minutes later, they were unloading their belongings from the trunk of the car in front of the main door of Tea for Two when Bob walked up the drive.

"Oh!" Jan said. "Hello. I wasn't expecting you until this evening."

"Need a hand?"

Jan smiled and nodded, and he drew her in for a leisurely kiss. "Important things first," he said. "I missed you."

He turned to Elaine and grinned. "And you."

"Yeah, yeah," Elaine said, chuckling. "I hear you." She hefted one of the boxes they were bringing home from the tea presentation. But before she could start for the kitchen, a familiar black Cadillac turned into the driveway and pulled to a stop just behind Elaine's Malibu.

"Nathan!" she said. She dropped the box back into the trunk unceremoniously and rushed around to the driver's door as a lean figure unfolded himself from the car and held out his arms. "I thought you wouldn't be back until tonight," she said, kissing him enthusiastically.

"I thought I wouldn't be back this early either," Nathan said, smiling down at her with his arms linked behind her waist. "But I knew you'd be home by midafternoon, and the second sale didn't sound nearly as appealing as being with you on your only day off, so I flew by the first sale, placed a couple of absentee bids, and headed home. Looks like my timing was perfect."

"It was." Elaine's face was glowing. "Can you stay for dinner? Both of you?" She looked over at Bob as she spoke.

"Sure," Nathan said as Bob nodded.

Jan clapped her hands. "And maybe we can play a game after dinner."

Elaine rolled her eyes. "Haven't we had enough of games for the weekend?"

"And we solved a...what?" Jan asked Elaine. "A puzzle? A mystery? A problem?"

"All of the above," Elaine said in a wry tone.

"This sounds interesting." Bob headed for the trunk. "Why don't we help you bring everything in and put it away, while you tell us about it?"

As he reached for a box, a pickup turned off Main Street into the driveway behind Nathan's car.

"It's Archie." Jan started for the truck. "Hey, you. Not that I'm not delighted to see you, but it's your day off."

"I thought you and Gloria were going to that concert up in Bar Harbor," Elaine added.

"This is more important," Archie informed her. "I was hoping you'd be here, because I have some news I couldn't wait to share."

"Is it about your father?" Both cousins were excited.

He nodded. He put the truck in park, then turned it off and stepped from the driver's side, waving a piece of paper. "I finally made contact with that chap, and he e-mailed me the letter, as well as some other information he went to the trouble to uncover. I'm as sure as I can be from a copy that this letter is my father's handwriting," he reported. He looked calm, but his voice betrayed his excitement.

"The authenticator told me he felt certain it was, but I had to see it for myself. Look." He showed Jan and Elaine the copy of a handwritten note. At the bottom, in addition to his signature, was the distinctive emblem the painter had used to sign his work, including the painting the cousins had purchased.

"What does it say?" Jan's voice was hushed.

"I'll read it to you," Archie said. "It's addressed to Geraldine's mother—who was his first wife, it seems, and likely the woman in the painting." His voice quavered, and he stopped, swallowed, and cleared his throat. "The chap was so interested in my case that he did a little research on his own, which he included for me. My father's first wife died in a bombing raid during the war, and his daughter was assumed to have perished with her. That's why he never claimed Geraldine after the war—he didn't know she was alive!"

Jan put up a comforting hand and patted his back lightly as he went on. "So here's the pertinent part of the letter: *I cannot express how much I look forward to the day I return from this war. I long to see you. I love you. Kiss my Geraldine for me and tell her Daddy loves her. I pray for the day we are reunited.'*" He glanced up, his eyes shining. "You know we felt certain we were siblings, but this"—he shook the paper—"this is proof positive."

"That's wonderful," Elaine said. "Congratulations!"

"Thank you," he said, and there was a tremor in his voice. "There's more. The authenticator did some research through a few old contacts in the art world, and he wanted to let me know that, as I'd suspected, my father was injured in the war. That was the reason he never painted again. Apparently, he tried not long after he first was hurt, but he no longer had the ability to paint with the same precision he once had. The authenticator speculated that he may have lost his creative desire in his grief."

"That must have been very distressing," Elaine said softly.

Archie nodded. "I can't imagine losing all one's family, along with such a gift. That must have been very hard."

"So he never painted again?" Jan asked.

Archie shook his head. "That certainly explains why I knew nothing about his talent. And I can only assume that likewise, he couldn't bear to speak of his first family. I called Geraldine and told her everything." Now his eyes were shining and he smiled. "It's one thing to believe you have found a blood relative, but it's quite another to *know* it. Thank you both, so very much, for pursuing my father's signature and for helping me find my sister."

"We couldn't have done it if you hadn't recognized your father's symbol in the painting," Jan said. "I prefer to think there may have been some divine guidance involved."

"And two very determined, very curious amateur sleuths," Archie said with a laugh. "I can't wait to see what you two get up to next."

ABOUT THE AUTHOR

Anne Marie Rodgers has written more than twenty novels for Guideposts and nearly five dozen stories in her twenty-five-year publishing career, including a number of best-sellers and award winners. Anne Marie is deeply committed to animal rescue and wildlife rehabilitation and has become a bat care specialist in her Savannah, Georgia, community. One of her greatest joys in life is her growing family, which includes two grandchildren and another on the way.

From the Tea for Two Kitchen

No-Wait Friendship Bread

Traditional Amish friendship bread requires patience, time, and a little maintenance. Here is a simple version that offers the taste without the time.

"Starter"

¾ cup sugar

¾ cup milk

¾ cup flour

Bread

1 cup oil (or substitute a cup of apple sauce if preferred)

½ cup milk

3 whole eggs

1 teaspoon vanilla extract

2 cups flour

1 cup sugar

1½ teaspoons baking powder

2 teaspoons cinnamon

½ teaspoon salt

½ teaspoon baking soda

15⅛ ounce box instant vanilla pudding (or try butterscotch for a variation)

1 cup chopped nuts (optional)

cinnamon and sugar

Preheat oven to 325 degrees. Mix together the "starter" ingredients until smooth, then stir in oil, milk, eggs, and vanilla with the "starter."

In a separate bowl, whisk together flour, sugar, baking powder, cinnamon, salt, baking soda, pudding mix, and nuts.

Add to liquid mixture and blend thoroughly. Pour into two large well-greased 9x5 inch loaf pans, one Bundt pan, or 48 muffin tins. Sprinkle the batter generously with cinnamon and sugar.

Bake bread for one hour or until done (insert a toothpick to check). Bake 30–35 minutes if making muffins. Cool and enjoy!

Read on for an exciting sneak peek
into the next volume of Tearoom Mysteries!

Tearoom in a Tempest
by Leslie Gould

As Elaine Cook approached Tea for Two, her windshield wipers sped back and forth across the windshield, clearing a small path through the driving rain. She paused for a moment, gazing out on Chickadee Lake, where the waves rode high and choppy and the April rain bounced up and then back down against the still-frigid surface.

Fortunately Elaine had too many fun events planned in the next few days to give in to the gloom. She pulled in to the driveway, turned off the wipers, and then shut off the engine. Bracing herself against the sleety rain, she grabbed the paper bag of groceries, the plastic bag with printer ink and a new blank notebook, and her purse from the passenger seat, then climbed out of her red Chevy Malibu, kicked the door shut behind her, and then dashed toward the house.

The rain beat against her face as she sloshed through the mud puddles in her waterproof boots. Ahead was the Victorian house that she and her cousin Jan had turned into a tearoom over two years ago.

Elaine had left their employee Rose Young in charge while she ran errands and Jan finished up the baking. Their other employee, Archie, had left with his wife, Gloria, and his sister, Geraldine, for a visit to England, where they were from. She and Jan had received a postcard the day before saying they were having a wonderful time, visiting museums where Archie and Geraldine's father's works of art were displayed. Elaine was thrilled for Archie, but it meant a little more planning on her part to coordinate schedules and keep the tearoom running smoothly.

Yes, there was a lot going on but no more than usual. Elaine was looking forward to spending the evening with her mother in Augusta, and then in three days, on Monday, her daughter, Sasha, would return to Maine from her time of training in Vermont, and stay until the Monday after Mother's Day. Sasha had combined her vacation days and a leave of absence from her job as a fitness trainer in Colorado for some time off.

As Elaine stepped into the house, the sound of spoons clinking against cups and the chatter of the customers greeted her. It was music to her ears and further lifted her spirits.

Rose smiled from the cash register as she rang up an order for an elderly woman. Elaine could see customers sitting at several of the tables covered with lace and linen and set with china. The tearoom appeared to be much busier than she'd anticipated it would be on a rainy Friday afternoon.

Rose nodded at Elaine's inquiring expression, making the wheat-colored bun atop her head wiggle a little. She motioned toward the dining room. "We've got a group in there too."

"Lovely," Elaine said. "I'll help you fill orders."

Rose smiled in appreciation.

Elaine made her way to the kitchen, put the groceries on the kitchen counter, hung up her coat, brushed her fingers through her short, damp hair, and then placed the ink and notebook on her desk in her office. After she rolled up the sleeves of her sweater, put on an apron, and scrubbed her hands, she began steeping a pot of Earl Grey tea and then placed two chocolate almond scones on a plate. Next she started a pot of orange spice tea and plated cranberry and white chocolate cookies.

Together, she and Rose quickly filled the orders. When Rose returned after delivering the next-to-last one, Elaine had a chance to ask where Jan was.

Rose, standing at the kitchen island, placed teacups on a tray. "She went with Bob to help friends with a cabin on the lake. A tree uprooted and fell across their garage and damaged their car. Bob was going to give them a ride into town. When he stopped by here, we weren't busy so I told Jan to ride along, that I'd be fine."

"What horrible weather to be out in." Elaine glanced out the kitchen window through the screened porch, hoping the rain had slowed. It hadn't, and the lake was churning even more. There wasn't a single boat on the water.

"More rain is predicted," Rose said. "I didn't think we'd have much business today, but almost everyone who's come in commented they just wanted a hot cup of tea to combat the dreariness. Mostly locals though," she added. "I think the tourists are staying away."

Elaine hoped it wasn't raining as hard in Augusta. For a moment she wondered if she shouldn't drive in the storm, but she planned to include Jan's granddaughter Avery in the outing and hated to cancel. Elaine was looking forward to taking the girl to visit her great-great-aunt, Elaine's mother. She didn't want to disappoint either one of them.

Rose interrupted Elaine's thoughts. "I almost forgot. A woman dropped off a package for you and Jan. She said she was remodeling her house and found something."

Elaine placed a pot of peppermint tea on Rose's tray. "Oh?"

"Yeah, it was kind of weird. She said she wanted the 'Pritchard cousins' to have what's inside."

"What *is* inside?" Elaine asked.

Rose shrugged. "I have no idea, and she didn't say. But the package is about the size of a small book." She nodded through the kitchen doorway toward the cash register cabinet as she lifted the tray and headed out to the floor. She called out over her shoulder, "The package is on the bottom shelf."

Curious, Elaine stepped to the counter and retrieved the parcel. She unwound the thick brown paper, revealing a small leather-bound book with the title *Evangeline: A Tale of Acadie* imprinted on the cover and the author's name, Henry Wadsworth Longfellow.

"Oh my," Elaine said out loud. Every Mainer knew Henry Wadsworth Longfellow. He was one of the state's most beloved authors. But why would someone gift the book to the "Pritchard cousins"? And who even remembered that she and Jan used to go by that designation? It was Jan's maiden name and also Elaine's mother's maiden name, but once Jan's parents died there wasn't anyone with that last name left in the area. Not more than a handful of people would make the connection to Jan and Elaine, except perhaps Jan's cousin Lori, who lived in Portland.

Elaine opened the cover, which was in remarkably good condition. On the title page of the epic poem was the name of the publishing company, *Boston: Ticknor & Company,* and the year, *1847.* Then an autograph. *Henry W. Longfellow.* Her heart sped—could the signature possibly be genuine? It was surprisingly easy to read even though it was written in that ornate, old-fashioned script of so long ago.

She turned to the next page. Faintly at the top right-hand side was a name, written in pencil. She squinted. *Lena Foret.* She was sure of it. That was the name of her and Jan's Grandmother Pritchard—their Nana—before she married their grandfather.

Elaine wanted to hug the book to her chest, but she feared damaging it so she held it in front of her. Their grandmother wasn't born until 1901, so obviously the book would have been given to her years after it was published.

As she leafed through the pages, Elaine struggled to remember what she could about the story of Evangeline. She couldn't come up with much more than it was about a girl, born in Nova Scotia, during the Great Upheaval of the Acadians, sometime in the 1700s.

Elaine reached the back of the book, where a piece of white paper was affixed to the last page with something written on it. The ink had faded and the script was old-fashioned with lots of swirls—and not easy to read the way the autograph had been. She could make out the letter *L*, a few words in the one paragraph—*recover* and *book* and *hurt,* and then a lone *T* at the end. What in the world could the note be about?

She closed the book and pulled out her cell phone from the pocket of her sweater and snapped a photo of the front, then the title page with the autograph, Lena Foret's name, and the note, and sent a quick text to Jan with the photos attached. Maybe Jan had some memory of the book since she'd been in the Maine area all those years while Elaine was traveling the world.

Rose stepped out of the dining room with the empty tray. "What is it?" she asked.

Elaine pointed to the counter. "A book." She glanced at Rose. "As you'd guessed. It appears that it belonged to our grandmother."

"Wow," Rose said. "That's really cool."

"Tell me again who dropped it off?"

Rose's face reddened. "She didn't give her name. And we were really busy right then, so I'm afraid I didn't think to ask."

"That's okay," Elaine said. "I understand. But you didn't recognize her?"

"No." Rose frowned. "She was probably around your age. Shoulder-length white hair. Slender." She shrugged. "I'm sorry."

As Rose retreated to the kitchen, Elaine thought about what to do. She didn't have much time today, but a quick visit next door at the Bookworm with the owner, Bristol Payson, was in order. Perhaps she'd at least be able to tell Elaine the best way to care for the book while she tried to figure out where it had come from.

FROM THE
GUIDEPOSTS ARCHIVES

This story, by Mary Margaret Kern of Noblesville,
Indiana, originally appeared in *Guideposts*.

This is silly," I said to my husband as we walked into the Jefferson High gymnasium for my twenty-fifth high-school reunion. "I don't know why I let you talk me into coming. I mean, who cares what we thought or did so many years ago?"

"You might be surprised," said Herb.

Everywhere we looked were faded reminders of the past: wall-to-wall posters of former athletes, placards sporting old game scores, tables piled high with boxes of yellowed newspaper clippings and stacks of old yearbooks—a welter of memorabilia.

"Want to look it over?" asked Herb.

"No."

Standing at the edge of the crowd, I forced myself to appear interested in the small group of long-skirted, grown-heavier women and graying and balding men. Much to my dismay, someone spotted me.

"Don't I know you?" exclaimed a vaguely familiar face. "Aren't you...why, of course you are! Do come join us..."

Herb and I found ourselves included in a group.

"You haven't changed," said someone.

But that's not true, I thought.

"It's so nice to know your husband," commented another. "Tell me, where did you two meet?"

Finally, we excused ourselves.

"Herb," I whispered, as we moved away from the chattering crowd, "I hardly knew these people. This whole evening is just as bad as I thought it would be. Unless we find someone I really shared something with, we might as well go home."

Then, from the corner of my eye, I saw her coming. My heart jumped. It was Carol. And she was headed toward me.

Of all people, I thought. We'd shared something, all right. We'd shared a place on the election ballot as opposing candidates for secretary of the senior class. Carol had won. It had been the biggest disappointment of my high-school life. My senior year, as a result of that defeat, had been spent like all the others—on the fringe of school activities, but never quite "in." But for people like Carol...

She was standing in front of me now, her bright blue dinner dress swirling around her petite, still trim figure.

"How wonderful to see you!" she beamed. "I hoped you would come."

Her smile was warm and friendly. Her brown eyes, crinkled partly shut, seemed to dance. She was—no doubt about it—as charming and enchanting as ever. Herb was entranced.

As I stooped to press my cheek against hers in greeting, long-forgotten feelings of inferiority came flooding back. It didn't matter that now I had a happy marriage, beautiful children and a successful writing career; how tall and ungainly I had always felt compared to Carol. How unpopular and dull. I felt my face grow hot.

Trying not to let my feelings show, I introduced Herb. Carol explained that her husband was caught in the crowd; that she would go find him presently. But first, she insisted, we should talk. When was the last time we'd seen each other?

I couldn't recall.

"Well, this may surprise you," said Carol, suddenly thoughtful, "but my most vivid memory of you is hearing your voice over the telephone."

"What?"

"The time you phoned me after that class secretary election," she said. "Don't you remember?"

Again my heart lurched and I was back in high school at the close of an assembly, anxiously waiting for the principal to announce the election results...

"Please, God," I had prayed frantically. "Please, let it be me."

Moments later, while all the other girls were squealing and clustering around Carol, I was racing blindly for my locker and home. When I tossed my books on the hall table, they skidded off and clattered to the floor. The noise brought my mother in from the kitchen. She saw my face.

"Is something wrong?"

"Yes!" I blurted. "Carol won the election, that's what's wrong."

"I know how disappointed you must be," she said quietly.

"But Mother," I swallowed a sob, "you don't know. You just couldn't know how important this was. I—I even asked God to help. He didn't listen." I kept my eyes on the toes of my loafers. "He never listens."

"Mary," said my mother softly, "God always listens—and answers—but in His own time, and in His own way. You have to learn to trust in Him. Sometimes it's hard to understand."

It was obvious to me that my mother, and God, were the ones having trouble understanding. Still, as I stood there twisting a strand of long brown hair around my finger, I began to feel a little better.

Mother gently reached over and placed her hand on my shoulder. "The thing to do now," she said, leading me toward the kitchen, "is phone and congratulate Carol."

"Congratulate her?!" My whole body tensed.

The telephone hung on the wall not three feet away. Deep down inside, something told me it was the right thing to do.

"Dear God," I whispered, "please help me do this."

Still, I was full of resistance as I reached for the receiver. If only no one would be home, I thought. Or just so Carol isn't there.

I dialed. At the sound of Carol's voice, my hand gripped the phone so tightly my knuckles turned white. Somehow, however, I got the words out. In fact, I was surprised at how easily they came, once I started speaking.

Carol's reply was slow and quiet.

"How nice," I heard her say. "I never expected..." And, distinctly and fervently as she hung up, "Thank you very much."

Later, as we worked together in school activities, Carol always seemed especially friendly. After a while, I almost forgot how deeply the defeat had hurt me. Almost—but not quite.

So why, I thought irritably, did she have to bring it up now?

"Well," Carol was continuing, "I never forgot that phone call. In fact, this spring, when our daughter ran for a campus office in college and was defeated—guess what I did?" She smiled happily. "I persuaded her to telephone and congratu-late the winner—just as you did for me."

Just as you did for me.

"It...it wasn't all that much," I stammered. "Frankly," I had to be honest, "my mother twisted my arm."

"That doesn't matter," said Carol. "You did it."

She reached over and squeezed my hand. "And I've always remembered."

With that, Carol excused herself to find her husband.

Herb was regarding me quizzically. "Still sorry you came to the reunion?"

"No," I said, feeling a warm, wonderful glow of happiness. "I'm glad we came. Very glad."

A NOTE FROM THE EDITORS

We hope you enjoyed Tearoom Mysteries, published by the Books and Inspirational Media Division of Guideposts, a nonprofit organization that touches millions of lives every day through products and services that inspire, encourage, help you grow in your faith, and celebrate God's love.

Thank you for making a difference with your purchase of this book, which helps fund our many outreach programs to military personnel, prisons, hospitals, nursing homes, and educational institutions.

We also create many useful and uplifting online resources. Visit Guideposts.org to read true stories of hope and inspiration, access OurPrayer network, sign up for free newsletters, download free e-books, join our Facebook community, and follow our stimulating blogs.

To learn about other Guideposts publications, including the best-selling devotional *Daily Guideposts*, go to Guideposts.org/ Shop, call (800) 932-2145, or write to Guideposts, PO Box 5815, Harlan, Iowa 51593.

Sign up for the
Guideposts Fiction Newsletter
and stay up-to-date on the books you love!

You'll get sneak peeks of new releases, recommendations from other Guideposts readers, and special offers just for you . . .
and it's FREE!

Just go to Guideposts.org/Newsletters
today to sign up.

Find more inspiring fiction in these best-loved Guideposts series!

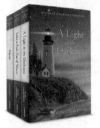

Mysteries of Martha's Vineyard
Come to the shores of this quaint and historic island and dig into a cozy mystery. When a recent widow inherits a lighthouse just off the coast of Massachusetts, she finds exciting adventures, new friends, and renewed hope.

Tearoom Mysteries
Mix one stately Victorian home, a charming lakeside town in Maine, and two adventurous cousins with a passion for tea and hospitality. Add a large scoop of intriguing mystery and sprinkle generously with faith, family, and friends, and you have the recipe for Tearoom Mysteries.

Sugarcreek Amish Mysteries
Be intrigued by the suspense and joyful "aha!" moments in these delightful stories. Each book in the series brings together two women of vastly different backgrounds and traditions, who realize there's much more to the "simple life" than meets the eye.

Mysteries of Silver Peak
Escape to the historic mining town of Silver Peak, Colorado, and discover how one woman's love of antiques helps her solve mysteries buried deep in the town's checkered past.

Patchwork Mysteries
Discover that life's little mysteries often have a common thread in a series where every novel contains an intriguing whodunit centered around a quilt located in a beautiful New England town.

To learn more about these books, visit Guideposts.org/Shop